# About the Author

Agatha Christie is the most widely published author of all time and in any language, outsold only by the Bible and Shakespeare. Her books have sold more than a billion copies in English and another billion in a hundred foreign languages. She is the author of eighty crime novels and short-story collections, nineteen plays, two memoirs, and six novels written under the name Mary Westmacott.

She first tried her hand at detective fiction while working in a hospital dispensary during World War I, creating the now legendary Hercule Poirot with her debut novel *The Mysterious Affair at Styles*. With *The Murder in the Vicarage*, published in 1930, she introduced another beloved sleuth, Miss Jane Marple. Additional series characters include the husband-and-wife crime-fighting team of Tommy and Tuppence Beresford, private investigator Parker Pyne, and Scotland Yard detectives Superintendent Battle and Inspector Japp.

Many of Christie's novels and short stories were adapted into plays, films, and television series. *The Mousetrap*, her most famous play of all, opened in 1952 and is the longest-running play in history. Among her best-known film adaptations are *Murder on the Orient Express* (1974) and *Death on the Nile* (1978), with Albert Finney and Peter Ustinov playing Hercule Poirot, respectively. On the small screen Poirot has been most memorably portrayed by David Suchet, and Miss Marple by Joan Hickson and subsequently Geraldine McEwan and Julia McKenzie.

Christie was first married to Archibald Christie and then to archaeologist Sir Max Mallowan, whom she accompanied on expeditions to countries that would also serve as the settings for many of her novels. In 1971 she achieved one of Britain's highest honors when she was made a Dame of the British Empire. She died in 1976 at the age of eighty-five. Her one hundred and twentieth anniversary was celebrated around the world in 2010.

www.AgathaChristie.com

# THE AGATHA CHRISTIE COLLECTION

The Man in the Brown Suit
The Secret of Chimneys
The Seven Dials Mystery
The Mysterious Mr. Quin
The Sittaford Mystery
Parker Pyne Investigates
Why Didn't They Ask Evans?
Murder Is Easy
The Regatta Mystery and
    Other Stories
And Then There Were None
Towards Zero
Death Comes as the End
Sparkling Cyanide
The Witness for the Prosecution and
    Other Stories
Crooked House
Three Blind Mice and Other Stories
They Came to Baghdad
Destination Unknown
Ordeal by Innocence
Double Sin and Other Stories
The Pale Horse
Star over Bethlehem: Poems and
    Holiday Stories
Endless Night
Passenger to Frankfurt
The Golden Ball and Other Stories
The Mousetrap and Other Plays
The Harlequin Tea Set and
    Other Stories

**The Hercule Poirot Mysteries**
The Mysterious Affair at Styles
The Murder on the Links
Poirot Investigates
The Murder of Roger Ackroyd
The Big Four
The Mystery of the Blue Train
Peril at End House
Lord Edgware Dies
Murder on the Orient Express
Three Act Tragedy
Death in the Clouds
The A.B.C. Murders
Murder in Mesopotamia
Cards on the Table
Murder in the Mews
Dumb Witness

Death on the Nile
Appointment with Death
Hercule Poirot's Christmas
Sad Cypress
One, Two, Buckle My Shoe
Evil Under the Sun
Five Little Pigs
The Hollow
The Labors of Hercules
Taken at the Flood
The Under Dog and Other Stories
Mrs. McGinty's Dead
After the Funeral
Hickory Dickory Dock
Dead Man's Folly
Cat Among the Pigeons
The Clocks
Third Girl
Hallowe'en Party
Elephants Can Remember
Curtain: Poirot's Last Case

**The Miss Marple Mysteries**
The Murder at the Vicarage
The Body in the Library
The Moving Finger
A Murder Is Announced
They Do It with Mirrors
A Pocket Full of Rye
4:50 from Paddington
The Mirror Crack'd from Side to Side
A Caribbean Mystery
At Bertram's Hotel
Nemesis
Sleeping Murder
Miss Marple: The Complete
    Short Stories

**The Tommy and
Tuppence Mysteries**
The Secret Adversary
Partners in Crime
N or M?
By the Pricking of My Thumbs
Postern of Fate

**Memoirs**
An Autobiography
Come, Tell Me How You Live

*Agatha Christie*

# The Secret of Chimneys

### WILLIAM MORROW

*An Imprint of* HarperCollins*Publishers*

AGATHA CHRISTIE® THE SECRET OF CHIMNEYS™. Copyright © 1925 Agatha Christie Limited (a Chorion company). All rights reserved.

THE SECRET OF CHIMNEYS © 1925. Published by permission of G.P. Putnam's Sons, a member of Penguin Group (USA) Inc. All rights reserved. Printed in the United States of America. No part of this book may be used or reproduced in any manner whatsoever without written permission except in the case of brief quotations embodied in critical articles and reviews. For information, address HarperCollins Publishers, 195 Broadway, New York, NY 10007.

HarperCollins books may be purchased for educational, business, or sales promotional use. For information, please email Special Markets Department at SPsales@harpercollins.com.

For more information about educational use, teachers should visit www.HarperAcademic.com.

FIRST WILLIAM MORROW PAPERBACK EDITION PUBLISHED 2012.

Designed by Michael P. Correy

Library of Congress Cataloging-in-Publication Data is available upon request.

ISBN 978-0-06-207415-7

18  19  20  21  22  23  24    LSC    10  9  8  7  6  5

*To my nephew*

*In memory of an inscription*
*at Compton Castle and a day*
*at the zoo*

# One

## ANTHONY CADE SIGNS ON

"Gentleman Joe!"

"Why, if it isn't old Jimmy McGrath."

Castle's Select Tour, represented by seven depressed-looking females and three perspiring males, looked on with considerable interest. Evidently their Mr. Cade had met an old friend. They all admired Mr. Cade so much, his tall lean figure, his suntanned face, the lighthearted manner with which he settled disputes and cajoled them all into good temper. This friend of his now—surely rather a peculiar-looking man. About the same height as Mr. Cade, but thickset and not nearly so good-looking. The sort of man one read about in books, who probably kept a saloon. Interesting though. After all, that was what one came abroad for—to see all these peculiar things one read about in books. Up to now they had been rather bored with Bulawayo. The sun was unbearably hot, the hotel was uncomfortable, there seemed to be nowhere particular to go until the moment should arrive to motor to the Matoppos. Very fortunately, Mr. Cade had suggested picture postcards. There was an excellent supply of picture postcards.

Anthony Cade and his friend had stepped a little apart.

"What the hell are you doing with this pack of females?" demanded McGrath. "Starting a harem?"

"Not with this little lot," grinned Anthony. "Have you taken a good look at them?"

"I have that. Thought maybe you were losing your eyesight."

"My eyesight's as good as ever it was. No, this is a Castle's Select Tour. I'm Castle—the local Castle, I mean."

"What the hell made you take on a job like that?"

"A regrettable necessity for cash. I can assure you it doesn't suit my temperament."

Jimmy grinned.

"Never a hog for regular work, were you?"

Anthony ignored this aspersion.

"However, something will turn up soon, I expect," he remarked hopefully. "It usually does." Jimmy chuckled.

"If there's any trouble brewing, Anthony Cade is sure to be in it sooner or later, I know that," he said. "You've an absolute instinct for rows—*and* the nine lives of a cat. When can we have a yarn together?"

Anthony sighed.

"I've got to take these cackling hens to see Rhodes' grave."

"That's the stuff," said Jimmy approvingly. "They'll come back bumped black and blue with the ruts in the road, and clamouring for bed to rest the bruises on. Then you and I will have a spot or two and exchange the news."

"Right. So long, Jimmy."

Anthony rejoined his flock of sheep. Miss Taylor, the youngest and most skittish of the party, instantly attacked him.

"Oh, Mr. Cade, was that an old friend of yours?"

"It was, Miss Taylor. One of the friends of my blameless youth."

Miss Taylor giggled.

"I thought he was such an interesting-looking man."

"I'll tell him you said so."

"Oh, Mr. Cade, how can you be so naughty! The very idea! What was that name he called you?"

"Gentleman Joe?"

"Yes. Is your name Joe?"

"I thought you knew it was Anthony, Miss Taylor."

"Oh, go on with you!" cried Miss Taylor coquettishly.

Anthony had by now well mastered his duties. In addition to making the necessary arrangements of travel, they included soothing down irritable old gentlemen when their dignity was ruffled, seeing that elderly matrons had ample opportunities to buy picture postcards, and flirting with everything under a catholic forty years of age. The last task was rendered easier for him by the extreme readiness of the ladies in question to read a tender meaning into his most innocent remarks.

Miss Taylor returned to the attack.

"Why does he call you Joe, then?"

"Oh, just because it isn't my name."

"And why Gentleman Joe?"

"The same kind of reason."

"Oh, Mr. Cade," protested Miss Taylor, much distressed, "I'm sure you shouldn't say that. Papa was only saying last night what gentlemanly manners you had."

"Very kind of your father, I'm sure, Miss Taylor."

"And we are all agreed that you are quite the gentleman."

"I'm overwhelmed."

"No, really, I mean it."

"Kind hearts are more than coronets," said Anthony vaguely, without a notion of what he meant by the remark, and wishing fervently it was lunchtime.

"That's such a beautiful poem, I always think. Do you know much poetry, Mr. Cade?"

"I might recite 'The boy stood on the burning deck' at a pinch. 'The boy stood on the burning deck, whence all but he had fled.' That's all I know, but I can do that bit with action if you like. 'The boy stood on the burning deck'—whoosh—whoosh—whoosh— (the flames, you see) 'Whence all but he had fled'—for that bit I run to and fro like a dog."

Miss Taylor screamed with laughter.

"Oh, do look at Mr. Cade! Isn't he funny?"

"Time for morning tea," said Anthony briskly. "Come this way. There is an excellent café in the next street."

"I presume," said Mrs. Caldicott in her deep voice, "that the expense is included in the Tour?"

"Morning tea, Mrs. Caldicott," said Anthony, assuming his professional manner, "is an extra."

"Disgraceful."

"Life is full of trials, isn't it?" said Anthony cheerfully.

Mrs. Caldicott's eyes gleamed, and she remarked with the air of one springing a mine:

"I suspected as much, and in anticipation I poured off some tea into a jug at breakfast this morning! I can heat that up on the spirit lamp. Come, Father."

Mr. and Mrs. Caldicott sailed off triumphantly to the hotel, the lady's back complacent with successful forethought.

"Oh, Lord," muttered Anthony, "what a lot of funny people it does take to make a world."

He marshalled the rest of the party in the direction of the café. Miss Taylor kept by his side, and resumed her catechism.

"Is it a long time since you saw your friend?"

"Just over seven years."

"Was it in Africa you knew him?"

"Yes, not this part, though. The first time I ever saw Jimmy McGrath he was all trussed up ready for the cooking pot. Some of the tribes in the interior are cannibals, you know. We got there just in time."

"What happened?"

"Very nice little shindy. We potted some of the beggars, and the rest took to their heels."

"Oh, Mr. Cade, what an adventurous life you must have led."

"Very peaceful, I assure you."

But it was clear that the lady did not believe him.

It was about ten o'clock that night when Anthony Cade walked into the small room where Jimmy McGrath was busy manipulating various bottles.

"Make it strong, James," he implored. "I can tell you, I need it."

"I should think you did, my boy. I wouldn't take on that job of yours for anything."

"Show me another, and I'll jump out of it fast enough."

McGrath poured out his own drink, tossed it off with a practised hand and mixed a second one. Then he said slowly:

"Are you in earnest about that, old son?"

"About what?"

"Chucking this job of yours if you could get another?"

"Why? You don't mean to say that you've got a job going begging? Why don't you grab it yourself?"

"I have grabbed it—but I don't much fancy it, that's why I'm trying to pass it on to you."

Anthony became suspicious.

"What's wrong with it? They haven't engaged you to teach in a Sunday school, have they?"

"Do you think anyone would choose me to teach in a Sunday school?"

"Not if they knew you well, certainly."

"It's a perfectly good job—nothing wrong with it whatsoever."

"Not in South America by any lucky chance? I've rather got my eye on South America. There's a very tidy little revolution coming off in one of those little republics soon."

McGrath grinned.

"You always were keen on revolutions—anything to be mixed up in a really good row."

"I feel my talents might be appreciated out there. I tell you, Jimmy, I can be jolly useful in a revolution—to one side or the other. It's better than making an honest living any day."

"I think I've heard that sentiment from you before, my son. No, the job isn't in South America—it's in England."

"England? Return of hero to his native land after many long

years. They can't dun you for bills after seven years, can they, Jimmy?"

"I don't think so. Well, are you on for hearing more about it?"

"I'm on all right. The thing that worries me is why you're not taking it on yourself."

"I'll tell you. I'm after gold, Anthony—far up in the interior."

Anthony whistled and looked at him.

"You've always been after gold, Jimmy, ever since I knew you. It's your weak spot—your own particular little hobby. You've followed up more wildcat trails than anyone I know."

"And in the end I'll strike it. You'll see."

"Well, everyone his own hobby. Mine's rows, yours is gold."

"I'll tell you the whole story. I suppose you know all about Herzoslovakia?"

Anthony looked up sharply.

"Herzoslovakia?" he said, with a curious ring in his voice.

"Yes. Know anything about it?"

There was quite an appreciable pause before Anthony answered. Then he said slowly:

"Only what everyone knows. It's one of the Balkan States, isn't it? Principal rivers, unknown. Principal mountains, also unknown, but fairly numerous. Capital, Ekarest. Population, chiefly brigands. Hobby, assassinating kings and having revolutions. Last king, Nicholas IV, assassinated about seven years ago. Since then it's been a republic. Altogether a very likely spot. You might have mentioned before that Herzoslovakia came into it."

"It doesn't except indirectly."

Anthony gazed at him more in sorrow than in anger.

"You ought to do something about this, James," he said. "Take a correspondence course, or something. If you'd told a story like this in the good old Eastern days, you'd have been hung up by the heels and bastinadoed or something equally unpleasant."

Jimmy pursued this course quite unmoved by these strictures.

"Ever heard of Count Stylptitch?"

"Now you're talking," said Anthony. "Many people who have never heard of Herzoslovakia would brighten at the mention of Count Stylptitch. The Grand Old Man of the Balkans. The Greatest Statesman of Modern Times. The biggest villain unhung. The point of view all depends on which newspaper you take in. But be sure of this, Count Stylptitch will be remembered long after you and I are dust and ashes, James. Every move and countermove in the Near East for the last twenty years has had Count Stylptitch at the bottom of it. He's been a dictator and a patriot and a statesman—and nobody knows exactly what he has been, except that he's been a perfect king of intrigue. Well, what about him?"

"He was Prime Minister of Herzoslovakia—that's why I mentioned it first."

"You've no sense of proportion, Jimmy. Herzoslovakia is of no importance at all compared to Stylptitch. It just provided him with a birthplace and a post in public affairs. But I thought he was dead?"

"So he is. He died in Paris about two months ago. What I'm telling you about happened some years ago."

"The question is," said Anthony, "what *are* you telling me about?"

Jimmy accepted the rebuke and hastened on.

"It was like this. I was in Paris—just four years ago, to be exact. I was walking along one night in rather a lonely part, when I saw half a dozen French toughs beating up a respectable-looking old gentleman. I hate a one-sided show, so I promptly butted in and proceeded to beat up the toughs. I guess they'd never been hit really hard before. They melted like snow!"

"Good for you, James," said Anthony softly. "I'd like to have seen that scrap."

"Oh, it was nothing much," said Jimmy modestly. "But the old boy was no end grateful. He'd had a couple, no doubt about that, but he was sober enough to get my name and address out of me, and he came along and thanked me next day. Did the thing in style, too. It was then that I found out it was Count Stylptitch I'd rescued. He'd got a house up by the Bois."

Anthony nodded.

"Yes, Stylptitch went to live in Paris after the assassination of King Nicholas. They wanted him to come back and be president later, but he wasn't taking any. He remained sound to his monarchical principles, though he was reported to have his finger in all the backstairs pies that went on in the Balkans. Very deep, the late Count Stylptitch."

"Nicholas IV was the man who had a funny taste in wives, wasn't he?" said Jimmy suddenly.

"Yes," said Anthony. "And it did for him, too, poor beggar. She was some little guttersnipe of a music hall artiste in Paris—not even suitable for a morganatic alliance. But Nicholas had a frightful crush on her, and she was all out for being a queen. Sounds fantastic, but they managed it somehow. Called her the Countess Popoffsky, or something, and pretended she had Romanoff blood in her veins. Nicholas married her in the cathedral at Ekarest with a couple of unwilling archbishops to do the job, and she was crowned as Queen Varaga. Nicholas squared his ministers, and I suppose he thought that was all that mattered—but he forgot to reckon with the populace. They're very aristocratic and reactionary in Herzoslovakia. They like their kings and queens to be the genuine article. There were mutterings and discontent, and the usual ruthless suppressions, and the final uprising which stormed the palace, murdered the King and Queen, and proclaimed a republic. It's been a republic ever since—but things still manage to be pretty lively there, so I've heard. They've assassinated a president or two, just to keep their hand in. But *revenons à nos moutons*. You had got to where Count Stylptitch was hailing you as his preserver."

"Yes. Well, that was the end of that business. I came back to Africa and never thought of it again until about two weeks ago I got a queer-looking parcel which had been following me all over the place for the Lord knows how long. I'd seen in a paper that Count Stylptitch had recently died in Paris. Well, this parcel contained his memoirs—or reminiscences, or whatever you call the things. There was a note enclosed to the effect that if I delivered the manuscript at a certain firm of publishers in London on or before October 13th, they were instructed to hand me a thousand pounds."

"A thousand pounds? Did you say a thousand pounds, Jimmy?"

"I did, my son. I hope to God it's not a hoax. Put not your trust in princes or politicians, as the saying goes. Well, there it is. Owing to the way the manuscript had been following me around, I had no time to lose. It was a pity, all the same. I'd just fixed up this trip to the interior, and I'd set my heart on going. I shan't get such a good chance again."

"You're incurable, Jimmy. A thousand pounds in the hand is worth a lot of mythical gold."

"And supposing it's all a hoax? Anyway, here I am, passage

booked and everything, on the way to Cape Town—and then you blow along!"

Anthony got up and lit a cigarette.

"I begin to perceive your drift, James. You go gold hunting as planned, and I collect the thousand pounds for you. How much do I get out of it?"

"What do you say to a quarter?"

"Two hundred and fifty pounds free of income tax, as the saying goes?"

"That's it."

"Done, and just to make you gnash your teeth I'll tell you that I would have gone for a hundred! Let me tell you, James McGrath, *you* won't die in your bed counting up your bank balance."

"Anyway, it's a deal?"

"It's a deal all right. I'm on. And confusion to Castle's Select Tours."

They drank the toast solemnly.

# Two

## A Lady in Distress

"So that's that," said Anthony, finishing off his glass and replacing it on the table. "What boat were you going on?"

"*Granarth Castle.*"

"Passage booked in your name, I suppose, so I'd better travel as James McGrath. We've outgrown the passport business, haven't we.

"No odds either way. You and I are totally unlike, but we'd probably have the same description on one of those blinking things. Height six feet, hair brown, eyes blue, nose ordinary, chin ordinary—"

"Not so much of this 'ordinary' stunt. Let me tell you that Castle's selected me out of several applicants solely on account of my pleasing appearance and nice manners."

Jimmy grinned.

"I noticed your manners this morning."

"The devil you did."

Anthony rose and paced up and down the room. His brow was slightly wrinkled, and it was some minutes before he spoke.

"Jimmy," he said at last. "Stylptitch died in Paris. What's the point of sending a manuscript from Paris to London via Africa?"

Jimmy shook his head helplessly.

"I don't know."

"Why not do it up in a nice little parcel and send it by post?"

"Sounds a damn sight more sensible, I agree."

"Of course," continued Anthony, "I know that kings and queens and government officials are prevented by etiquette from doing anything in a simple, straightforward fashion. Hence King's Messengers and all that. In medieval days you gave a fellow a signet ring as a sort of open sesame. 'The King's Ring! Pass, my lord!' And usually it was the other fellow who had stolen it. I always wonder why some bright lad never hit on the expedient of copying the ring—making a dozen or so, and selling them at a hundred ducats apiece. They seem to have had no initiative in the Middle Ages."

Jimmy yawned.

"My remarks on the Middle Ages don't seem to amuse you. Let us get back to Count Stylptitch. From France to England via Africa seems a bit thick even for a diplomatic personage. If he merely wanted to ensure that you should get a thousand pounds he could have left it you in his will. Thank God neither you nor I are too proud to accept a legacy! Stylptitch must have been barmy."

"You'd think so, wouldn't you?"

Anthony frowned and continued his pacing.

"Have you read the thing at all?" he asked suddenly.

"Read what?"

"The manuscript."

"Good Lord, no. What do you think I want to read a thing of that kind for?"

Anthony smiled.

"I just wondered, that's all. You know a lot of trouble has been caused by memoirs. Indiscreet revelations, that sort of thing. People who have been close as an oyster all their lives seem positively to relish causing trouble when they themselves shall be comfortably dead. It gives them a kind of malicious glee. Jimmy, what sort of a man was Count Stylptitch? You met him and talked to him, and you're a pretty good judge of raw human nature. Could you imagine him being a vindictive old devil?"

Jimmy shook his head.

"It's difficult to tell. You see, that first night he was distinctly canned, and the next day he was just a high-toned old boy with the most beautiful manners overwhelming me with compliments till I didn't know where to look."

"And he didn't say anything interesting when he was drunk?"

Jimmy cast his mind back, wrinkling his brows as he did so.

"He said he knew where the Koh-i-noor was," he volunteered doubtfully.

"Oh, well," said Anthony, "we all know that. They keep it in the Tower, don't they? Behind thick plate glass and iron bars, with a lot of gentlemen in fancy dress standing round to see you don't pinch anything."

"That's right," agreed Jimmy.

"Did Stylptitch say anything else of the same kind? That he knew which city the Wallace Collection was in, for instance?"

Jimmy shook his head.

"Hm!" said Anthony.

He lit another cigarette, and once more began pacing up and down the room.

"You never read the papers, I suppose, you heathen?" he threw out presently.

"Not very often," said McGrath simply. "They're not about anything that interests me as a rule."

"Thank heaven I'm more civilized. There have been several mentions of Herzoslovakia lately. Hints at a royalist restoration."

"Nicholas IV didn't leave a son," said Jimmy. "But I don't suppose for a minute that the Obolovitch dynasty is extinct. There are probably shoals of young 'uns knocking about, cousins and second cousins and third cousins once removed."

"So that there wouldn't be any difficulty in finding a king?"

"Not in the least, I should say," replied Jimmy. "You know, I don't wonder at their getting tired of republican institutions. A full-blooded, virile people like that must find it awfully tame to pot at presidents after being used to kings. And talking of kings, that reminds me of something else old Stylptitch let out that night. He said he knew the gang that was after him. They were King Victor's people, he said."

"What?" Anthony wheeled round suddenly.

A short grin widened on McGrath's face.

"Just a mite excited, aren't you, Gentleman Joe?" he drawled.

"Don't be an ass, Jimmy. You've just said something rather important."

He went over to the window and stood there looking out.

"Who is this King Victor, anyway?" demanded Jimmy. "Another Balkan monarch?"

"No," said Anthony slowly. "He isn't that kind of a king."

"What is he, then?"

There was a pause, and then Anthony spoke.

"He's a crook, Jimmy. The most notorious jewel thief in the world. A fantastic, daring fellow, not to be daunted by anything. King Victor was the nickname he was known by in Paris. Paris was the headquarters of his gang. They caught him there and put him away for seven years on a minor charge. They couldn't prove the more important things against him. He'll be out soon—or he may be out already."

"Do you think Count Stylptitch had anything to do with putting him away? Was that why the gang went for him? Out of revenge?"

"I don't know," said Anthony. "It doesn't seem likely on the face of it. King Victor never stole the crown jewels of Herzoslovakia as far as I've heard. But the whole thing seems rather suggestive, doesn't it? The death of Stylptitch, the memoirs, and the rumours in the papers—all vague but interesting. And there's a further rumour to the effect that they've found oil in Herzoslovakia. I've a feeling in my bones, James, that people are getting ready to be interested in that unimportant little country."

"What sort of people?"

"Hebraic people. Yellow-faced financiers in city offices."

"What are you driving at with all this?"

"Trying to make an easy job difficult, that's all."

"You can't pretend there's going to be any difficulty in handing over a simple manuscript at a publisher's office?"

"No," said Anthony regretfully. "I don't suppose there'll be anything difficult about that. But shall I tell you, James, where I propose to go with my two hundred and fifty pounds?"

"South America?"

"No, my lad, Herzoslovakia. I shall stand in with the republic, I think. Very probably I shall end up as president."

"Why not announce yourself as the principal Obolovitch and be a king whilst you're about it?"

"No, Jimmy. Kings are for life. Presidents only take on the job for four years or so. It would quite amuse me to govern a kingdom like Herzoslovakia for four years."

"The average for kings is even less, I should say," interpolated Jimmy.

"It will probably be a serious temptation to me to embezzle your share of the thousand pounds. You won't want it, you know, when you get back weighed down with nuggets. I'll invest it for you in Herzoslovakian oil shares. You know, James, the more I think of it, the more pleased I am with this idea of yours. I should never have thought of Herzoslovakia if you hadn't mentioned it. I shall spend one day in London, collecting the booty, and then away by the Balkan Express!"

"You won't get off quite as fast as that. I didn't mention it before, but I've got another little commission for you."

Anthony sank into a chair and eyed him severely.

"I knew all along that you were keeping something dark. This is where the catch comes in."

"Not a bit. It's just something that's got to be done to help a lady."

"Once and for all, James, I refuse to be mixed up in your beastly love affairs."

"It's not a love affair. I've never seen the woman. I'll tell you the whole story."

"If I've got to listen to more of your long, rambling stories, I shall have to have another drink."

His host complied hospitably with this demand, then began the tale.

"It was when I was up in Uganda. There was a dago there whose life I had saved—"

"If I were you, Jimmy, I should write a short book entitled 'Lives I have Saved.' This is the second I've heard of this evening."

"Oh, well, I didn't really do anything this time. Just pulled the dago out of the river. Like all dagos, he couldn't swim."

"Wait a minute, has this story anything to do with the other business?"

"Nothing whatever, though, oddly enough, now I remember it, the man was a Herzoslovakian. We always called him Dutch Pedro, though."

Anthony nodded indifferently.

"Any name's good enough for a dago," he remarked. "Get on with the good work, James."

"Well, the fellow was sort of grateful about it. Hung around like a dog. About six months later he died of fever. I was with him. Last thing, just as he was pegging out, he beckoned me and whispered some excited jargon about a secret—a gold mine, I thought he said. Shoved an oilskin packet into my hand which he'd always worn next his skin. Well, I didn't think much of it at the time. It wasn't until a week afterwards that I opened the packet. Then I was curious, I must confess. I shouldn't have thought that Dutch Pedro would have had the sense to know a gold mine when he saw it—but there's no accounting for luck—"

"And at the mere thought of gold, your heart beat pitterpat as always," interrupted Anthony.

"I was never so disgusted in my life. Gold mine, indeed! I daresay it may have been a gold mine to him, the dirty dog. Do you know what it was? A woman's letters—yes, a woman's letters, and an Englishwoman at that. The skunk had been blackmailing her—and he had the impudence to pass on his dirty bag of tricks to me."

"I like to see your righteous heat, James, but let me point out to you that dagos will be dagos. He meant well. You had saved his life, he bequeathed to you a profitable source of raising money—your high-minded British ideals did not enter his horizon."

"Well, what the hell was I to do with the things? Burn 'em, that's what I thought at first. And then it occurred to me that there would be that poor dame, not knowing they'd been destroyed, and always living in a quake and a dread lest that dago should turn up again one day."

"You've more imagination than I gave you credit for, Jimmy," observed Anthony, lighting a cigarette. "I admit that the case presented more difficulties than were at first apparent. What about just sending them to her by post?"

"Like all women, she'd put no date and no address on most of the letters. There was a kind of address on one—just one word. 'Chimneys.' "

Anthony paused in the act of blowing out his match, and he dropped it with a quick jerk of the wrist as it burned his finger.

"Chimneys?" he said. "That's rather extraordinary."

"Why, do you know it?"

"It's one of the stately homes of England, my dear James. A

place where kings and queens go for weekends, and diplomatists forgather and diplome."

"That's one of the reasons why I'm so glad that you're going to England instead of me. You know all these things," said Jimmy simply. "A josser like myself from the backwoods of Canada would be making all sorts of bloomers. But someone like you who's been to Eton and Harrow—"

"Only one of them," said Anthony modestly.

"Will be able to carry it through. Why didn't I send them to her, you say? Well, it seemed to me dangerous. From what I could make out, she seemed to have a jealous husband. Suppose he opened the letter by mistake. Where would the poor dame be then? Or she might be dead—the letters looked as though they'd been written some time. As I figured it out, the only thing was for someone to take them to England and put them into her own hands."

Anthony threw away his cigarette, and coming across to his friend, clapped him affectionately on the back.

"You're a real knight-errant, Jimmy," he said. "And the backwoods of Canada should be proud of you. I shan't do the job half as prettily as you would."

"You'll take it on, then?"

"Of course."

McGrath rose, and going across to a drawer, took out a bundle of letters and threw them on the table.

"Here you are. You'd better have a look at them."

"Is it necessary? On the whole, I'd rather not."

"Well, from what you say about this Chimneys place, she may have been staying there only. We'd better look through the letters and see if there's any clue as to where she really hangs out."

"I suppose you're right."

They went through the letters carefully, but without finding what they had hoped to find. Anthony gathered them up again thoughtfully.

"Poor little devil," he remarked. "She was scared stiff."

Jimmy nodded.

"Do you think you'll be able to find her all right?" he asked anxiously.

"I won't leave England till I have. You're very concerned about this unknown lady, James?"

Jimmy ran his finger thoughtfully over the signature.

"It's a pretty name," he said apologetically. *"Virginia Revel."*

# Three

## Anxiety in High Places

"Quite so, my dear fellow, quite so," said Lord Caterham.

He had used the same words three times already, each time in the hope that they would end the interview and permit him to escape. He disliked very much being forced to stand on the steps of the exclusive London club to which he belonged and listen to the interminable eloquence of the Hon. George Lomax.

Clement Edward Alistair Brent, ninth Marquis of Caterham, was a small gentleman, shabbily dressed, and entirely unlike the popular conception of a marquis. He had faded blue eyes, a thin melancholy nose,and a vague but courteous manner.

The principal misfortune of Lord Caterham's life was to have succeeded his brother, the eighth marquis, four years ago. For the previous Lord Caterham had been a man of mark, a household word all over England. At one time Secretary of State for Foreign Affairs, he had always bulked largely in the counsels of the Empire, and his country seat, Chimneys, was famous for its hospitality. Ably seconded by his wife, a daughter of the Duke of Perth, history had been made and unmade at informal weekend parties at Chimneys, and there was hardly anyone of note in England—or indeed in Europe—who had not, at one time or another, stayed there.

That was all very well. The ninth Marquis of Caterham had the utmost respect and esteem for the memory of his brother. Henry had done that kind of thing magnificently. What Lord Caterham objected to was the assumption that Chimneys was a national possession rather than a private country house. There was nothing that bored Lord Caterham more than politics—unless it was politicians. Hence his impatience under the continued eloquence of George Lomax. A robust man, George Lomax, inclined to *embonpoint,* with a red face and protuberant eyes, and an immense sense of his own importance.

"You see the point, Caterham? We can't—we simply can't afford a scandal of any kind just now. The position is one of the utmost delicacy."

"It always is," said Lord Caterham, with a flavour of irony.

"My dear fellow, I'm in a position to *know!*"

"Oh, quite so, quite so," said Lord Caterham, falling back upon his previous line of defence.

"One slip over this Herzoslovakian business and we're done. It is most important that the oil concessions should be granted to a British company. You must see that?"

"Of course, of course."

"Prince Michael Obolovitch arrives the end of the week, and the whole thing can be carried through at Chimneys under the guise of a shooting party."

"I was thinking of going abroad this week," said Lord Caterham.

"Nonsense, my dear Caterham, no one goes abroad in early October."

"My doctor seems to think I'm in rather a bad way," said Lord Caterham, longingly eyeing a taxi that was crawling past.

He was quite unable to make a dash for liberty, however, since Lomax had the unpleasant habit of retaining a hold upon a person with whom he was engaged in serious conversation—doubtless the result of long experience. In this case, he had a firm grip of the lapel of Lord Caterham's coat.

"My dear man, I put it to you imperially. In a moment of national crisis, such as is fast approaching—"

Lord Caterham wriggled uneasily. He felt suddenly that he would rather give any number of house parties than listen to George Lomax quoting from one of his own speeches. He knew by experience that Lomax was quite capable of going on for twenty minutes without a stop.

"All right," he said hastily, "I'll do it. You'll arrange the whole thing, I suppose."

"My dear fellow, there's nothing to arrange. Chimneys, quite apart from its historic associations, is ideally situated. I shall be at the Abbey, less than seven miles away. It wouldn't do, of course, for me to be actually a member of the house party."

"Of course not," agreed Lord Caterham, who had no idea why it would not do, and was not interested to learn.

"Perhaps you wouldn't mind having Bill Eversleigh, though. He'd be useful to run messages."

"Delighted," said Lord Caterham, with a shade more animation. "Bill's quite a decent shot, and Bundle likes him."

"The shooting, of course, is not really important. It's only the pretext, as it were."

Lord Caterham looked depressed again.

"That will be all, then. The Prince, his suite, Bill Eversleigh, Herman Isaacstein—"

"Who?"

"Herman Isaacstein. The representative of the syndicate I spoke to you about."

"The all-British syndicate?

"Yes. Why?"

"Nothing—nothing—I only wondered, that's all. Curious names these people have."

"Then, of course, there ought to be one or two outsiders—just to give the thing a *bona fide* appearance. Lady Eileen could see to that—young people, uncritical, and with no idea of politics."

"Bundle would attend to that all right, I'm sure."

"I wonder now." Lomax seemed struck by an idea. "You remember the matter I was speaking about just now?"

"You've been speaking about so many things."

"No, no, I mean this unfortunate contretemps"—he lowered his voice to a mysterious whisper—"the memoirs—Count Stylptitch's memoirs."

"I think you're wrong about that," said Lord Caterham, suppressing a yawn. "People *like* scandal. Damn it all, I read reminiscences myself—and enjoy 'em too."

"The point is not whether people will read them or not—they'll read them fast enough—but their publication at this juncture might ruin everything—everything. The people of Herzoslovakia wish to restore the monarchy, and are prepared to offer the crown to Prince

Michael, who has the support and encouragement of His Majesty's Government—"

"And who is prepared to grant concessions to Mr. Ikey Hermanstein and Co. in return for the loan of a million or so to set him on the throne—"

"Caterham, Caterham," implored Lomax in an agonized whisper. "Discretion, I beg of you. Above all things, discretion."

"And the point is," continued Lord Caterham, with some relish, though he lowered his voice in obedience to the other's appeal, "that some of Stylptitch's reminiscences may upset the applecart. Tyranny and misbehaviour of the Obolovitch family generally, eh? Questions asked in the House. Why replace the present broad-minded and democratic form of government by an obsolete tyranny? Policy dictated by the bloodsucking capitalists. Down with the Government. That kind of thing—eh?"

Lomax nodded.

"And there might be worse still," he breathed. "Suppose—only suppose that some reference should be made to—to that unfortunate disappearance—you know what I mean."

Lord Caterham stared at him.

"No, I don't. What disappearance?"

"You must have heard of it? Why, it happened while they were at Chimneys. Henry was terribly upset about it. It almost ruined his career."

"You interest me enormously," said Lord Caterham. "Who or what disappeared?"

Lomax leant forward and put his mouth to Lord Caterham's ear. The latter withdrew it hastily.

"For God's sake, don't hiss at me."

"You heard what I said?"

"Yes, I did," said Lord Caterham reluctantly. "I remember now hearing something about it at the time. Very curious affair. I wonder who did it. It was never recovered?"

"Never. Of course we had to go about the matter with the utmost discretion. No hint of the loss could be allowed to leak out. But Stylptitch was there at the time. He knew something. Not all, but something. We were at loggerheads with him once or twice over the Turkish question. Suppose that in sheer malice he has set the whole thing down for the world to read. Think of the scandal—of the far-reaching results. Everyone would say—why was it hushed up?"

"Of course they would," said Lord Caterham, with evident enjoyment.

Lomax, whose voice had risen to a high pitch, took a grip on himself.

"I must keep calm," he murmured. "I must keep calm. But I ask you this, my dear fellow. If he didn't mean mischief, why did he send the manuscript to London in this roundabout way?"

"It's odd, certainly. You are sure of your facts?"

"Absolutely. We—er—had our agents in Paris. The memoirs were conveyed away secretly some weeks before his death."

"Yes, it looks as though there's something in it," said Lord Caterham, with the same relish he had displayed before.

"We have found out that they were sent to a man called Jimmy, or James, McGrath, a Canadian at present in Africa."

"Quite an Imperial affair, isn't it?" said Lord Caterham cheerily.

"James McGrath is due to arrive by the *Granarth Castle* tomorrow—Thursday."

"What are you going to do about it?"

"We shall, of course, approach him at once, point out the possibly serious consequences, and beg him to defer publication of the memoirs for at least a month, and in any case to permit them to be judiciously—er—edited."

"Supposing that he says 'No, sir,' or 'I'll goddarned well see you in hell first,' or something bright and breezy like that?" suggested Lord Caterham.

"That's just what I'm afraid of," said Lomax simply. "That's why it suddenly occurred to me that it might be a good thing to ask him down to Chimneys as well. He'd be flattered, naturally, at being asked to meet Prince Michael, and it might be easier to handle him."

"I'm not going to do it," said Lord Caterham hastily. "I don't get on with Canadians, never did—especially those that have lived much in Africa!"

"You'd probably find him a splendid fellow—a rough diamond, you know."

"No, Lomax. I put my foot down there absolutely. Somebody else has got to tackle him."

"It has occurred to me," said Lomax, "that a woman might be very useful here. Told enough and not too much, you understand. A woman could handle the whole thing delicately and with tact—put the position before him, as it were, without getting his back up. Not that I approve of women in politics—St. Stephen's is ruined, absolutely ruined, nowadays. But woman in her own sphere can do wonders. Look at Henry's wife and what she did for him. Marcia was magnificent, unique, a perfect political hostess."

"You don't want to ask Marcia down for this party, do you?" asked Lord Caterham faintly, turning a little pale at the mention of his redoubtable sister-in-law.

"No, no, you misunderstand me. I was speaking of the influence of women in general. No, I suggest a young woman, a woman of charm, beauty, intelligence?"

"Not Bundle? Bundle would be no use at all. She's a red-hot Socialist if she's anything at all, and she'd simply scream with laughter at the suggestion."

"I was not thinking of Lady Eileen. Your daughter, Caterham, is charming, simply charming, but quite a child. We need some one with *savoir faire,* poise, knowledge of the world—Ah, of course, the very person. My cousin Virginia."

"Mrs. Revel?" Lord Caterham brightened up. He began to feel that he might possibly enjoy the party after all. "A very good suggestion of yours, Lomax. The most charming woman in London."

"She is well up in Herzoslovakian affairs too. Her husband was at the Embassy there, you remember. And, as you say, a woman of great personal charm."

"A delightful creature," murmured Lord Caterham.

"That is settled, then."

Mr. Lomax relaxed his hold on Lord Caterham's lapel, and the latter was quick to avail himself of the chance.

"Bye-bye, Lomax, you'll make all the arrangements, won't you?"

He dived into a taxi. As far as it is possible for one upright Christian gentleman to dislike another upright Christian gentleman, Lord Caterham disliked the Hon. George Lomax. He disliked his puffy red face, his heavy breathing, and his prominent earnest blue eyes. He thought of the coming weekend and sighed. A nuisance, an abominable nuisance. Then he thought of Virginia Revel and cheered up a little.

"A delightful creature," he murmured to himself. "A most delightful creature."

# Four

## Introducing a Very Charming Lady

George Lomax returned straightway to Whitehall. As he entered the sumptuous apartment in which he transacted affairs of State, there was a scuffling sound.

Mr. Bill Eversleigh was assiduously filing letters, but a large armchair near the window was still warm from contact with a human form.

A very likeable young man, Bill Eversleigh. Age at a guess, twenty-five, big and rather ungainly in his movements, a pleasantly ugly face, a splendid set of white teeth and a pair of honest brown eyes.

"Richardson sent up that report yet?"

"No, sir. Shall I get on to him about it?"

"It doesn't matter. Any telephone messages?"

"Miss Oscar is dealing with most of them. Mr. Isaacstein wants to know if you can lunch with him at the Savoy tomorrow."

"Tell Miss Oscar to look in my engagement book. If I'm not engaged, she can ring up and accept."

"Yes, sir."

"By the way, Eversleigh, you might ring up a number for me now. Look it up in the book. Mrs. Revel, 487 Pont Street."

"Yes, sir."

Bill seized the telephone book, ran an unseeing eye down a column of M's, shut the book with a bang and moved to the instrument on the desk. With his hand upon it, he paused, as though in sudden recollection.

"Oh, I say, sir, I've just remembered. Her line's out of order. Mrs. Revel's, I mean. I was trying to ring her up just now."

George Lomax frowned.

"Annoying," he said, "distinctly annoying." He tapped the table undecidedly.

"If it's anything important, sir, perhaps I might go round there now in a taxi. She is sure to be in at this time in the morning."

George Lomax hesitated, pondering the matter. Bill waited expectantly, poised for instant flight, should the reply be favourable.

"Perhaps that would be the best plan," said Lomax at last. "Very well, then, take a taxi there, and ask Mrs. Revel if she will be at home this afternoon at four o'clock as I am very anxious to see her about an important matter."

"Right, sir."

Bill seized his hat and departed.

Ten minutes later, a taxi deposited him at 487 Pont Street. He rang the bell and executed a loud rat-tat on the knocker. The door was opened by a grave functionary to whom Bill nodded with the ease of long acquaintance.

"Morning, Chilvers, Mrs. Revel in?"

"I believe, sir, that she is just going out."

"Is that you, Bill?" called a voice over the banisters. "I thought I recognized that muscular knock. Come up and talk to me."

Bill looked up at the face that was laughing down on him, and which was always inclined to reduce him—and not him alone—to a state of babbling incoherency. He took the stairs two at a time and clasped Virginia Revel's outstretched hands tightly in his.

"Hullo, Virginia!"

"Hullo, Bill!"

Charm is a very peculiar thing; hundreds of young women, some of them more beautiful than Virginia Revel, might have said "Hullo, Bill," with exactly the same intonation, and yet have produced no effect whatever. But those two simple words, uttered by Virginia, had the most intoxicating effect upon Bill.

Virginia Revel was just twenty-seven. She was tall and of an exquisite slimness—indeed, a poem might have been written to her slimness, it was so exquisitely proportioned. Her hair was of real bronze, with the greenish tint in its gold; she had a determined little chin, a lovely nose, slanting blue eyes that showed a gleam of deepest cornflower between the half-closed lids, and a delicious and quite indescribable mouth that tilted ever so slightly at one corner in what is known as "the signature of Venus." It was a wonderfully expressive face, and there was a sort of radiant vitality about her that always challenged attention. It would have been quite impossible ever to ignore Virginia Revel.

She drew Bill into the small drawing room which was all pale mauve and green and yellow, like crocuses surprised in a meadow.

"Bill, darling," said Virginia, "isn't the Foreign Office missing you? I thought they couldn't get on without you."

"I've brought a message for you from Codders."

Thus irreverently did Bill allude to his chief.

"And by the way, Virginia, in case he asks, remember that your telephone was out of order this morning."

"But it hasn't been."

"I know that. But I said it was."

"Why? Enlighten me as to this Foreign Office touch." Bill threw her a reproachful glance.

"So that I could get here and see you, of course."

"Oh, darling Bill, how dense of me! And how perfectly sweet of you!"

"Chilvers said you were going out."

"So I was—to Sloane Street. There's a place there where they've got a perfectly wonderful new hip band."

"A hip band?"

"Yes, Bill, H-I-P hip, B-A-N-D band. A band to confine the hips. You wear it next the skin."

"I blush for you Virginia. You shouldn't describe your underwear to a young man to whom you are not related. It isn't delicate."

"But, Bill dear, there's nothing indelicate about hips. We've all got hips—although we poor women are trying awfully hard to pretend we haven't. This hip band is made of red rubber and comes to just above the knees, and it's simply impossible to walk in it."

"How awful!" said Bill. "Why do you do it?"

"Oh, because it gives one such a noble feeling to suffer for one's silhouette. But don't let's talk about my hip band. Give me George's message."

"He wants to know whether you'll be in at four o'clock this afternoon."

"I shan't. I shall be at Ranelagh. Why this sort of formal call? Is he going to propose to me, do you think?"

"I shouldn't wonder."

"Because, if so, you can tell him that I much prefer men who propose on impulse."

"Like me?"

"It's not an impulse with you, Bill. It's habit."

"Virginia, won't you ever—"

"No, no, no, Bill. I won't have it in the morning before lunch. Do try and think of me as a nice motherly person approaching middle age who has your interests thoroughly at heart."

"Virginia, I do love you so."

"I know, Bill, I know. And I simply love being loved. Isn't it wicked and dreadful of me? I should like every nice man in the world to be in love with me."

"Most of them are, I expect," said Bill gloomily.

"But I hope George isn't in love with me. I don't think he can be. He's so wedded to his career. What else did he say?"

"Just that it was very important."

"Bill, I'm getting intrigued. The things that George thinks important are so awfully limited. I think I must chuck Ranelagh. After all, I can go to Ranelagh any day. Tell George that I shall be awaiting him meekly at four o'clock."

Bill looked at his wristwatch.

"It seems hardly worthwhile to go back before lunch. Come out and chew something, Virginia."

"I'm going out to lunch somewhere or other."

"That doesn't matter. Make a day of it, and chuck everything all round."

"It would be rather nice," said Virginia, smiling at him.

"Virginia, you're a darling. Tell me, you do like me rather, don't you? Better than other people."

"Bill, I adore you. If I had to marry someone—simply had to—I mean if it was in a book and a wicked mandarin said to me, 'Marry someone or die by slow torture,' I should choose you at once—I should indeed. I should say, 'Give me little Bill.' "

"Well, then—"

"Yes, but I haven't got to marry anyone. I love being a wicked widow."

"You could do all the same things still. Go about, and all that. You'd hardly notice me about the house."

"Bill, you don't understand. I'm the kind of person who marries enthusiastically if they marry at all."

Bill gave a hollow groan.

"I shall shoot myself one of these days, I expect," he murmured gloomily.

"No, you won't, Bill darling. You'll take a pretty girl out to supper—like you did the night before last."

Mr. Eversleigh was momentarily confused.

"If you mean Dorothy Kirkpatrick, the girl who's in *Hooks and Eyes,* I—well, dash it all, she's a thoroughly nice girl, straight as they make 'em. There was no harm in it."

"Bill darling, of course there wasn't. I love you to enjoy yourself. But don't pretend to be dying of a broken heart, that's all."

Mr. Eversleigh recovered his dignity.

"You don't understand at all, Virginia," he said severely. "Men—"

"Are polygamous! I know they are. Sometimes I have a shrewd suspicion that I am polyandrous. If you really love me, Bill, take me out to lunch quickly."

# Five

There is often a flaw in the best-laid plans. George Lomax had made one mistake—there was a weak spot in his preparations. The weak spot was Bill.

Bill Eversleigh was an extremely nice lad. He was a good cricketer and a scratch golfer, he had pleasant manners, and an amiable disposition, but his position in the Foreign Office had been gained, not by brains, but by good connexions. For the work he had to do he was quite suitable. He was more or less George's dog. He did no responsible or brainy work. His part was to be constantly at George's elbow, to interview unimportant people whom George didn't want to see, to run errands, and generally to make himself useful. All this Bill carried out faithfully enough. When George was absent, Bill stretched himself out in the biggest chair and read the sporting news, and in so doing he was merely carrying out a time-honoured tradition.

Being accustomed to send Bill on errands, George had dispatched him to the Union Castle offices to find out when the *Granarth Castle* was due in. Now, in common with most well-educated young Englishmen, Bill had a pleasant but quite inaudible voice. Any elocution master would have found fault with his pronunciation of the word Granarth. It might have been anything. The clerk took it to be Carnfrae.

The *Carnfrae Castle* was due in on the following Thursday. He said so. Bill thanked him and went out. George Lomax accepted the information and laid his plans accordingly. He knew nothing about Union Castle liners, and took it for granted that James McGrath would duly arrive on Thursday.

Therefore, at the moment he was buttonholing Lord Caterham on the steps of the club on Wednesday morning, he would have been greatly surprised to learn that the *Granarth Castle* had docked at Southampton the preceding afternoon. At two o'clock that afternoon Anthony Cade, travelling under the name of Jimmy McGrath, stepped out of the boat train at Waterloo, hailed a taxi, and after a moment's hesitation, ordered the driver to proceed to the Blitz Hotel.

"One might as well be comfortable," said Anthony to himself as he looked with some interest out of the taxi windows.

It was exactly fourteen years since he had been in London.

He arrived at the hotel, booked a room, and then went for a short stroll along the Embankment. It was rather pleasant to be back in London again. Everything was changed of course. There had been a little restaurant there—just past Blackfriars Bridge—where he had dined fairly often, in company with other earnest lads. He had been a Socialist then, and worn a flowing red tie. Young—very young.

He retraced his steps back to the Blitz. Just as he was crossing the road, a man jostled against him, nearly making him lose his balance. They both recovered themselves, and the man muttered an apology, his eyes scanning Anthony's face narrowly. He was a short, thickset man of the working classes, with something foreign in his appearance.

Anthony went on into the hotel, wondering, as he did so, what had inspired that searching glance. Nothing in it probably. The deep tan of his face was somewhat unusual looking amongst these pallid Londoners and it had attracted the fellow's attention. He went up to his room and, led by a sudden impulse, crossed to the looking glass and stood studying his face in it. Of the few friends of the old days—just a chosen few—was it likely that any of them would recognize him now if they were to meet him face to face? He shook his head slowly.

When he had left London he had been just eighteen—a fair, slightly chubby boy, with a misleadingly seraphic expression. Small chance that that boy would be recognized in the lean, brown-faced man with the quizzical expression.

The telephone beside the bed rang, and Anthony crossed to the receiver.

"Hullo!"

The voice of the desk clerk answered him.

"Mr. James McGrath?"

"Speaking."

"A gentleman has called to see you."

Anthony was rather astonished.

"To see *me?*"

"Yes, sir, a foreign gentleman."

"What's his name?"

There was a slight pause, and then the clerk said:

"I will send up a page boy with his card."

Anthony replaced the receiver and waited. In a few minutes there was a knock on the door and a small page appeared bearing a card upon a salver.

Anthony took it. The following was the name engraved upon it.

*Baron Lolopretjzyl*

He now fully appreciated the desk clerk's pause.

For a moment or two he stood studying the card, and then made up his mind.

"Show the gentleman up."

"Very good, sir."

In a few minutes the Baron Lolopretjzyl was ushered into the room, a big man with an immense fan-like black beard and a high, bald forehead.

He brought his heels together with a click, and bowed.

"Mr. McGrath," he said.

Anthony imitated his movements as nearly as possible.

"Baron," he said. Then, drawing forward a chair, "Pray sit down. I have not, I think had the pleasure of meeting you before?"

"That is so," agreed the Baron, seating himself. "It is my misfortune," he added politely.

"And mine also," responded Anthony, on the same note.

"Let us now to business come," said the Baron. "I represent in London the Loyalist party of Herzoslovakia."

"And represent it admirably, I am sure," murmured Anthony.

The Baron bowed in acknowledgement of the compliment.

"You are too kind," he said stiffly. "Mr. McGrath, I will not from you conceal anything. The moment has come for the restoration of the monarchy, in abeyance since the martyrdom of His Most Gracious Majesty King Nicholas IV of blessed memory."

"Amen," murmured Anthony. "I mean hear, hear."

"On the throne will be placed His Highness Prince Michael, who the support of the British Government has."

"Splendid," said Anthony. "It's very kind of you to tell me all this."

"Everything arranged is—when you come here to trouble make."

The Baron fixed him with a stern eye.

"My dear Baron," protested Anthony.

"Yes, yes, I know what I am talking about. You have with you the memoirs of the late Count Stylptitch."

He fixed Anthony with an accusing eye.

"And if I have? What have the memoirs of Count Stylptitch to do with Prince Michael?"

"They will cause scandals."

"Most memoirs do that," said Anthony soothingly.

"Of many secrets he the knowledge had. Should he reveal but the quarter of them, Europe into war plunged may be."

"Come, come," said Anthony. "It can't be as bad as all that."

"An unfavourable opinion of the Obolovitch will abroad be spread. So democratic is the English spirit."

"I can quite believe," said Anthony, "that the Obolovitch may have been a trifle high-handed now and again. It runs in the blood.

But people in England expect that sort of thing from the Balkans. I don't know why they should, but they do."

"You do not understand," said the Baron. "You do not understand at all. And my lips sealed are." He sighed.

"What exactly are you afraid of?" asked Anthony.

"Until I have read the memoirs I do not know," explained the Baron simply. "But there is sure to be something. These great diplomats are always indiscreet. The applecart upset will be, as the saying goes."

"Look here," said Anthony kindly. "I'm sure you're taking altogether too pessimistic a view of the thing. I know all about publishers—they sit on manuscripts and hatch 'em like eggs. It will be at least a year before the thing is published."

"Either a very deceitful or a very simple young man you are. All is arranged for the memoirs in a Sunday newspaper to come out immediately.

"Oh!" Anthony was somewhat taken aback. "But you can always deny everything," he said hopefully.

The Baron shook his head sadly.

"No, no, through the hat you talk. Let us to business come. One thousand pounds you are to have, is it not so? You see, I have the good information got."

"I certainly congratulate the Intelligence Department of the Loyalists."

"Then I to you offer fifteen hundred."

"Anthony stared at him in amazement, then shook his head ruefully.

"I'm afraid it can't be done," he said, with regret.

"Good. I to you offer two thousand."

"You tempt me, Baron, you tempt me. But I still say it can't be done."

"Your own price name, then."

"I'm afraid you don't understand the position. I'm perfectly willing to believe that you are on the side of the angels, and that these memoirs may damage your cause. Nevertheless, I've undertaken the job, and I've got to carry it through. See? I can't allow myself to be bought off by the other side. That kind of thing isn't done."

The Baron listened very attentively. At the end of Anthony's speech he nodded his head several times.

"I see. Your honour as an Englishman it is?"

"Well, we don't put it that way ourselves," said Anthony. "But I daresay, allowing for a difference in vocabulary, that we both mean much the same thing."

The Baron rose to his feet.

"For the English honour I much respect have," he announced. "We must another way try. I wish you good morning."

He drew his heels together, clicked, bowed and marched out of the room, holding himself stiffly erect.

"Now I wonder what he meant by that," mused Anthony. "Was it a threat? Not that I'm in the least afraid of old Lollipop. Rather a good name for him, that, by the way. I shall call him Baron Lollipop."

He took a turn or two up and down the room, undecided on his next course of action. The date stipulated upon for delivering the manuscript was a little over a week ahead. Today was the 5th of October. Anthony had no intention of handing it over before the last moment. Truth to tell, he was by now feverishly anxious to read these memoirs. He had meant to do so on the boat coming over, but had been laid low with a touch of fever, and not at all in the mood for deciphering crabbed and illegible handwriting, for none of the manuscript was typed. He was now more than ever determined to see what all the fuss was about.

There was the other job too.

On an impulse, he picked up the telephone book and looked up the name of Revel. There were six Revels in the book: Edward Henry Revel, surgeon, of Harley Street; and James Revel and Co., saddlers; Lennox Revel of Abbotbury Mansions, Hampstead; Miss Mary Revel with an address in Ealing; Hon. Mrs. Timothy Revel of 487 Pont Street; and Mrs. Willis Revel of 42 Cadogan Square. Eliminating the saddlers and Miss Mary Revel, that gave him four names to investigate—and there was no reason to suppose that the lady lived in London at all! He shut up the book with a short shake of the head.

"For the moment I'll leave it to chance," he said. "Something usually turns up."

The luck of the Anthony Cades of this world is perhaps in some measure due to their own belief in it. Anthony found what he was after not half an hour later, when he was turning over the pages of an illustrated paper. It was a representation of some tableaux organized by the Duchess of Perth. Below the central figure, a woman in Eastern dress, was the inscription:

*The Hon. Mrs. Timothy Revel as Cleopatra. Before her marriage, Mrs. Revel was the Hon. Virginia Cawthron, a daughter of Lord Edgbaston.*

Anthony looked at the picture some time, slowly pursing up his lips as though to whistle. Then he tore out the whole page, folded it up and put it in his pocket. He went upstairs again, unlocked his suitcase and took out the packet of letters. He took out the folded page from his pocket and slipped it under the string that held them together.

Then at a sudden sound behind him, he wheeled round sharply. A man was standing in the doorway, the kind of man whom Anthony had fondly imagined existed only in the chorus of a comic opera. A sinister-looking figure, with a squat brutal head and lips drawn back in an evil grin.

"What the devil are you doing here?" asked Anthony. "And who let you come up?"

"I pass where I please," said the stranger. His voice was guttural and foreign, though his English was idiomatic enough.

"Another dago," thought Anthony.

"Well, get out, do you hear?" he went on aloud.

The man's eyes were fixed on the packet of letters which Anthony had caught up.

"I will get out when you have given me what I have come for."

"And what's that, may I ask?"

The man took a step nearer.

"The memoirs of Count Stylptitch," he hissed.

"It's impossible to take you seriously," said Anthony. "You're so completely the stage villain. I like your getup very much. Who sent you here? Baron Lollipop?"

"Baron?—" The man jerked out a string of harsh sounding consonants.

"So that's how you pronounce it, is it? A cross between gargling and barking like a dog. I don't think I could say it myself—my throat's not made that way. I shall have to go on calling him Lollipop. So he sent you, did he?"

But he received a vehement negative. His visitor went so far as to spit upon the suggestion in a very realistic manner. Then he drew from his pocket a sheet of paper which he threw upon the table.

"Look," he said. "Look and tremble, accursed Englishman."

Anthony looked with some interest, not troubling to fulfil the latter part of the command. On the paper was traced the crude design of a human hand in red.

"It looks like a hand," he remarked. "But, if you say so, I'm quite prepared to admit that it's a Cubist picture of Sunset at the North Pole."

"It is the sign of the Comrades of the Red Hand. I am a Comrade of the Red Hand."

"You don't say so," said Anthony, looking at him with much interest. "Are the others all like you? I don't know what the Eugenic Society would have to say about it."

The man snarled angrily.

"Dog," he said. "Worse than dog. Paid slave of an effete monarchy. Give me the memoirs, and you shall go unscathed. Such is the clemency of the Brotherhood."

"It's very kind of them, I'm sure," said Anthony, "but I'm afraid that both they and you are labouring under a misapprehension. My instructions are to deliver the manuscript—not to your amiable society, but to a certain firm of publishers."

"Pah!" laughed the other. "Do you think you will ever be permitted to reach that office alive? Enough of this fool's talk. Hand over the papers, or I shoot."

He drew a revolver from his pocket and brandished it in the air.

But there he misjudged his Anthony Cade. He was not used to men who could act as quickly—or quicker than they could think. Anthony did not wait to be covered by the revolver. Almost as soon as the other got it out of his pocket, Anthony had sprung forward and knocked it out of his hand. The force of the blow sent the man swinging round, so that he presented his back to his assailant.

The chance was too good to be missed. With one mighty, well-directed kick, Anthony sent the man flying through the doorway into the corridor, where he collapsed in a heap.

Anthony stepped out after him, but the doughty Comrade of the Red Hand had had enough. He got nimbly to his feet and fled down the passage. Anthony did not pursue him, but went back into his own room.

"So much for the Comrades of the Red Hand," he remarked. "Picturesque appearance, but easily routed by direct action. How the hell did that fellow get in, I wonder? There's one thing that stands out pretty clearly—this isn't going to be quite such a soft job as I thought. I've already fallen foul of both the Loyalist and the Revolutionary parties. Soon, I suppose, the Nationalists and the Independent Liberals will be sending up a delegation. One thing's fixed. I start on that manuscript tonight."

Looking at his watch, Anthony discovered that it was nearly nine o'clock, and he decided to dine where he was. He did not anticipate any more surprise visits, but he felt that it was up to him to be on his guard. He had no intention of allowing his suitcase to be rifled whilst he was downstairs in the Grill Room. He rang the bell and asked for the menu, selected a couple of dishes and ordered a bottle of Chambertin. The waiter took the order and withdrew.

Whilst he was waiting for the meal to arrive, he got out the package of manuscript and put it on the table with the letters.

There was a knock at the door, and the waiter entered with a small table and the accessories of the meal. Anthony had strolled over to the mantelpiece. Standing there with his back to the room, he was directly facing the mirror, and idly glancing in it he noticed a curious thing.

The waiter's eyes were glued on the parcel of manuscript. Shooting little glances sideways at Anthony's immovable back, he moved softly round the table. His hands were twitching and he kept passing his tongue over his dry lips. Anthony observed him more closely. He was a tall man, supple like all waiters, with a clean-shaven, mobile face. An Italian, Anthony thought, not a Frenchman.

At the critical moment Anthony wheeled round abruptly. The waiter started slightly, but pretended to be doing something with the saltcellar.

"What's your name?" asked Anthony abruptly.

"Giuseppe, monsieur."

"Italian, eh?"

"Yes, monsieur."

Anthony spoke to him in that language, and the man answered fluently enough. Finally Anthony dismissed him with a nod, but all the while he was eating the excellent meal which Giuseppe served to him, he was thinking rapidly.

Had he been mistaken? Was Giuseppe's interest in the parcel just ordinary curiosity? It might be so, but remembering the feverish intensity of the man's excitement, Anthony decided against that theory. All the same, he was puzzled.

"Dash it all," said Anthony to himself, "everyone can't be after the blasted manuscript. Perhaps I'm fancying things."

Dinner concluded and cleared away, he applied himself to the perusal of the memoirs. Owing to the illegibility of the late Count's handwriting, the business was a slow one. Anthony's yawns succeeded one another with suspicious rapidity. At the end of the fourth chapter, he gave it up.

So far, he had found the memoirs insufferably dull, with no hint of scandal of any kind.

He gathered up the letters and the wrapping of the manuscript which were lying in a heap together on the table and locked them up in the suitcase. Then he locked the door, and as an additional precaution put a chair against it. On the chair he placed the water bottle from the bathroom.

Surveying these preparations with some pride, he undressed and got into bed. He had one more shot at the Count's memoirs, but felt his eyelids drooping, and stuffing the manuscript under his pillow, he switched out the light and fell asleep almost immediately.

It must have been some four hours later that he awoke with a start. What had awakened him he did not know—perhaps a sound, perhaps only the consciousness of danger which in men who have led an adventurous life is very fully developed.

For a moment he lay quite still, trying to focus his impressions. He could hear a very stealthy rustle, and then he became aware of a denser blackness somewhere between him and the window—on the floor by the suitcase.

With a sudden spring, Anthony jumped out of bed, switching

the light on as he did so. A figure sprang up from where it had been kneeling by the suitcase.

It was the waiter, Giuseppe. In his right hand gleamed a long thin knife. He hurled himself straight upon Anthony, who was by now fully conscious of his own danger. He was unarmed and Giuseppe was evidently thoroughly at home with his own weapon.

Anthony sprang to one side, and Giuseppe missed him with the knife. The next minute the two men were rolling on the floor together, locked in a close embrace. The whole of Anthony's faculties were centred on keeping a close grip of Giuseppe's right arm so that he would be unable to use the knife. He bent it slowly back. At the same time he felt the Italian's other hand clutching at his windpipe, stifling him, choking. And still, desperately, he bent the right arm back.

There was a sharp tinkle as the knife fell on the floor. At the same time, the Italian extricated himself with a swift twist from Anthony's grasp. Anthony sprang up too, but made the mistake of moving towards the door to cut off the other's retreat. He saw, too late, that the chair and the water bottle were just as he had arranged them.

Giuseppe had entered by the window, and it was the window he made for now. In the instant's respite given him by Anthony's move towards the door, he had sprung out on the balcony, leaped over to the adjoining balcony and had disappeared through the adjoining window.

Anthony knew well enough that it was of no use to pursue him. His way of retreat was doubtless fully assured. Anthony would merely get himself into trouble.

He walked over to the bed, thrusting his hand beneath the pillow and drawing out the memoirs. Lucky that they had been there and not in the suitcase. He crossed over to the suitcase and looked inside, meaning to take out the letters.

Then he swore softly under his breath.

The letters were gone.

# Six

## The Gentle Art of Blackmail

It was exactly five minutes to four when Virginia Revel, rendered punctual by a healthy curiosity, returned to the house in Pont Street. She opened the door with her latchkey, and stepped into the hall to be immediately confronted by the impassive Chilvers.

"I beg pardon, ma'am, but a—a person has called to see you—"

For the moment, Virginia did not pay attention to the subtle phraseology whereby Chilvers cloaked his meaning.

"Mr. Lomax? Where is he? In the drawing room?"

"Oh, no, ma'am, not Mr. Lomax." Chilvers' tone was faintly reproachful. "A person—I was reluctant to let him in, but he said his business was most important—connected with the late Captain, I understood him to say. Thinking therefore that you might wish to see him, I put him—er—in the study."

Virginia stood thinking for a minute. She had been a widow now for some years, and the fact that she rarely spoke of her husnd was taken by some to indicate that below her careless de-meanour was a still-aching wound. By others it was taken to mean the exact opposite, that Virginia had never really cared for Tim Revel, and that she found it insincere to profess a grief she did not feel.

"I should have mentioned, ma'am," continued Chilvers, "that the man appears to be some kind of foreigner."

Virginia's interest heightened a little. Her husband had been in the Diplomatic Service, and they had been together in Herzoslova-kia just before the sensational murder of the King and Queen. This man might probably be a Herzoslovakian, some old servant who had fallen on evil days.

"You did quite right, Chilvers," she said with a quick, approv-ing nod. "Where did you say you put him? In the study?"

She crossed the hall with her light buoyant step, and opened the door of the small room that flanked the dining room.

The visitor was sitting in a chair by the fireplace. He rose on her entrance and stood looking at her. Virginia had an excellent memory for faces, and she was at once quite sure that she had never seen the man before. He was tall and dark, supple in figure, and quite unmistakably a foreigner; but she did not think he was of Slavonic origin. She put him down as Italian or possibly Spanish.

"You wish to see me?" she asked. "I am Mrs. Revel."

The man did not answer for a minute or two. He was looking her slowly over, as though appraising her narrowly. There was a veiled insolence in his manner which she was quick to feel.

"Will you please state your business?" she said, with a touch of impatience.

"You are Mrs. Revel? Mrs. Timothy Revel?"

"Yes. I told you so just now."

"Quite so. It is a good thing that you consented to see me, Mrs. Revel. Otherwise, as I told your butler, I should have been compelled to do business with your husband."

Virginia looked at him in astonishment, but some impulse quelled the retort that sprang to her lips. She contented herself by remarking dryly:

"You might have found some difficulty in doing that."

"I think not. I am very persistent. But I will come to the point. Perhaps you recognize this?"

He flourished something in his hand. Virginia looked at it without much interest.

"Can you tell me what it is, madame?"

"It appears to be a letter," replied Virginia, who was by now convinced that she had to do with a man who was mentally unhinged.

"And perhaps you note to whom it is addressed," said the man significantly, holding it out to her.

"I can read," Virginia informed him pleasantly. "It is addressed to a Captain O'Neill at Rue de Quenelles No. 15 Paris."

The man seemed searching her face hungrily for something he did not find.

"Will you read it, please?"

Virginia took the envelope from him, drew out the enclosure and glanced at it, but almost immediately she stiffened and held it out to him again.

"This is a private letter—certainly not meant for my eyes."

The man laughed sardonically.

"I congratulate you, Mrs. Revel, on your admirable acting. You play your part to perfection. Nevertheless, I think that you will hardly be able to deny the signature!"

"The signature?"

Virginia turned the letter over—and was struck dumb with astonishment. The signature, written in a delicate slanting hand, was Virginia Revel. Checking the exclamation of astonishment that rose to her lips, she turned again to the beginning of the letter and deliberately read the whole thing through. Then she stood a minute lost in thought. The nature of the letter made it clear enough what was in prospect.

"Well, madame?" said the man. "That is your name, is it not?"

"Oh, yes," said Virginia. "It's my name."

"But not my handwriting," she might have added.

Instead she turned a dazzling smile upon her visitor.

"Supposing," she said sweetly, "we sit down and talk it over?"

He was puzzled. Not so had he expected her to behave. His instinct told him that she was not afraid of him.

"First of all, I should like to know how you found me out?"

"That was easy."

He took from his pocket a page torn from an illustrated paper, and handed it to her. Anthony Cade would have recognized it.

She gave it back to him with a thoughtful little frown.

"I see," she said. "It was very easy."

"Of course you understand, Mrs. Revel, that that is not the only letter. There are others."

"Dear me," said Virginia, "I seem to have been frightfully indiscreet."

Again she could see that her light tone puzzled him. She was by now thoroughly enjoying herself.

"At any rate," she said, smiling sweetly at him, "it's very kind of you to call and give them back to me."

There was a pause as he cleared his throat.

"I am a poor man, Mrs. Revel," he said at last, with a good deal of significance in his manner.

"As such you will doubtless find it easier to enter the Kingdom of Heaven, or so I have always heard."

"I cannot afford to let you have these letters for nothing."

"I think you are under a misapprehension. Those letters are the property of the person who wrote them."

"That may be the law, madame, but in this country you have a saying 'Possession is nine points of the law.' And, in any case, are you prepared to invoke the aid of the law?"

"The law is a severe one for blackmailers," Virginia reminded him.

"Come, Mrs. Revel, I am not quite a fool. I have read these letters—the letters of a woman to her lover, one and all breathing dread of discovery by her husband. Do you want me to take them to your husband?"

"You have overlooked one possibility. Those letters were written some years ago. Supposing that since then—I have become a widow."

He shook his head with confidence.

"In that case—if you had nothing to fear—you would not be sitting here making terms with me."

Virginia smiled.

"What is your price?" she asked in a businesslike manner.

"For one thousand pounds I will hand the whole packet over to you. It is very little that I am asking there; but, you see, I do not like the business."

"I shouldn't dream of paying you a thousand pounds," said Virginia with decision.

"Madame, I never bargain. A thousand pounds, and I will place the letters in your hands."

Virginia reflected.

"You must give me a little time to think it over. It will not be easy for me to get such a sum together."

"A few pounds on account perhaps—say fifty—and I will call again."

Virginia looked up at the clock. It was five minutes past four, and she fancied that she had heard the bell.

"Very well," she said hurriedly. "Come back tomorrow, but later than this. About six."

She crossed over to a desk that stood against the wall, unlocked one of the drawers, and took out an untidy handful of notes.

"There is about forty pounds here. That will have to do for you."

He snatched at it eagerly.

"And now go at once, please," said Virginia.

He left the room obediently enough. Through the open door, Virginia caught a glimpse of George Lomax in the hall, just being ushered upstairs by Chilvers. As the front door closed, Virginia called to him.

"Come in here, George. Chilvers, bring us tea in here, will you please?"

She flung open both windows, and George Lomax came into the room to find her standing erect with dancing eyes and wind-blown hair.

"I'll shut them in a minute, George, but I felt the room ought to be aired. Did you fall over the blackmailer in the hall?"

"The what?"

"Blackmailer, George. B-L-A-C-K-M-A-I-L-E-R: black-mailer. One who blackmails."

"My dear Virginia, you can't be serious!"

"Oh, but I am, George."

"But who did he come here to blackmail?"

"Me, George."

"But, my dear Virginia, what have you been doing?"

"Well, just for once, as it happens, I hadn't been doing any-thing. The good gentleman mistook me for someone else."

"You rang up the police, I suppose?"

"No, I didn't. I suppose you think I ought to have done so."

"Well—" George considered weightily. "No, no, perhaps not—perhaps you acted wisely. You might be mixed up in some unpleas-ant publicity in connexion with the case. You might even have had to give evidence—"

"I should have liked that," said Virginia. "I would love to be summoned, and I should like to see if judges really do make all the rotten jokes you read about. It would be most exciting. I was at Vine Street the other day to see about a diamond brooch I had lost, and there was the most perfectly lovely inspector—the nicest man I ever met."

George, as was his custom, let all irrelevancies pass.

"But what did you do about this scoundrel?"

"Well, George, I'm afraid I let him do it."

"Do what?"

"Blackmail me."

George's face of horror was so poignant that Virginia had to bite her underlip.

"You mean—do I understand you to mean—that you did not correct the misapprehension under which he was labouring?"

Virginia shook her head, shooting a sideways glance at him.

"Good heavens, Virginia, you must be mad."

"I suppose it would seem that way to you."

"But why? In God's name, why?"

"Several reasons. To begin with, he was doing it so beautifully—blackmailing me, I mean—I hate to interrupt an artist when he's doing his job really well. And then, you see, I'd never been blackmailed—"

"I should hope not, indeed."

"And I wanted to see what it felt like."

"I am quite at a loss to comprehend you, Virginia."

"I knew you wouldn't understand."

"You did not give him money, I hope?"

"Just a trifle," said Virginia apologetically.

"How much?"

"Forty pounds."

"Virginia!"

"My dear George, it's only what I pay for an evening dress. It's just as exciting to buy a new experience as it is to buy a new dress—more so, in fact."

George Lomax merely shook his head, and Chilvers appearing at that moment with the tea urn, he was saved from having to express his outraged feelings. When tea had been brought in, and Virginia's deft fingers were manipulating the heavy silver teapot, she spoke again on the subject.

"I had another motive too, George—a brighter and better one. We women are usually supposed to be cats, but at any rate I'd done another woman a good turn this afternoon. This man isn't likely to go off looking for another Virginia Revel. He thinks he's found his bird all right. Poor little devil, she was in a blue funk when she wrote that letter. Mr. Blackmailer would have had the easiest job in his life there. Now, though he doesn't know it, he's up against a tough proposition. Starting with the great advantage of having led a blameless life, I shall toy with him to his undoing—as they say in books. Guile, George, lots of guile."

George still shook his head.

"I don't like it," he persisted. "I don't like it."

"Well, never mind, George dear. You didn't come here to talk about blackmailers. What did you come here for, by the way? Correct answer: 'To see *you!*' Accent on the you, and press her hand with significance unless you happen to have been eating heavily buttered muffin, in which case it must all be done with the eyes."

"I did come to see you," replied George seriously. "And I am glad to find you alone."

" 'Oh, George, this is so sudden.' Says she, swallowing a currant."

"I wanted to ask a favour of you. I have always considered you, Virginia, as a woman of considerable charm."

"Oh, George!"

"And also as a woman of intelligence!"

"Not really? How well the man knows me."

"My dear Virginia, there is a young fellow arriving in England tomorrow whom I should like you to meet."

"All right, George, but it's your party—let that be clearly understood."

"You could, I feel sure, if you chose, exercise your considerable charm."

Virginia cocked her head a little on one side.

"George dear, I don't 'charm' as a profession, you know. Often I like people—and then, well, they like me. But I don't think I could set out in cold blood to fascinate a helpless stranger. That sort of thing isn't done, George, it really isn't. There are professional sirens who would do it much better than I should."

"That is out of the question, Virginia. This young man, he is a Canadian, by the way, of the name of McGrath—"

" 'A Canadian of Scottish descent.' Says she, deducing brilliantly."

"Is probably quite unused to the higher walks of English society. I should like him to appreciate the charm and distinction of a real English gentlewoman."

"Meaning me?"

"Exactly."

"Why?"

"I beg your pardon?"

"I said why? You don't boom the real English gentlewoman with every stray Canadian who sets foot upon our shores. What is the deep idea, George? To put it vulgarly, what do *you* get out of it?"

"I cannot see that that concerns you, Virginia."

"I couldn't possibly go out for an evening and fascinate unless I knew all the whys and wherefores."

"You have a most extraordinary way of putting things, Virginia. Anyone would think—"

"Wouldn't they? Come on, George, part with a little more information."

"My dear Virginia, matters are likely to be a little strained shortly in a certain Central European nation. It is important, for reasons which are immaterial, that this—Mr.—er—McGrath should be brought to realize that the restoring of the monarchy in Herzoslovakia is imperative to the peace of Europe."

"The part about the peace of Europe is all bosh," said Virginia calmly, "but I'm all for monarchies every time, especially for a picturesque people like the Herzoslovakians. So you're running a king in the Herzoslovakian Stakes, are you? Who is he?"

George was reluctant to answer, but did not see his way to avoid the question. The interview was not going at all as he had planned. He had foreseen Virginia as a willing, docile tool, receiving his hints gratefully, and asking no awkward questions. This was far from being the case. She seemed determined to know all about it and this George, ever doubtful of female discretion, was determined at all costs to avoid. He had made a mistake. Virginia was not the woman for the part. She might, indeed, cause serious trouble. Her account of her interview with the blackmailer had caused him grave apprehension. A most undependable creature, with no idea of treating serious matters seriously.

"Prince Michael Obolovitch," he replied, as Virginia was obviously waiting for an answer to her question. "But please let that go no further."

"Don't be absurd, George. There are all sorts of hints in the papers already, and articles cracking up the Obolovitch dynasty and talking about the murdered Nicholas IV as though he were a cross between a saint and a hero instead of a stupid little man besotted by a third-rate actress."

George winced. He was more than ever convinced that he had made a mistake in enlisting Virginia's aid. He must stave her off quickly.

"You are right, my dear Virginia," he said hastily, as he rose to his feet to bid her farewell. "I should not have made the suggestion I did to you. But we are anxious for the Dominions to see eye to eye with us on this Herzoslovakian crisis, and McGrath has, I believe, influence in journalistic circles. As an ardent monarchist, and with your knowledge of the country, I thought it a good plan for you to meet him."

"So that's the explanation, is it?"

"Yes, but I daresay you wouldn't have cared for him."

Virginia looked at him for a second and then she laughed.

"George," she said, "you're a rotten liar."

"Virginia!"

"Rotten, absolutely rotten! If I had had your training, I could have managed a better one than that—one that had a chance of being believed. But I shall find out all about it, my poor George. Rest assured of that. The Mystery of Mr. McGrath. I shouldn't wonder if I got a hint or two at Chimneys this weekend."

"At Chimneys? You are going to Chimneys?"

George could not conceal his perturbation. He had hoped to reach Lord Caterham in time for the invitation to remain unissued.

"Bundle rang up and asked me this morning."

George made a last effort.

"Rather a dull party, I believe," he said. "Hardly in your line, Virginia."

"My poor George, why didn't you tell me the truth and trust me? It's still not too late."

George took her hand and dropped it again limply.

"I have told you the truth," he said coldly, and he said it without a blush.

"That's a better one," said Virginia approvingly. "But it's still not good enough. Cheer up, George, I shall be at Chimneys all right, exerting my considerable charm—as you put it. Life has become suddenly very much more amusing. First a blackmailer, and then George in diplomatic difficulties. Will he tell all to the beautiful woman who asks for his confidence so pathetically? No, he will reveal nothing until the last chapter. Good-bye, George. One last fond look before you go? No? Oh, George, dear, don't be sulky about it!"

Virginia ran to the telephone as soon as George had departed with a heavy gait through the front door.

She obtained the number she required and asked to speak to Lady Eileen Brent.

"Is that you, Bundle? I'm coming to Chimneys all right tomorrow. What? Bore me? No, it won't. Bundle, wild horses wouldn't keep me away! So there!"

# Seven

## MR. MCGRATH REFUSES AN INVITATION

The letters were gone!

Having once made up his mind to the fact of their disappearance, there was nothing to do but accept it. Anthony realized very well that he could not pursue Giuseppe through the corridors of the Blitz Hotel. To do so was to court undesired publicity, and in all probability to fail in his object all the same.

He came to the conclusion that Giuseppe had mistaken the packets of letters, enclosed as they were in the other wrappings, for the memoirs themselves. It was likely therefore that when he discovered his mistake he would make another attempt to get hold of the memoirs. For this attempt Anthony intended to be fully prepared.

Another plan that occurred to him was to advertise discreetly for the return of the package of letters. Supposing Giuseppe to be an emissary of the Comrades of the Red Hand, or, which seemed to Anthony more probable, to be employed by the Loyalist party, the letters could have no possible interest for either employer and he would probably jump at the chance of obtaining a small sum of money for their return.

Having thought out all this, Anthony returned to bed and slept peacefully until morning. He did not fancy that Giuseppe would be anxious for a second encounter that night.

Anthony got up with his plan of campaign fully thought-out. He had a good breakfast, glanced at the papers which were full of the new discoveries of oil in Herzoslovakia, and then demanded an interview with the manager and being Anthony Cade, with a gift for getting his own way by means of quiet determination he obtained what he asked for.

The manager, a Frenchman with an exquisitely suave manner, received him in his private office.

"You wished to see me, I understand, Mr.—er—McGrath?"

"I did. I arrived at your hotel yesterday afternoon and I had dinner served to me in my own rooms by a waiter whose name was Giuseppe."

He paused.

"I daresay we have a waiter of that name," agreed the manager indifferently.

"I was struck by something unusual in the man's manner, but thought nothing more of it at the time. Later, in the night, I was awakened by the sound of someone moving softly about the room. I switched on the light, and found this same Giuseppe in the act of rifling my leather suitcase."

The manager's indifference had completely disappeared now.

"But I have heard nothing of this," he exclaimed. "Why was I not informed sooner?"

"The man and I had a brief struggle—he was armed with a knife, by the way. In the end he succeeded in making off by way of the window."

"What did you do then, Mr. McGrath?"

"I examined the contents of my suitcase."

"Had anything been taken?"

"Nothing of—importance," said Anthony slowly.

The manager leaned back with a sigh.

"I am glad of that," he remarked. "But you will allow me to say, Mr. McGrath, that I do not quite understand your attitude in the matter. You made no attempt to arouse the hotel? To pursue the thief?"

Anthony shrugged his shoulders.

"Nothing of value had been taken, as I tell you. I am aware, of course, that strictly speaking it is a case for the police—"

He paused, and the manager murmured without any particular enthusiasm:

"For the police—of course—"

"In any case, I was fairly certain that the man would manage to make good his escape, and since nothing was taken, why bother with the police?"

The manager smiled a little.

"I see that you realize, Mr. McGrath, that I am not at all anxious to have the police called in. From my point of view it is always disastrous. If the newspapers can get hold of anything connected with a big fashionable hotel such as this, they always run it for all it is worth, no matter how insignificant the real subject may be."

"Quite so," agreed Anthony. "Now I told you that nothing of value had been taken, and that was perfectly true in a sense. Nothing of any value to the thief was taken, but he got hold of something which is of considerable value to me."

"Ah?"

"Letters, you understand."

An expression of superhuman discretion, only to be achieved by a Frenchman, settled down upon the manager's face.

"I comprehend," he murmured. "But perfectly. Naturally, it is not a matter for the police."

"We are quite agreed upon that point. But you will understand that I have every intention of recovering these letters. In the part of the world where I come from, people are used to doing things for themselves. What I require from you therefore is the fullest possible information you can give me about this waiter, Giuseppe."

"I see no objection to that," said the manager after a moment or two's pause. "I cannot give you the information offhand, of course, but if you will return in half an hour's time I will have everything ready to lay before you."

"Thank you very much. That will suit me admirably."

In half an hour's time, Anthony returned to the office again to find that the manager had been as good as his word. Jotted down on a piece of paper were all the relevant facts known about Giuseppe Manelli.

"He came to us, you see, about three months ago. A skilled and experienced waiter. Has given complete satisfaction. He has been in England about five years."

Together the two men ran over a list of the hotels and restaurants where the Italian had worked. One fact struck Anthony as being possibly of significance. At two of the hotels in question there had been serious robberies during the time that Giuseppe was employed there, though no suspicion of any kind had attached to him in either case. Still, the fact was significant.

Was Giuseppe merely a clever hotel thief? Had his search of Anthony's suitcase been only part of his habitual professional tactics? He might just possibly have had the packet of letters in his hand at the moment when Anthony switched on the light, and have shoved it into his pocket mechanically so as to have his hands free. In that case, the thing was mere plain or garden robbery.

Against that, there was to be put the man's excitement of the evening before when he had caught sight of the papers lying on the table. There had been no money or object of value there such as would excite the cupidity of an ordinary thief.

No, Anthony felt convinced that Giuseppe had been acting as a tool for some outside agency. With the information supplied to him by the manager, it might be possible to learn something about Giuseppe's private life and so finally track him down. He gathered up the sheet of paper and rose.

"Thank you very much indeed. It's quite unnecessary to ask, I suppose, whether Giuseppe is still in the hotel?"

The manager smiled.

"His bed was not slept in, and all his things have been left behind. He must have rushed straight out after his attack upon you. I don't think there is much chance of our seeing him again."

"I imagine not. Well, thank you very much indeed. I shall be staying on here for the present."

"I hope you will be successful in your task, but I confess that I am rather doubtful."

"I always hope for the best."

One of Anthony's first proceedings was to question some of

the other waiters who had been friendly with Giuseppe, but he obtained very little to go upon. He wrote out an advertisement on the lines he had planned, and had it sent to five of the most widely read newspapers. He was just about to go out and visit the restaurant at which Giuseppe had been previously employed when the telephone rang. Anthony took up the receiver.

"Hullo, what is it?"

A toneless voice replied.

"Am I speaking to Mr. McGrath?"

"You are. Who are you?"

"This is Messrs. Balderson and Hodgkins. Just a minute, please. I will put you through to Mr. Balderson."

"Our worthy publishers," thought Anthony. "So they are getting worried too, are they? They needn't. There's a week to run still."

A hearty voice struck suddenly upon his ear.

"Hullo! That Mr. McGrath?"

"Speaking."

"I'm Mr. Balderson of Balderson and Hodgkins. What about that manuscript, Mr. McGrath?"

"Well," said Anthony, "what about it?"

"Everything about it. I understand, Mr. McGrath, that you have just arrived in this country from South Africa. That being so, you can't possibly understand the position. There's going to be trouble about that manuscript, Mr. McGrath, big trouble. Sometimes I wish we'd never said we'd handle it."

"Indeed?"

"I assure you it's so. At present I'm anxious to get it into my possession as quickly as possible, so as to have a couple of copies made. Then, if the original is destroyed—well, no harm will be done."

"Dear me," said Anthony.

"Yes, I expect it sounds absurd to you, Mr. McGrath. But, I assure you, you don't appreciate the situation. There's a determined effort being made to prevent its ever reaching this office. I say to you quite frankly and without humbug that if you attempt to bring it yourself it's ten to one that you'll never get here."

"I doubt that," said Anthony. "When I want to get anywhere, I usually do."

"You're up against a very dangerous lot of people. I wouldn't have believed it myself a month ago. I tell you, Mr. McGrath, we've been bribed and threatened and cajoled by one lot and another until we don't know whether we're on our heads or our heels. My suggestion is that you do not attempt to bring the manuscript here. One of our people will call upon you at the hotel and take possession of it."

"And supposing the gang does him in?" asked Anthony.

"The responsibility would then be ours—not yours. You would have delivered it to our representative and obtained a written discharge. The cheque for—er—a thousand pounds which we are instructed to hand to you will not be available until Wednesday next by the terms of our agreement with the executors of the late—er—author—you know whom I mean, but if you insist I will send my own cheque for that amount by the messenger."

Anthony reflected for a minute or two. He had intended to keep the memoirs until the last day of grace, because he was anxious to see for himself what all the fuss was about. Nevertheless, he realized the force of the publisher's arguments.

"All right," he said, with a little sigh. "Have it your own way.

Send your man along. And if you don't mind sending that cheque as well I'd rather have it now, as I may be going out of England before next Wednesday."

"Certainly, Mr. McGrath. Our representative will call upon you first thing tomorrow morning. It will be wiser not to send anyone direct from the office. Our Mr. Holmes lives in South London. He will call in on his way to us, and will give you a receipt for the package. I suggest that tonight you should place a dummy packet in the manager's safe. Your enemies will get to hear of this, and it will prevent any attack being made upon your apartments tonight."

"Very well, I will do as you direct."

Anthony hung up the receiver with a thoughtful face.

Then he went on with his interrupted plan of seeking news of the slippery Giuseppe. He drew a complete blank, however. Giuseppe had worked at the restaurant in question, but nobody seemed to know anything of his private life or associates.

"But I'll get you, my lad," murmured Anthony, between his teeth. "I'll get you yet. It's only a matter of time."

His second night in London was entirely peaceful.

At nine o'clock the following morning, the card of Mr. Holmes from Messrs. Balderson and Hodgkins was sent up, and Mr. Holmes followed it. A small, fair man with a quiet manner. Anthony handed over the manuscript, and received in exchange a cheque for a thousand pounds. Mr. Holmes packed up the manuscript in the small brown bag he carried, wished Anthony good morning, and departed. The whole thing seemed very tame.

"But perhaps he'll be murdered on the way there," Anthony murmured aloud, as he stared idly out of the window. "I wonder now—I very much wonder."

He put the cheque in an envelope, enclosed a few lines of writing with it, and sealed it up carefully. Jimmy, who had been more or less in funds at the time of his encounter with Anthony at Bulawayo, had advanced him a substantial sum of money which was, as yet, practically untouched.

"If one job's done with, the other isn't," said Anthony to himself. "Up to now, I've bungled it. But never say die. I think that, suitably disguised, I shall go and have a look at 487 Pont Street."

He packed his belongings, went down and paid his bill, and ordered his luggage to be put on a taxi. Suitably rewarding those who stood in his path, most of whom had done nothing whatever materially to add to his comfort, he was on the point of being driven off, when a small boy rushed down the steps with a letter.

"Just come for you, this very minute, sir."

With a sigh, Anthony produced yet another shilling. The taxi groaned heavily and jumped forward with a hideous crashing of gears, and Anthony opened the letter.

It was rather a curious document. He had to read it four times before he could be sure of what it was all about. Put in plain English (the letter was not in plain English, but in the peculiar involved style common to missives issued by government officials) it presumed that Mr. McGrath was arriving in England from South Africa today—Thursday, it referred obliquely to the memoirs of Count Stylptitch, and begged Mr. McGrath to do nothing in the matter until he had had a confidential conversation with Mr. George Lomax, and certain other parties whose magnificence was vaguely hinted at. It also contained a definite invitation to go down to Chimneys as the guest of Lord Caterham, on the following day, Friday.

A mysterious and thoroughly obscure communication. Anthony enjoyed it very much.

"Dear old England," he murmured affectionately. "Two days behind the times, as usual. Rather a pity. Still, I can't go down to Chimneys under false pretences. I wonder, though, if there's an inn handy? Mr. Anthony Cade might stay at the inn without anyone being the wiser."

He leaned out of the window, and gave new directions to the taxi driver, who acknowledged them with a snort of contempt.

The taxi drew up before one of London's more obscure hostelries. The fare, however, was paid on a scale befitting its point of departure.

Having booked a room in the name of Anthony Cade, Anthony passed into a dingy writing room, took out a sheet of notepaper stamped with the legend Hotel Blitz, and wrote rapidly.

He explained that he had arrived on the preceding Tuesday, that he had handed over the manuscript in question to Messrs. Balderson and Hodgkins, and he regretfully declined the kind invitation of Lord Caterham as he was leaving England almost immediately. He signed the letter "Yours faithfully, James McGrath."

And now," said Anthony, as he affixed the stamp to the envelope. "To business. Exit James McGrath, and Enter Anthony Cade."

# Eight

## A Dead Man

On that same Thursday afternoon Virginia Revel had been playing tennis at Ranelagh. All the way back to Pont Street, as she lay back in the long, luxurious limousine, a little smile played upon her lips as she rehearsed her part in the forthcoming interview. Of course it was within the bounds of possibility that the blackmailer might not reappear, but she felt pretty certain that he would. She had shown herself an easy prey. Well, perhaps this time there would be a little surprise for him!

When the car drew up at the house, she turned to speak to the chauffeur before going up the steps.

"How's your wife, Walton? I forgot to ask."

"Better I think, ma'am. The doctor said he'd look in and see her about half past six. Will you be wanting the car again?"

Virginia reflected for a minute.

"I shall be away for the weekend. I'm going by the 6:40 from Paddington, but I shan't need you again—a taxi will do for that. I'd rather you saw the doctor. If he thinks it would do your wife good to go away for the weekend, take her somewhere, Walton. I'll stand the expense."

Cutting short the man's thanks with an impatient nod of the head, Virginia ran up the steps, delved into her bag in search of her latchkey, remembered she hadn't got it with her, and hastily rang the bell.

It was not answered at once, but as she waited there a young man came up the steps. He was shabbily dressed, and carried in his hand a sheaf of leaflets. He held one out to Virginia with the legend on it plainly visible: "Why Did I Serve My Country?" In his left hand he held a collecting box.

"I can't buy two of those awful poems in one day," said Virginia pleadingly. "I bought one this morning. I did, indeed, honour bright."

The young man threw back his head and laughed. Virginia laughed with him. Running her eyes carelessly over him, she thought him a more pleasing specimen than usual of London's unemployed. She liked his brown face, and the lean hardness of him. She went so far as to wish she had a job for him.

But at that moment the door opened, and immediately Virginia forgot all about the problem of the unemployed, for to her astonishment the door was opened by her own maid, Elise.

"Where's Chilvers?" she demanded sharply, as she stepped into the hall.

"But he is gone, madame, with the others."

"What others? Gone where?"

"But to Datchet, madame—to the cottage, as your telegram said."

"My telegram?" said Virginia, utterly at sea.

"Did not madame send a telegram? Surely there can be no mistake. It came but an hour ago."

"I never sent any telegram. What did it say?"

"I believe it is still on the table *là-bas*."

Elise retired, pouncing upon it, and brought it to her mistress in triumph.

"*Voilà*, madame!"

The telegram was addressed to Chilvers and ran as follows:

"Please take household down to cottage at once, and make preparations for weekend party there. Catch 5:49 train."

There was nothing unusual about it, it was just the sort of message she herself had frequently sent before, when she had arranged a party at her riverside bungalow on the spur of the moment. She always took the whole household down, leaving an old woman as caretaker. Chilvers would not have seen anything wrong with the message, and like a good servant had carried out his orders faithfully enough.

"Me, I remained," explained Elise, "knowing that madame would wish me to pack for her."

"It's a silly hoax," cried Virginia, flinging down the telegram angrily. "You know perfectly well, Elise, that I am going to Chimneys. I told you so this morning."

"I thought madame had changed her mind. Sometimes that does happen, does it not, madame?"

Virginia admitted the truth of the accusation with a half-smile.

She was busy trying to find a reason for this extraordinary practical joke. Elise put forward a suggestion.

*"Mon Dieu!"* she cried, clasping her hands. "If it should be the malefactors, the thieves! They send the bogus telegram and get the *domestiques* all out of the house, and then they rob it."

"I suppose that might be it," said Virginia doubtfully.

"Yes, yes madame, that is without a doubt. Every day you read in the papers of such things. Madame will ring up the police at once—at once—before they arrive and cut our throats."

"Don't get so excited, Elise. They won't come and cut our throats at six o'clock in the afternoon."

"Madame, I implore you, let me run out and fetch a policeman now, at once."

"What on earth for? Don't be silly, Elise. Go up and pack my things for Chimneys, if you haven't already done it. The new Cailleaux evening dress, and the white crêpe marocain, and—yes, the black velvet—black velvet is so political, is it not?"

"Madame looks ravishing in the eau de nil satin," suggested Elise, her professional instincts reasserting themselves.

"No, I won't take that. Hurry up, Elise, there's a good girl. We've got very little time. I'll send a wire to Chilvers at Datchet, and I'll speak to the policeman on the beat as we go out and tell him to keep an eye on the place. Don't start rolling your eyes again, Elise—if you get so frightened before anything has happened, what would you do if a man jumped out from some dark corner and stuck a knife into you?"

Elise gave vent to a shrill squeak, and beat a speedy retreat up the stairs, darting nervous glances over her shoulder as she went.

Virginia made a face at her retreating back, and crossed the hall to the little study where the telephone was. Elise's suggestion of ringing up the police station seemed to her a good one, and she intended to act upon it without any further delay.

She opened the study door and crossed to the telephone. Then, with her hand on the receiver, she stopped. A man was sitting in the big armchair, sitting in a curious huddled position. In the stress of the moment, she had forgotten all about her expected visitor. Apparently he had fallen asleep whilst waiting for her.

She came right up to the chair, a slightly mischievous smile upon her face. And then suddenly the smile faded.

The man was not asleep. *He was dead.*

She knew it at once, knew it instinctively even before her eyes had seen and noted the small shining pistol lying on the floor, the little singed hole just above the heart with the dark stain round it, and the horrible dropped jaw.

She stood quite still, her hands pressed to her sides. In the silence she heard Elise running down the stairs.

"Madame! Madame!"

"Well, what is it?"

She moved quickly to the door. Her whole instinct was to conceal what had happened—for the moment anyway—from Elise. Elise would promptly go into hysterics, she knew that well enough, and she felt a great need for calm and quiet in which to think things out.

"Madame, would it not be better if I should draw the chain across the door? These malefactors, at any minute they may arrive."

"Yes, if you like. Anything you like."

She heard the rattle of the chain, and then Elise running up-stairs again, and drew a long breath of relief.

She looked at the man in the chair and then at the telephone. Her course was quite clear, she must ring up the police at once.

But still she did not do so. She stood quite still, paralysed with horror and with a host of conflicting ideas rushing through her brain. The bogus telegram! Had it something to do with this? Supposing Elise had not stayed behind? She would have let herself in—that is, presuming she had had her latchkey with her as usual to find herself alone in the house with a murdered man—a man whom she had permitted to blackmail her on a former occasion. Of course she had an explanation of that; but thinking of that explanation she was not quite easy in her mind. She remembered how frankly incredible George had found it. Would other people think the same? Those letters now—of course, she hadn't written them, but would it be so easy to prove that?

She put her hands on her forehead, squeezing them tight together.

"I must think," said Virginia. "I simply must think."

Who had let the man in? Surely not Elise. If she had done so, she would have been sure to have mentioned the fact at once. The whole thing seemed more and more mysterious as she thought about it. There was really only one thing to be done—ring up the police.

She stretched out her hand to the telephone, and suddenly she thought of George. A man—that was what she wanted—an ordinary levelheaded, unemotional man who would see things in their proper proportion and point out to her the best course to take.

Then she shook her head. Not George. The first thing George would think of would be his own position. He would hate being mixed up in this kind of business. George wouldn't do at all.

Then her face softened. Bill, of course! Without more ado, she rang up Bill.

She was informed that he had left half an hour ago for Chimneys.

"Oh, damn!" cried Virginia, jamming down the receiver. It was horrible to be shut up with a dead body and to have no one to speak to.

And at that minute the front doorbell rang.

Virginia jumped. In a few minutes it rang again. Elise, she knew, was upstairs packing and wouldn't hear it.

Virginia went out in the hall, drew back the chain, and undid all the bolts that Elise had fastened in her zeal. Then, with a long breath, she threw open the door. On the steps was the unemployed young man.

Virginia plunged headlong with a relief born of overstrung nerves.

Come in," she said. "I think perhaps I've got a job for you."

She took him into the dining room, pulled forward a chair for him, sat herself facing him, and stared at him very attentively.

"Excuse me," she said, "but are you—I mean—"

"Eton and Oxford," said the young man. "That's what you wanted to ask me, wasn't it?"

"Something of the kind," admitted Virginia.

"Come down in the world entirely through my own incapacity to stick to regular work. This isn't regular work you're offering me, I hope?"

A smile hovered for a moment on her lips.

"It's very irregular."

"Good," said the young man in a tone of satisfaction.

Virginia noted his bronzed face and long lean body with approval.

"You see," she explained. "I'm in rather a hole, and most of my friends are—well, rather high up. They've all got something to lose."

"I've nothing whatever to lose. So go ahead. What's the trouble?"

"There's a dead man in the next room," said Virginia. "He's been murdered, and I don't know what to do about it."

She blurted out the words as simply as a child might have done. The young man went up enormously in her estimation by the way he accepted her statement. He might have been used to hearing a similar announcement made every day of his life.

"Excellent," he said, with a trace of enthusiasm. "I've always wanted to do a bit of amateur detective work. Shall we go and view the body, or will you give me the facts first?"

"I think I'd better give you the facts." She paused for a moment to consider how best to condense her story, and then began speaking quietly and concisely:

"This man came to the house for the first time yesterday and asked to see me. He had certain letters with him—love letters, signed with my name—"

"But which weren't written by you," put in the young man quietly.

Virginia looked at him in some astonishment.

"How did you know that?"

"Oh, I deduced it. But go on."

"He wanted to blackmail me—and I—well, I don't know if you'll understand, but I—let him."

She looked at him appealingly, and he nodded his head reassuringly.

"Of course I understand. You wanted to see what it felt like."

"How frightfully clever of you! That's just what I did feel."

"I *am* clever," said the young man modestly. "But, mind you, very few people would understand that point of view. Most people, you see, haven't got any imagination."

"I suppose that's so. I told this man to come back today—at six o'clock. I arrived home from Ranelagh to find that a bogus telegram had got all the servants except my maid out of the house. Then I walked into the study and found the man shot."

"Who let him in?"

"I don't know. I think if my maid had done so she would have told me."

"Does she know what has happened?"

"I have told her nothing."

The young man nodded, and rose to his feet.

"And now to view the body," he said briskly. "But I'll tell you this—on the whole it's always best to tell the truth. One lie involves you in such a lot of lies—and continuous lying is so monotonous."

"Then you advise me to ring up the police?"

"Probably. But we'll just have a look at the fellow first."

Virginia led the way out of the room. On the threshold she paused, looking back at him.

"By the way," she said, "you haven't told me your name yet?"

"My name? My name's Anthony Cade."

# Nine

## ANTHONY DISPOSES OF A BODY

Anthony followed Virginia out of the room, smiling a little to himself. Events had taken quite an unexpected turn. But as he bent over the figure in the chair he grew grave again.

"He's still warm," he said sharply. "He was killed less than half an hour ago."

"Just before I came in?"

"Exactly."

He stood upright, drawing his brows together in a frown. Then he asked a question of which Virginia did not at once see the drift:

"Your maid's not been in this room, of course?"

"No."

"Does she know that you've been into it?"

"Why—yes. I came to the door to speak to her."

"After you'd found the body?"

"Yes."

"And you said nothing?"

"Would it have been better if I had? I thought she would go into hysterics—she's French, you know, and easily upset—I wanted to think over the best thing to do."

Anthony nodded, but did not speak.

"You think it a pity, I can see?"

"Well, it was rather unfortunate, Mrs. Revel. If you and the maid had discovered the body together, immediately on your return, it would have simplified matters very much. The man would then definitely have been shot *before* your return to the house."

"Whilst now they might say he was shot *after*—I see—"

He watched her taking in the idea, and was confirmed in his first impression of her, formed when she had spoken to him on the steps outside. Besides beauty, she possessed courage and brains.

Virginia was so engrossed in the puzzle presented to her that it did not occur to her to wonder at this strange man's ready use of her name.

"Why didn't Elise hear the shot, I wonder?" she murmured.

Anthony pointed to the open window, as a loud backfire came from a passing car.

"There you are. London's not the place to notice a pistol shot."

Virginia turned with a little shudder to the body in the chair.

"He looks like an Italian," she remarked curiously.

"He is an Italian," said Anthony. "I should say that his regular profession was that of a waiter. He only did blackmailing in his spare time. His name might very possibly be Giuseppe."

"Good heavens!" cried Virginia. "Is this Sherlock Holmes?"

"No," said Anthony regretfully. "I'm afraid it's just plain or garden cheating. I'll tell you all about it presently. Now you say this man showed you some letters and asked you for money. Did you give him any?"

"Yes, I did."

"How much?"

"Forty pounds."

"That's bad," said Anthony, but without manifesting any undue surprise. "Now let's have a look at the telegram."

Virginia picked it up from the table and gave it to him. She saw his face grow grave as he looked at it.

"What's the matter?"

He held it out, pointing silently to the place of origin.

"Barnes," he said. "And you were at Ranelagh this afternoon. What's to prevent you having sent it off yourself?"

Virginia felt fascinated by his words. It was as though a net was closing tighter and tighter round her. He was forcing her to see all the things which she had felt dimly at the back of her mind.

Anthony took out his handkerchief and wound it round his hand, then he picked up the pistol.

"We criminals have to be so careful," he said apologetically. "Fingerprints, you know."

Suddenly she saw his whole figure stiffen. His voice, when he spoke, had altered. It was terse and curt.

"Mrs. Revel," he said, "have you ever seen this pistol before?"

"No," said Virginia wonderingly.

"Are you sure of that?"

"Quite sure."

"Have you a pistol of your own?"

"No."

"Have you ever had one?"

"No, never."

"You are sure of that?"

"Quite sure."

He stared at her steadily for a minute, and Virginia stared back in complete surprise at his tone.

Then, with a sigh, he relaxed.

"That's odd," he said. "How do you account for this?"

He held out the pistol. It was a small, dainty article, almost a toy—though capable of doing deadly work. Engraved on it was the name Virginia.

"Oh, it's impossible!" cried Virginia.

Her astonishment was so genuine that Anthony could but believe in it.

"Sit down," he said quietly. "There's more in this than there seemed to be first go off. To begin with, what's our hypothesis? There are only two possible ones. There is, of course, the real Virginia of the letters. She may have somehow or other tracked him down, shot him, dropped the pistol, stolen the letters, and taken herself off. That's quite possible, isn't it?"

"I suppose so," said Virginia unwillingly.

"The other hypothesis is a good deal more interesting. Whoever wished to kill Giuseppe, wished also to incriminate you—in fact, that may have been their main object. They could get *him* easily enough anywhere, but they took extraordinary pains and trouble to get him *here*, and whoever they were they knew all about you, your cottage at Datchet, your usual household arrangements, and the fact that you were at Ranelagh this afternoon. It seems an absurd question, but have you any enemies, Mrs. Revel?"

"Of course I haven't—not that kind, anyway."

"The question is," said Anthony, "what are we going to do now? There are two courses open to us. A: ring up the police, tell the whole story, and trust to your unassailable position in the world and your hitherto blameless life. B: an attempt on my part to dispose successfully of the body. Naturally my private inclinations urge me to B. I've always wanted to see if I couldn't conceal a crime with the necessary cunning, but have had a squeamish objection to shedding blood. On the whole, I expect A's the soundest. Then here's a sort of bowdlerized A. Ring up the police, etc, but suppress the pistol and the blackmailing letters—that is, if they are on him still."

Anthony ran rapidly through the dead man's pockets.

"He's been stripped clean," he announced. "There's not a thing on him. There'll be dirty work at the crossroads over those letters yet. Hullo, what's this? Hole in the lining—something got caught there, torn roughly out, and a scrap of paper left behind."

He drew out the scrap of paper as he spoke, and brought it over to the light. Virginia joined him.

"Pity we haven't got the rest of it," he muttered. "Chimneys 11:45 Thursday—Sounds like an appointment."

"Chimneys?" cried Virginia. "How extraordinary!"

"Why extraordinary? Rather high-toned for such a low fellow?"

"I'm going to Chimneys this evening. At least I was."

Anthony wheeled round on her.

"What's that? Say that again."

"I was going to Chimneys this evening," repeated Virginia.

Anthony stared at her.

"I begin to see. At least, I may be wrong—but it's an idea. Suppose someone wanted badly to prevent your going to Chimneys?"

"My cousin George Lomax does," said Virginia with a smile. "But I can't seriously suspect George of murder."

Anthony did not smile. He was lost in thought.

"If you ring up the police, its good-bye to any idea of getting to Chimneys today—or even tomorrow. And I should like you to go to Chimneys. I fancy it will disconcert our unknown friends. Mrs. Revel, will you put yourself in my hands?"

"It's to be Plan B, then?"

"It's to be Plan B. The first thing is to get that maid of yours out of the house. Can you manage that?"

"Easily."

Virginia went out in the hall and called up the stairs.

"Elise. Elise."

"Madame?"

Anthony heard a rapid colloquy, and then the front door opened and shut. Virginia came back into the room.

"She's gone. I sent her for some special scent—told her the shop in question was open until eight. It won't be, of course. She's to follow after me by the next train without coming back here."

"Good," said Anthony approvingly. "We can now proceed to the disposal of the body. It's a timeworn method, but I'm afraid I shall have to ask you if there's such a thing in the house as a trunk?"

"Of course there is. Come down to the basement and take your choice."

There was a variety of trunks in the basement. Anthony selected a solid affair of suitable size.

"I'll attend to this part of it," he said tactfully. "You go upstairs and get ready to start."

Virginia obeyed. She slipped out of her tennis kit, put on a soft brown travelling dress and a delightful little orange hat, and came down to find Anthony waiting in the hall with a neatly strapped trunk beside him.

"I should like to tell you the story of my life," he remarked, "but it's going to be rather a busy evening. Now this is what you've got to do. Call a taxi, have your luggage put on it, including the trunk. Drive to Paddington. There have the trunk put in the Left Luggage Office. I shall be on the platform. As you pass me, drop the cloakroom ticket. I will pick it up and return it to you, but in reality I shall keep it. Go on to Chimneys, and leave the rest to me."

"It's awfully good of you," said Virginia. "It's really dreadful of me saddling a perfect stranger with a dead body like this."

"I like it," returned Anthony nonchalantly. "If one of my friends, Jimmy McGrath, were here, he'd tell you that anything of this kind suits me down to the ground."

Virginia was staring at him.

"What name did you say? Jimmy McGrath?"

Anthony returned her glance keenly.

"Yes. Why? Have you heard of him?"

"Yes—and quite lately." She paused irresolutely, and then went on. "Mr. Cade, I must talk to you. Can't you come down to Chimneys?"

"You'll see me before very long, Mrs. Revel—I'll tell you that. Now, exit Conspirator A by back door slinkingly. Exit Conspirator B in blaze of glory by front door to taxi."

The plan went through without a hitch. Anthony, having picked up a second taxi, was on the platform and duly retrieved the fallen ticket. He then departed in search of a somewhat battered secondhand Morris Cowley which he had acquired earlier in the day in case it should be necessary to his plans.

Returning to Paddington in this, he handed the ticket to the porter, who got the trunk out of the cloakroom and wedged it securely at the back of the car. Anthony drove off.

His objective now was out of London. Through Notting Hill, Shepherd's Bush, down Goldhawk Road, through Brentford and Hounslow till he came to the long stretch of road midway between Hounslow and Staines. It was a well-frequented road, with motors passing continuously. No footmarks or tyremarks were likely to show. Anthony stopped the car at a certain spot. Getting down, he first obscured the number plate with mud. Then, waiting until he heard no car coming in either direction, he opened the trunk, heaved out Giuseppe's body, and laid it neatly down by the side of the road, on the inside of a curve, so that the headlights of passing motors would not strike on it.

Then he entered the car again and drove away. The whole business had occupied exactly one minute and a half. He made a detour to the right, returning to London by way of Burnham Beeches. There again he halted the car, and choosing a giant of the forest he deliberately climbed the huge tree. It was something of a feat, even for Anthony. To one of the topmost branches he affixed a small brown-paper parcel, concealing it in a little niche close to the bole.

"A very clever way of disposing of the pistol," said Anthony to himself with some approval. "Everybody hunts about on the ground, and drags ponds. But there are very few people in England who could climb that tree."

Next, back to London and Paddington Station. Here he left the trunk—at the other cloakroom this time, the one on the Arrival side. He thought longingly of such things as good rump steaks, juicy chops, and large masses of fried potatoes. But he shook his head ruefully, glancing at his wristwatch. He fed the Morris with a fresh supply of petrol, and then took the road once more. North this time.

It was just after half past eleven that he brought the car to rest in the road adjoining the park of Chimneys. Jumping out he scaled the wall easily enough, and set out towards the house. It took him longer than he thought, and presently he broke into a run. A great grey mass loomed up out of the darkness—the venerable pile of Chimneys. In the distance a stable clock chimed the three-quarters.

11:45—the time mentioned on the scrap of paper. Anthony was on the terrace now, looking up at the house. Everything seemed dark and quiet.

"They go to bed early, these politicians," he murmured to himself.

And suddenly a sound smote upon his ears—the sound of a shot. Anthony spun round quickly. The sound had come from within the house—he was sure of that. He waited a minute, but everything was still as death. Finally he went up to one of the long French windows from where he judged the sound that had startled him had come. He tried the handle. It was locked. He tried some of the other windows, listening intently all the while. But the silence remained unbroken.

In the end he told himself that he must have imagined the sound, or perhaps mistaken a stray shot coming from a poacher in the woods. He turned and retraced his steps across the park, vaguely dissatisfied and uneasy.

He looked back at the house, and whilst he looked a light sprang up in one of the windows on the first floor. In another minute it went out again, and the whole place was in darkness once more.

# Ten

## CHIMNEYS

Inspector Badgworthy in his office. Time, 8:30 a.m. A tall portly man, Inspector Badgworthy, with a heavy regulation tread. Inclined to breathe hard in moments of professional strain. In attendance Constable Johnson, very new to the Force, with a downy unfledged look about him, like a human chicken.

The telephone on the table rang sharply, and the inspector took it up with his usual portentous gravity of action.

"Yes. Police station Market Basing. Inspector Badgworthy speaking. What?"

Slight alteration in the inspector's manner. As he is greater than Johnson, so others are greater than Inspector Badgworthy.

"Speaking, my lord. I beg your pardon, my lord? I didn't quite hear what you said?"

Long pause, during which the inspector listens, quite a variety of expressions passing over his usually impassive countenance. Finally he lays down the receiver, after a brief "At once, my lord."

He turned to Johnson, seeming visibly swelled with importance.

"From his lordship—at Chimneys—murder."

"Murder," echoed Johnson, suitably impressed.

"Murder it is," said the inspector, with great satisfaction.

"Why, there's never been a murder here—not that I've ever heard of—except the time that Tom Pearse shot his sweetheart."

"And that, in a manner of speaking, wasn't murder at all, but drink," said the inspector, deprecatingly.

"He weren't hanged for it," agreed Johnson gloomily. "But this is the real thing, is it, sir?"

"It is, Johnson. One of his lordship's guests, a foreign gentleman, discovered shot. Open window, and footprints outside."

"I'm sorry it were a foreigner," said Johnson, with some regret.

It made the murder seem less real. Foreigners, Johnson felt, were liable to be shot.

"His lordship's in a rare taking," continued the inspector. "We'll get hold of Dr. Cartwright and take him up with us right away. I hope to goodness no one will get messing with those footprints."

Badgworthy was in a seventh heaven. A murder! At Chimneys! Inspector Badgworthy in charge of the case. The police have a clue. Sensational arrest. Promotion and kudos for the aforementioned inspector.

"That is," said Inspector Badgworthy to himself, "if Scotland Yard doesn't come butting in."

The thought damped him momentarily. It seemed so extremely likely to happen under the circumstances.

They stopped at Dr. Cartwright's, and the doctor, who was a

comparatively young man, displayed a keen interest. His attitude was almost exactly that of Johnson.

"Why, bless my soul," he exclaimed. "We haven't had a murder here since the time of Tom Pearse."

All three of them got into the doctor's little car, and started off briskly for Chimneys. As they passed the local inn, the Jolly Cricketers, the doctor noticed a man standing in the doorway.

"Stranger," he remarked. "Rather a nice-looking fellow. Wonder how long he's been here, and what he's doing staying at the Cricketers? I haven't seen him about at all. He must have arrived last night."

"He didn't come by train," said Johnson.

Johnson's brother was the local railway porter, and Johnson was therefore always well up in arrivals and departures.

"Who was here for Chimneys yesterday?" asked the inspector.

"Lady Eileen, she come down by the 3:40, and two gentlemen with her, an American gent and a young Army chap—neither of them with valets. His lordship come down with a foreign gentleman, the one that's been shot as likely as not, by the 5:40, and the foreign gentleman's valet. Mr. Eversleigh come by the same train. Mrs. Revel came by the 7:25, and another foreign-looking gentleman came by it too, one with a bald head and a hook nose. Mrs. Revel's maid came by the 8:56."

Johnson paused, out of breath.

"And there was no one for the Cricketers?"

Johnson shook his head.

"He must have come by car then," said the inspector. "Johnson, make a note to institute inquiries at the Cricketers on your way back. We want to know all about any strangers. He was very sunburnt, that gentleman. Likely as not, he's come from foreign parts too."

The inspector nodded his head with great sagacity, as though to imply that that was the sort of wide-awake man he was—not to be caught napping under any consideration.

The car passed in through the park gates of Chimneys. Descriptions of that historic place can be found in any guidebook. It is also No. 3 in *Historic Homes of England*, price 21*s*. On Thursday, coaches come over from Middlingham and view those portions of it which are open to the public. In view of all these facilities, to describe Chimneys would be superfluous.

They were received at the door by a white-headed butler whose demeanour was perfect.

"We are not accustomed," it seemed to say, "to having murder committed within these walls. But these are evil days. Let us meet disaster with perfect calm, and pretend with our dying breath that nothing out of the usual has occurred."

"His lordship," said the butler, "is expecting you. This way, if you please."

He led them to a small cosy room which was Lord Caterham's refuge from the magnificence elsewhere, and announced them.

"The police, my lord, and Dr. Cartwright."

Lord Caterham was pacing up and down in a visibly agitated state.

"Ha! Inspector, you've turned up at last. I'm thankful for that. How are you, Cartwright? This is the very devil of a business, you know. The very devil of a business."

And Lord Caterham, running his hands through his hair in

a frenzied fashion until it stood upright in little tufts, looked even less like a peer of the realm than usual.

"Where's the body?" asked the doctor, in curt businesslike fashion.

Lord Caterham turned to him as though relieved at being asked a direct question.

"In the Council Chamber—just where it was found—I wouldn't have it touched. I believed—er—that that was the correct thing to do."

"Quite right, my lord," said the inspector approvingly.

He produced a notebook and pencil.

"And who discovered the body? Did you?"

"Good Lord, no," said Lord Caterham. "You don't think I usually get up at this unearthly hour in the morning, do you? No, a housemaid found it. She screamed a good deal, I believe. I didn't hear her myself. Then they came to me about it, and of course I got up and came down—and there it was, you know."

"You recognized the body as that of one of your guests?"

"That's right, Inspector."

"By name?"

This perfectly simple question seemed to upset Lord Caterham. He opened his mouth once or twice, and then shut it again. Finally he asked feebly:

"Do you mean—do you mean—what was his name?"

"Yes, my lord."

"Well," said Lord Caterham, looking slowly round the room, as though hoping to gain inspiration. "His name was—I should say it was—yes, decidedly so—Count Stanislaus."

There was something so odd about Lord Caterham's manner, that the inspector ceased using his pencil and stared at him instead. But at that moment a diversion occurred which seemed highly welcome to the embarrassed peer.

The door opened and a girl came into the room. She was tall, slim and dark, with an attractive boyish face, and a very determined manner. This was Lady Eileen Brent, commonly known as Bundle, Lord Caterham's eldest daughter. She nodded to the others, and addressed her father directly.

"I've got him," she announced.

For a moment the inspector was on the point of starting forward under the impression that the young lady had captured the murderer red-handed, but almost immediately he realized that her meaning was quite different.

Lord Caterham uttered a sigh of relief.

"That's a good job. What did he say?"

"He's coming over at once. We are to 'use the utmost discretion.'"

Her father made a sound of annoyance.

"That's just the sort of idiotic thing George Lomax would say. However, once he comes, I shall wash my hands of the whole affair."

He appeared to cheer up a little at the prospect.

"And the name of the murdered man was Count Stanislaus?" queried the doctor.

A lightning glance passed between father and daughter, and then the former said with some dignity:

"Certainly. I said so just now."

"I asked because you didn't seem quite sure about it before," explained Cartwright.

There was a faint twinkle in his eye, and Lord Caterham looked at him reproachfully.

"I'll take you to the Council Chamber," he said more briskly.

They followed him, the inspector bringing up the rear, and darting sharp glances all around him as he went, much as though he expected to find a clue in a picture frame, or behind a door.

Lord Caterham took a key from his pocket and unlocked a door, flinging it open. They all passed into a big room panelled in oak, with three French windows giving on the terrace. There was a long refectory table and a good many oak chests, and some beautiful old chairs. On the walls were various paintings of dead and gone Caterhams and others.

Near the left-hand wall, about halfway between the door and the window, a man was lying on his back, his arms flung wide.

Dr. Cartwright went over and knelt down by the body. The inspector strode across to the windows, and examined them in turn. The centre one was closed, but not fastened. On the steps outside were footprints leading up to the window, and a second set going away again.

"Clear enough," said the inspector, with a nod. "But there ought to be footprints on the inside as well. They'd show up plain on this parquet floor."

"I think I can explain that," interposed Bundle. "The housemaid had polished half the floor this morning before she saw the body. You see, it was dark when she came in here. She went straight across to the windows, drew the curtains, and began on the floor, and naturally didn't see the body which is hidden from that side of the room by the table. She didn't see it until she came right on top of it."

The inspector nodded.

"Well," said Lord Caterham, eager to escape. "I'll leave you here, Inspector. You'll be able to find me if you—er—want me. But Mr. George Lomax is coming over from Wyvern Abbey shortly, and he'll be able to tell you far more than I could. It's his business really. I can't explain, but he will when he comes."

Lord Caterham beat a precipitate retreat without waiting for a reply.

"Too bad of Lomax," he complained. "Letting me in for this. What's the matter, Tredwell?"

The white-haired butler was hovering deferentially at his elbow.

"I have taken the liberty, my lord, of advancing the breakfast hour as far as you are concerned. Everything is ready in the dining room."

"I don't suppose for a minute I can eat anything," said Lord Caterham gloomily, turning his footsteps in that direction. "Not for a moment."

Bundle slipped her hand through his arm, and they entered the dining room together. On the sideboard were half a score of heavy silver dishes, ingeniously kept hot by patent arrangements.

"Omelet," said Lord Caterham, lifting each lid in turn. "Eggs and bacon, kidneys, devilled bird, haddock, cold ham, cold pheasant. I don't like any of these things, Tredwell. Ask the cook to poach me an egg, will you?"

"Very good, my lord."

Tredwell withdrew. Lord Caterham, in an absentminded fashion, helped himself plentifully to kidneys and bacon, poured himself out a cup of coffee, and sat down at the long table. Bundle was already busy with a plateful of eggs and bacon.

"I'm damned hungry," said Bundle with her mouth full. "It must be the excitement."

"It's all very well for you," complained her father. "You young people like excitement. But I'm in a very delicate state of health. Avoid all worry, that's what Sir Abner Willis said—avoid all worry. So easy for a man sitting in his consulting room in Harley Street to say that. How can I avoid worry when that ass Lomax lands me with a thing like this? I ought to have been firm at the time. I ought to have put my foot down."

With a sad shake of the head, Lord Caterham rose and carved himself a plate of ham.

"Codders has certainly done it this time," observed Bundle cheerfully. "He was almost incoherent over the telephone. He'll be here in a minute or two, spluttering nineteen to the dozen about discretion and hushing it up."

Lord Caterham groaned at the prospect.

"Was he up?" he asked.

"He told me," replied Bundle, "that he had been up and dictating letters and memoranda ever since seven o'clock."

"Proud of it, too," remarked her father. "Extraordinarily selfish, these public men. They make their wretched secretaries get up at the most unearthly hours in order to dictate rubbish to them. If a law was passed compelling them to stop in bed until eleven, what a benefit it would be to the nation! I wouldn't mind so much if they didn't talk such balderdash. Lomax is always talking to me of my 'position.' As if I had any. Who wants to be a peer nowadays?"

"Nobody," said Bundle. "They'd much rather keep a prosperous public house."

Tredwell reappeared silently with two poached eggs in a little silver dish which he placed on the table in front of Lord Caterham.

"What's that, Tredwell?" said the latter, looking at them with faint distaste.

"Poached eggs, my lord."

"I hate poached eggs," said Lord Caterham peevishly. "They're so insipid. I don't like to look at them even. Take them away, will you, Tredwell?"

"Very good, my lord."

Tredwell and the poached eggs withdrew as silently as they came.

"Thank God no one gets up early in this house," remarked Lord Caterham devoutly. "We shall have to break this to them when they do, I suppose."

He sighed.

"I wonder who murdered him," said Bundle. "And why?"

"That's not our business, thank goodness," said Lord Caterham. "That's for the police to find out. Not that Badgworthy will ever find anything. On the whole I rather hope it was Nosystein."

"Meaning—"

"The all-British syndicate."

"Why should Mr. Isaacstein murder him when he'd come down here on purpose to meet him?"

"High finance," said Lord Caterham vaguely. "And that reminds me, I shouldn't be at all surprised if Isaacstein wasn't an early riser. He may blow in upon us at any minute. It's a habit in the city. I believe that, however rich you are, you always catch the 9:17."

The sound of a motor being driven at great speed was heard through the open window.

"Codders," cried Bundle.

Father and daughter leaned out of the window and hailed the occupant of the car as it drew up before the entrance.

"In here, my dear fellow, in here," cried Lord Caterham, hastily swallowing his mouthful of ham.

George had no intention of climbing in through the window. He disappeared through the front door, and reappeared ushered in by Tredwell, who withdrew at once.

"Have some breakfast," said Lord Caterham, shaking him by the hand. "What about a kidney?"

George waved the kidney aside impatiently.

"This is a terrible calamity, terrible, terrible."

"It is indeed. Some haddock?"

"No, no. It must be hushed up—at all costs it must be hushed up."

As Bundle had prophesied, George began to splutter.

"I understand your feelings," said Lord Caterham sympathetically. "Try an egg and bacon, or some haddock."

"A totally unforeseen contingency—national calamity—concessions jeopardized—"

"Take time," said Lord Caterham. "And take some food. What you need is some food, to pull you together. Poached eggs now? There were some poached eggs here a minute or two ago."

"I don't want any food," said George. "I've had breakfast, and even if I hadn't had any I shouldn't want it. We must think what is to be done. You have told no one as yet?"

"Well, there's Bundle and myself. And the local police. And Cartwright. And all the servants of course."

George groaned.

"Pull yourself together, my dear fellow," said Lord Caterham kindly. "(I wish you'd have some breakfast.) You don't seem to realize that you can't hush up a dead body. It's got to be buried and all that sort of thing. Very unfortunate, but there it is."

George became suddenly calm.

"You are right, Caterham. You have called in the local police, you say? That will not do. We must have Battle."

"Battle, murder and sudden death," inquired Lord Caterham, with a puzzled face.

"No, no, you misunderstand me. I referred to Superintendent Battle of Scotland Yard. A man of the utmost discretion. He worked with us in that deplorable business of the Party funds."

"What was that?" asked Lord Caterham, with some interest.

But George's eye had fallen upon Bundle, as she sat half in and half out of the window, and he remembered discretion just in time. He rose.

"We must waste no time. I must send off some wires at once."

"If you write them out, Bundle will send them through the telephone."

George pulled out a fountain pen and began to write with incredible rapidity. He handed the first one to Bundle, who read it with a great deal of interest.

"God! what a name," she remarked. "Baron How Much?"

"Baron Lolopretjzyl."

Bundle blinked.

"I've got it, but it will take some conveying to the post office."

George continued to write. Then he handed his labours to Bundle and addressed the master of the house:

"The best thing that you can do, Caterham—"

"Yes," said Lord Caterham apprehensively.

"Is to leave everything in my hands."

"Certainly," said Lord Caterham, with alacrity. "Just what I was thinking myself. You'll find the police and Dr. Cartwright in the Council Chamber. With the—er—with the body, you know. My dear Lomax, I place Chimneys unreservedly at your disposal. Do anything you like."

"Thank you," said George. "If I should want to consult you—"

But Lord Caterham had faded unobtrusively through the farther door. Bundle had observed his retreat with a grim smile.

"I'll send off those telegrams at once," she said. "You know your way to the Council Chamber?"

"Thank you, Lady Eileen."

George hurried from the room.

# Eleven

## Superintendent Battle Arrives

So apprehensive was Lord Caterham of being consulted by George that he spent the whole morning making a tour of his estate. Only the pangs of hunger drew him homeward. He also reflected that by now the worst would surely be over.

He sneaked into the house quietly by a small side door. From there he slipped neatly into his sanctum. He flattered himself that his entrance had not been observed, but there he was mistaken. The watchful Tredwell let nothing escape him. He presented himself at the door.

"You'll excuse me, my lord—"

"What is it, Tredwell?"

"Mr. Lomax, my lord, is anxious to see you in the library as soon as you return."

By this delicate method Tredwell conveyed that Lord Caterham had not yet returned unless he chose to say so.

Lord Caterham sighed, and then rose.

"I suppose it will have to be done sooner or later. In the library, you say?"

"Yes, my lord."

Sighing again, Lord Caterham crossed the wide spaces of his ancestral home, and reached the library door. The door was locked. As he rattled the handle, it was unlocked from inside, opened a little way, and the face of George Lomax appeared, peering out suspiciously.

His face changed when he saw who it was.

"Ah, Caterham, come in. We were just wondering what had become of you."

Murmuring something vague about duties on the estate, repairs for tenants, Lord Caterham sidled in apologetically. There were two other men in the room. One was Colonel Melrose, the chief constable. The other was a squarely built middle-aged man with a face so singularly devoid of expression as to be quite remarkable.

"Superintendent Battle arrived half an hour ago," explained George. "He has been round with Inspector Badgworthy, and seen Dr. Cartwright. He now wants a few facts from us."

They all sat down, after Lord Caterham had greeted Melrose and acknowledged his introduction to Superintendent Battle.

"I need hardly tell you, Battle," said George, "that this is a case in which we must use the utmost discretion."

The superintendent nodded in an offhand manner that rather took Lord Caterham's fancy.

"That will be all right, Mr. Lomax. But no concealments from us. I understand that the dead gentleman was called Count

Stanislaus—at least, that that is the name by which the household knew him. Now was that his real name?"

"It was not."

"What was his real name?"

"Prince Michael of Herzoslovakia."

Battle's eyes opened just a trifle, otherwise he gave no sign.

"And what, if I may ask the question, was the purpose of his visit here? Just pleasure?"

"There was a further object, Battle. All this in the strictest confidence, of course."

"Yes, yes, Mr. Lomax."

"Colonel Melrose?"

"Of course."

"Well, then, Prince Michael was here for the express purpose of meeting Mr. Herman Isaacstein. A loan was to be arranged on certain terms."

"Which were?"

"I do not know the exact details. Indeed, they had not yet been arranged. But in the event of coming to the throne, Prince Michael pledged himself to grant certain oil concessions to those companies in which Mr. Isaacstein is interested. The British Government was prepared to support the claim of Prince Michael to the throne in view of his pronounced British sympathies."

"Well," said Superintendent Battle, "I don't suppose I need go further into it than that. Prince Michael wanted the money, Mr. Isaacstein wanted oil, and the British Government was ready to do the heavy father. Just one question. Was anyone else after those concessions?"

"I believe an American group of financiers had made overtures to His Highness."

"And been turned down, eh?"

But George refused to be drawn.

"Prince Michael's sympathies were entirely pro-British," he repeated.

Superintendent Battle did not press the point.

"Lord Caterham, I understand that this is what occurred yesterday. You met Prince Michael in town and journeyed down here in company with him. The Prince was accompanied by his valet, a Herzoslovakian named Boris Anchoukoff, but his equerry, Captain Andrassy, remained in town. The Prince, on arriving, declared himself greatly fatigued, and retired to the apartments set aside for him. Dinner was served to him there, and he did not meet the other members of the house party. Is that correct?"

"Quite correct."

"This morning a housemaid discovered the body at approximately 7:45 a.m. Dr. Cartwright examined the dead man and found that death was the result of a bullet fired from a revolver. No revolver was found, and no one in the house seems to have heard the shot. On the other hand the dead man's wristwatch was smashed by the fall, and marks the crime as having been committed at exactly a quarter to twelve. Now what time did you retire to bed last night?"

"We went early. Somehow or other the party didn't seem to 'go,' if you know what I mean, Superintendent. We went up about half past ten, I should say."

"Thank you. Now I will ask you, Lord Caterham, to give me a description of all the people staying in the house."

"But, excuse me, I thought the fellow who did it came from outside?"

Superintendent Battle smiled.

"I daresay he did. I daresay he did. But all the same I've got to know who was in the house. Matter of routine, you know."

"Well, there was Prince Michael and his valet and Mr. Herman Isaacstein. You know all about them. Then there was Mr. Eversleigh—"

"Who works in my department," put in George condescendingly.

"And who was acquainted with the real reason of Prince Michael's being here?"

"No, I should not say that," replied George weightily. "Doubtless he realized that something was in the wind, but I did not think it necessary to take him fully into my confidence."

"I see. Will you go on, Lord Caterham?"

"Let me see, there was Mr. Hiram Fish."

"Who is Mr. Hiram Fish?"

"Mr. Fish is an American. He brought over a letter of introduction from Mr. Lucius Gott—you've heard of Lucius Gott?"

Superintendent Battle smiled acknowledgement. Who had not heard of Lucius C. Gott, the multimillionaire?

"He was specially anxious to see my first editions. Mr. Gott's collection is, of course, unequalled, but I've got several treasures myself. This Mr. Fish was an enthusiast. Mr. Lomax had suggested that I ask one or two extra people down here this weekend to make things seem more natural, so I took the opportunity of asking Mr. Fish. That finishes the men. As for the ladies, there is only Mrs. Revel—and I expect she brought a maid or something like that. Then there was my daughter, and of course the children and their nurses and governesses and all the servants."

Lord Caterham paused and took a breath.

"Thank you," said the detective. "A mere matter of routine, but necessary as such."

"There is no doubt, I suppose," asked George ponderously, "that the murderer entered by the window?"

Battle paused for a minute before replying slowly.

"There were footsteps leading up to the window, and footsteps leading away from it. A car stopped outside the park at 11:40 last night. At twelve o'clock a young man arrived at the Jolly Cricketers in a car, and engaged a room. He put his boots outside to be cleaned—they were very wet and muddy, as though he had been walking through the long grass in the park."

George leant forward eagerly.

"Could not the boots be compared with the footprints?"

"They were."

"Well?"

"They exactly correspond."

"That settles it," cried George. "We have the murderer. This young man—what is his name, by the way?"

"At the inn he gave the name of Anthony Cade."

"This Anthony Cade must be pursued at once, and arrested."

"You won't need to pursue him," said Superintendent Battle.

"Why?"

"Because he's still there."

"What?"

"Curious, isn't it?"

Colonel Melrose eyed him keenly.

"What's in your mind, Battle? Out with it."

"I just say it's curious, that's all. Here's a young man who ought to cut and run, but he doesn't cut and run. He stays here, and gives us every facility for comparing footmarks."

"What do you think, then?"

"I don't know what to think. And that's a very disturbing state of mind."

"Do you imagine—" began Colonel Melrose, but broke off as a discreet knock came at the door.

George rose and went to it. Tredwell, inwardly suffering from having to knock at doors in this low fashion, stood dignified upon the threshold, and addressed his master.

"Excuse me, my lord, but a gentleman wishes to see you on urgent and important business, connected, I understand, with this morning's tragedy."

"What's his name?" asked Battle suddenly.

"His name, sir, is Mr. Anthony Cade, but he said it wouldn't convey anything to anybody."

It seemed to convey something to the four men present. They all sat up in varying degrees of astonishment.

Lord Caterham began to chuckle.

"I'm really beginning to enjoy myself. Show him in, Tredwell. Show him in at once."

# Twelve

## ANTHONY TELLS HIS STORY

"Mr. Anthony Cade," announced Tredwell. "Enter suspicious stranger from village inn," said Anthony.

He made his way towards Lord Caterham with a kind of instinct rare in strangers. At the same time he summed up the other three men in his own mind thus: "1, Scotland Yard. 2, local dignitary—probably chief constable. 3, harassed gentleman on the verge of apoplexy—possibly connected with the Government."

"I must apologize," continued Anthony, still addressing Lord Caterham. "For forcing my way in like this, I mean. But it was rumoured round the Jolly Dog, or whatever the name of your local pub may be, that you had had a murder up here, and as I thought I might be able to throw some light upon it I came along."

For a moment or two, no one spoke. Superintendent Battle because he was a man of ripe experience who knew how infinitely better it was to let everyone else speak if they could be persuaded upon to do so, Colonel Melrose because he was habitually taciturn, George because he was in the habit of having notice given to him of the question, Lord Caterham because he had not the least idea of what to say. The silence of the other three, however, and the fact that he had been directly addressed, finally forced speech upon the last named.

"Er—quite so—quite so," he said nervously. "Won't—you—er—sit down?"

"Thank you," said Anthony.

George cleared his throat portentously.

"Er—when you say you can throw light upon this matter, you mean?—"

"I mean," said Anthony, "that I was trespassing upon Lord Caterham's property (for which I hope he will forgive me) last night at about 11:45, and that I actually heard the shot fired. I can at any rate fix the time of the crime for you."

He looked round at the three in turn, his eyes resting longest on Superintendent Battle, the impassivity of whose face he seemed to appreciate.

"But I hardly think that that's news to you," he added gently.

"Meaning by that, Mr. Cade?" asked Battle.

"Just this. I put on shoes when I got up this morning. Later, when I asked for my boots, I couldn't have them. Some nice young constable had called round for them. So I naturally put two and two together, and hurried up here to clear my character if possible."

"A very sensible move," said Battle noncommittally.

Anthony's eyes twinkled a little.

"I appreciate your reticence, Inspector. It is Inspector, isn't it?"

Lord Caterham interposed. He was beginning to take a fancy to Anthony.

"Superintendent Battle of Scotland Yard. This is Colonel Melrose, our chief constable, and Mr. Lomax."

Anthony looked sharply at George.

"Mr. George Lomax?"

"Yes."

"I think, Mr. Lomax," said Anthony, "that I had the pleasure of receiving a letter from you yesterday."

George stared at him.

"I think not," he said coldly.

But he wished that Miss Oscar were here. Miss Oscar wrote all his letters for him, and remembered who they were to and what they were about. A great man like George could not possibly remember all these annoying details.

"I think, Mr. Cade," he hinted, "that you were about to give us some—er—explanation of what you were doing in the grounds last night at 11:45?"

His tone said plainly: "And whatever it may be, we are not likely to believe it."

"Yes, Mr. Cade, what *were* you doing?" said Lord Caterham with lively interest.

"Well," said Anthony regretfully, "I'm afraid it's rather a long story."

He drew out his cigarette case.

"May I?"

Lord Caterham nodded, and Anthony lit a cigarette, and braced himself for the ordeal.

He was aware, none better, of the peril in which he stood. In the short space of twenty-four hours, he had become embroiled in two separate crimes. His actions in connexion with the first would not bear looking into for a second. After deliberately disposing of one body and so defeating the aims of justice, he had arrived upon the scene of the second crime at the exact moment when it was being committed. For a young man looking for trouble, he could hardly have done better.

"South America," thought Anthony to himself, "simply isn't in it with this!"

He had already decided upon his course of action. He was going to tell the truth—with one trifling alteration, and one grave suppression.

"The story begins," said Anthony, "about three weeks ago—in Bulawayo. Mr. Lomax, of course, knows where that is—outpost of the Empire—'What do we know of England who only England know?' all that sort of thing. I was conversing with a friend of mine, a Mr. James McGrath—"

He brought out the name slowly, with a thoughtful eye on George. George bounded in his seat and repressed an exclamation with difficulty.

"The upshot of our conversation was that I came to England to carry out a little commission for Mr. McGrath, who was unable to go himself. Since the passage was booked in his name, I travelled as James McGrath. I don't know what particular kind of offence that was—the superintendent can tell me, I daresay, and run me in for so many months' hard if necessary."

"We'll get on with the story, if you please, sir," said Battle, but his eyes twinkled a little.

"On arrival in London I went to the Blitz Hotel, still as James McGrath. My business in London was to deliver a certain manuscript to a firm of publishers, but almost immediately I received deputations from the representatives of two political parties of a foreign kingdom. The methods of one were strictly constitutional, the methods of the other were not. I dealt with them both accordingly. But my troubles were not over. That night my room was broken into, and an attempt at burglary was made by one of the waiters at the hotel."

"That was not reported to the police, I think?" said Superintendent Battle.

"You are right. It was not. Nothing was taken, you see. But I did report the occurrence to the manager of the hotel, and he will confirm my story, and tell you that the waiter in question decamped rather abruptly in the middle of the night. The next day, the publishers rang me up, and suggested that one of their representatives would call upon me and receive the manuscript. I agreed to this, and the arrangement was duly carried out on the following morning. Since I have heard nothing further, I presume the manuscript reached them safely. Yesterday, still as James McGrath, I received a letter from Mr. Lomax—"

Anthony paused. He was by now beginning to enjoy himself. George shifted uneasily.

"I remember," he murmured. "Such a large correspondence. The name, of course, being different, I could not be expected to know. And I may say," George's voice rose a little, firm in assurance of moral stability, "that I consider this—this—masquerading as another man in the highest degree improper. I have no doubt, no doubt whatever that you have incurred a severe legal penalty."

"In this letter," continued Anthony, unmoved, "Mr. Lomax made various suggestions concerning the manuscript in my charge. He also extended an invitation to me from Lord Caterham to join the house party here."

"Delighted to see you, my dear fellow," said the nobleman. "Better late than never—eh?"

George frowned at him.

Superintendent Battle bent an unmoved eye upon Anthony.

"And is that your explanation of your presence here last night, sir?" he asked.

"Certainly not," said Anthony warmly. "When I am asked to stay at a country house, I don't scale the wall late at night, tramp across the park, and try the downstairs windows. I drive up to the front door, ring the bell and wipe my feet on the mat. I will proceed. I replied to Mr. Lomax's letter, explaining that the manuscript had passed out of my keeping, and therefore regretfully declining Lord Caterham's kind invitation. But after I had done so, I remembered something which had up till then escaped my memory." He paused. The moment had come for skating over thin ice. "I must tell you that in my struggle with the waiter Giuseppe, I had wrested from him a small bit of paper with some words scribbled on it. They had conveyed nothing to me at the time, but I still had them, and the mention of Chimneys recalled them to me. I got the torn scrap out and looked at it. It was as I had thought. Here is the piece of paper, gentlemen, you can see for yourselves. The words on it are 'Chimneys 11:45 Thursday.' "

Battle examined the paper attentively.

"Of course," continued Anthony, "the word Chimneys might have nothing whatever to do with this house. On the other hand, it might. And undoubtedly this Giuseppe was a thieving rascal. I made up my mind to motor down here last night, satisfy myself that all was as it should be, put up at the inn, and call upon Lord Caterham in the morning and put him on his guard in case some mischief should be intended during the weekend."

"Quite so," said Lord Caterham encouragingly. "Quite so."

"I was late getting here—had not allowed enough time. Consequently I stopped the car climbed over the wall and ran across the park. When I arrived on the terrace, the whole house was dark and silent. I was just turning away when I heard a shot. I fancied that it came from inside the house, and I ran back, crossed the terrace, and tried the windows. But they were fastened, and there was no sound of any kind from inside the house. I waited a while, but the whole place was as still as the grave, so I made up my mind that I had made a mistake, and that what I had heard was a stray poacher—quite natural conclusion to come to under the circumstances, I think."

"Quite natural," said Superintendent Battle expressionlessly.

"I went on to the inn, put up as I said—and heard the news this morning. I realized, of course, that I was a suspicious character—bound to be under the circumstances, and came up here to tell my story, hoping it wasn't going to be handcuffs for one."

There was a pause. Colonel Melrose looked sideways at Superintendent Battle.

"I think the story seems clear enough," he remarked.

"Yes," said Battle. "I don't think we'll be handing out any handcuffs this morning."

"Any questions, Battle?"

"There's one thing I'd like to know. What was this manuscript?"

He looked across at George, and the latter replied with a trace of unwillingness:

"The memoirs of the late Count Stylptitch. You see—"

"You needn't say anything more," said Battle. "I see perfectly."

He turned to Anthony.

"Do you know who it was that was shot, Mr. Cade?"

"At the Jolly Dog it was understood to be a Count Stanislaus or some such name."

"Tell him," said Battle laconically to George Lomax.

George was clearly reluctant, but he was forced to speak:

"The gentleman who was staying here incognito as Count Stanislaus was His Highness Prince Michael of Herzoslovakia."

Anthony whistled.

"That must be deuced awkward," he remarked.

Superintendent Battle, who had been watching Anthony closely, gave a short grunt as though satisfied of something, and rose abruptly to his feet.

"There are one or two questions I'd like to ask Mr. Cade," he announced. "I'll take him into the Council Chamber with me if I may."

"Certainly, certainly," said Lord Caterham. "Take him any-where you like."

Anthony and the detective went out together.

The body had been moved from the scene of the tragedy. There was a dark stain on the floor where it had lain, but otherwise there was nothing to suggest that a tragedy had ever occurred. The sun poured in through the three windows, flooding the room with light, and bringing out the mellow tone of the old panelling. Anthony looked around him with approval.

"Very nice," he commented. "Nothing much to beat old England, is there?"

"Did it seem to you at first that it was in this room the shot was fired?" asked the superintendent, not replying to Anthony's eulogium.

"Let me see."

"Anthony opened the window and went out on the terrace, looking up at the house.

"Yes, that's the room all right," he said. "It's built out, and occupies all the corner. If the shot had been fired anywhere else, it would have sounded from the *left*, but this was from behind me or to the right if anything. That's why I thought of poachers. It's at the extremity of the wing, you see."

He stepped back across the threshold, and asked suddenly, as though the idea had just struck him:

"But why do you ask? You know he was shot here, don't you?"

"Ah!" said the superintendent. "We never know as much as we'd like to know. But, yes, he was shot here all right. Now you said something about trying the windows, didn't you?"

"Yes. They were fastened from the inside."

"How many of them did you try?"

"All three of them."

"Sure of that, sir?"

"I'm in the habit of being sure. Why do you ask?"

"That's a funny thing," said the superintendent.

"What's a funny thing?"

"When the crime was discovered this morning, the middle one was open—not latched, that is to say."

"Whew!" said Anthony, sinking down on the window seat, and

taking out his cigarette case. "That's rather a blow. That opens up quite a different aspect of the case. It leaves us two alternatives. Either he was killed by someone in the house, and that someone unlatched the window after I had gone to make it look like an outside job—incidentally with me as Little Willie—or else, not to mince matters, I'm lying. I daresay you incline to the second possibility, but, upon my honour, you're wrong."

"Nobody's going to leave this house until I'm through with them, I can tell you that," said Superintendent Battle grimly.

Anthony looked at him keenly.

"How long have you had the idea that it might be an inside job?" he asked.

Battle smiled.

"I've had a notion that way all along. Your trail was a bit too—flaring, if I may put it that way. As soon as your boots fitted the footmarks, I began to have my doubts."

"I congratulate Scotland Yard," said Anthony lightly.

But at that moment, the moment when Battle apparently admitted Anthony's complete absence of complicity in the crime, Anthony felt more than ever the need of being upon his guard. Superintendent Battle was a very astute officer. It would not do to make any slip with Superintendent Battle about.

"That's where it happened, I suppose?" said Anthony, nodding towards the dark patch upon the floor.

"Yes."

"What was he shot with—a revolver?"

"Yes, but we shan't know what make until they get the bullet out at the autopsy."

"It wasn't found then?"

"No, it wasn't found."

"No clues of any kind?"

"Well, we've got this."

Rather after the manner of a conjurer, Superintendent Battle produced a half sheet of notepaper. And, as he did so, he again watched Anthony closely without seeming to do so.

But Anthony recognized the design upon it without any sign of consternation.

"Aha! Comrades of the Red Hand again. If they're going to scatter this sort of thing about, they ought to have it lithographed. It must be a frightful nuisance doing everyone separately. Where was this found?"

"Underneath the body. You've seen it before, sir?"

Anthony recounted to him in detail his short encounter with that public-spirited association.

"The idea is, I suppose, that the Comrades did him in."

"Do you think it likely, sir?"

"Well, it would be in keeping with their propaganda. But I've always found that those who talk most about blood have never actually seen it run. I shouldn't have said the Comrades had the guts myself. And they're such picturesque people too. I don't see one of them disguising himself as a suitable guest for a country house. Still, one never knows."

"Quite right, Mr. Cade. One never knows."

Anthony looked suddenly amused.

"I see the big idea now. Open window, trail of footprints, suspicious stranger at the village inn. But I can assure you, my dear Superintendent, that whatever I am, I am not the local agent of the Red Hand."

Superintendent Battle smiled a little. Then he played his last card.

"Would you have any objection to seeing the body?" he shot out suddenly.

"None whatever," rejoined Anthony.

Battle took a key from his pocket, and preceding Anthony down the corridor, paused at a door and unlocked it. It was one of the smaller drawing rooms. The body lay on a table covered with a sheet.

Superintendent Battle waited until Anthony was beside him, and then whisked away the sheet suddenly.

An eager light sprang into his eyes at the half-uttered exclamation and the start of surprise which the other gave.

"So you *do* recognize him, Mr. Cade?" he said, in a voice that he strove to render devoid of triumph.

"I've seen him before, yes," said Anthony, recovering himself. "But not as Prince Michael Obolovitch. He purported to come from Messrs. Balderson and Hodgkins, and he called himself Mr. Holmes."

# Thirteen

## The American Visitor

Superintendent Battle replaced the sheet with the slightly crest-fallen air of a man whose best point has fallen flat. Anthony stood with his hands in his pockets lost in thought.

"So that's what old Lollipop meant when he talked about 'other means,'" he murmured at last.

"I beg your pardon, Mr. Cade?"

"Nothing, Superintendent. Forgive my abstraction. You see I—or rather my friend, Jimmy McGrath, has been very neatly done out of a thousand pounds."

"A thousand pounds is a nice sum of money," said Battle.

"It isn't the thousand pounds so much," said Anthony, "though I agree with you that it's a nice sum of money. It's being done that maddens me. I handed over that manuscript like a little woolly lamb. It hurts, Superintendent, indeed it hurts."

The detective said nothing.

"Well, well," said Anthony. "Regrets are vain, and all may not yet be lost. I've only got to get hold of dear old Stylptitch's reminiscences between now and next Wednesday and all will be gas and gaiters."

"Would you mind coming back to the Council Chamber, Mr. Cade? There's one little thing I want to point out to you."

Back in the Council Chamber, the detective strode at once to the middle window.

"I've been thinking, Mr. Cade. This particular window is very stiff; very stiff indeed. You might have been mistaken in thinking that it was fastened. It might just have stuck. I'm sure—yes, I'm almost sure, that you *were* mistaken."

Anthony eyed him keenly.

"And supposing I say that I'm quite sure I was not?"

"Don't you think you could have been?" said Battle, looking at him very steadily.

"Well, to oblige you, Superintendent, yes."

Battle smiled in a satisfied fashion.

"You're quick in the uptake, sir. And you'll have no objection to saying so, careless like, at a suitable moment?"

"None whatever. I—"

He paused, as Battle gripped his arm. The superintendent was bent forward, listening.

Enjoining silence on Anthony with a gesture, he tiptoed noiselessly to the door, and flung it suddenly open.

On the threshold stood a tall man with black hair neatly parted in the middle, china-blue eyes with a particularly innocent expression, and a large placid face.

"Your pardon, gentlemen," he said in a slow drawling voice with a pronounced transatlantic accent. "But is it permitted to inspect the scene of the crime? I take it that you are both gentlemen from Scotland Yard?"

"I have not that honour," said Anthony. "But this gentleman is Superintendent Battle of Scotland Yard."

"Is that so?" said the American gentleman, with a great appearance of interest. "Pleased to meet you, sir. My name is Hiram P. Fish, of New York City."

"What was it you wanted to see, Mr. Fish?" asked the detective.

The American walked gently into the room, and looked with much interest at the dark patch on the floor.

"I am interested in crime, Mr. Battle. It is one of my hobbies. I have contributed a monograph to one of our weekly periodicals on the subject 'Degeneracy and the Criminal.' "

As he spoke, his eyes went gently round the room, seeming to note everything in it. They rested just a shade longer on the window.

"The body," said Superintendant Battle, stating a self-evident fact, "has been removed."

"Surely," said Mr. Fish. His eyes went on to the panelled walls. "Some remarkable pictures in this room, gentlemen. A Holbein, two Van Dycks, and, if I am not mistaken, a Velazquez. I am interested in pictures—and likewise in first editions. It was to see his first editions that Lord Caterham was so kind as to invite me down here."

He sighed gently.

"I guess that's all off now. It would show a proper feeling, I suppose, for the guests to return to town immediately?"

"I'm afraid that can't be done, sir," said Superintendent Battle. "Nobody must leave the house until after the inquest."

"Is that so? And when is the inquest?"

"May be tomorrow, may not be until Monday. We've got to arrange for the autopsy and see the coroner.

"I get you," said Mr. Fish. "Under the circumstances, though it will be a melancholy party."

Battle led the way to the door.

"We'd best get out of here," he said. "We're keeping it locked still."

He waited for the other two to pass through, and then turned the key and removed it.

"I opine," said Mr. Fish, "that you are seeking for fingerprints?"

"Maybe," said the superintendent laconically.

"I should say too, that, on a night such as last night, an intruder would have left footprints on the hardwood floor."

"None inside, plenty outside."

"Mine," explained Anthony cheerfully.

The innocent eyes of Mr. Fish swept over him.

"Young man," he said, "you surprise me."

They turned a corner, and came out into the big wide hall, panelled like the Council Chamber in old oak, and with a wide gallery above it. Two other figures came into sight at the far end.

"Aha!" said Mr. Fish. "Our genial host."

This was such a ludicrous description of Lord Caterham that Anthony had to turn his head away to conceal a smile.

"And with him," continued the American, "is a lady whose name I did not catch last night. But she is bright—she is very bright."

With Lord Caterham was Virginia Revel.

Anthony had been anticipating this meeting all along. He had no idea how to act. He must leave it to Virginia. Although he had full confidence in her presence of mind, he had not the slightest idea what line she would take. He was not long left in doubt.

"Why, it's Mr. Cade," said Virginia. She held out both hands to him. "So you found you could come down after all?"

"My dear Mrs. Revel, I had no idea Mr. Cade was a friend of yours," said Lord Caterham.

"He's a very old friend," said Virginia, smiling at Anthony, with a mischievous glint in her eye. "I ran across him in London unexpectedly yesterday, and told him I was coming down here."

Anthony was quick to give her her pointer.

"I explained to Mrs. Revel," he said, "that I had been forced to refuse your kind invitation—since it had really been extended to quite a different man. And I couldn't very well foist a perfect stranger on you under false pretences."

"Well, well, my dear fellow," said Lord Caterham, "that's all over and done with now. I'll send down to the Cricketers for your bag."

"It's very kind of you, Lord Caterham, but—"

"Nonsense, of course you must come to Chimneys. Horrible place, the Cricketers—to stay in, I mean."

"Of course, you must come, Mr. Cade," said Virginia softly.

Anthony realized the altered tone of his surroundings. Already Virginia had done much for him. He was no longer an ambiguous stranger. Her position was so assured and unassailable that anyone for whom she vouched was accepted as a matter of course. He thought of the pistol in the tree at Burnham Beeches, and smiled inwardly.

"I'll send for your traps," said Lord Caterham to Anthony. "I suppose, in the circumstances, we can't have any shooting. A pity. But there it is. And I don't know what the devil to do with Isaacstein. It's all very unfortunate."

The depressed peer sighed heavily.

"That's settled, then," said Virginia. "You can begin to be useful right away, Mr. Cade, and take me out on the lake. It's very peaceful there and far from crime and all that sort of thing. Isn't it awful for poor Lord Caterham having a murder done in his house? But it's George's fault really. This is George's party, you know."

"Ah!" said Lord Caterham. "But I should never have listened to him!"

He assumed the air of a strong man betrayed by a single weakness.

"One can't help listening to George," said Virginia. "He always holds you so that you can't get away. I'm thinking of patenting a detachable lapel."

"I wish you would," chuckled her host. "I'm glad you're coming to us, Cade. I need support."

"I appreciate your kindness very much, Lord Caterham," said Anthony. "Especially," he added, "when I'm such a suspicious character. But my staying here makes it easier for Battle."

"In what way, sir?" asked the superintendent.

"It won't be so difficult to keep an eye on me," explained Anthony gently.

And by the momentary flicker of the superintendent's eyelids he knew that his shot had gone home.

# Fourteen

## Mainly Political and Financial

Except for that involuntary twitch of the eyelids, Superintendent Battle's impassivity was unimpaired. If he had been surprised at Virginia's recognition of Anthony, he did not show it. He and Lord Caterham stood together and watched those two go out through the garden door. Mr. Fish also watched them.

"Nice young fellow, that," said Lord Caterham.

"Vurry nice for Mrs. Revel to meet an old friend," murmured the American. "They have been acquainted some time, presoomably?"

"Seems so," said Lord Caterham. "But I've never heard her mention him before. Oh, by the way, Battle, Mr. Lomax has been asking for you. He's in the Blue Morning room."

"Very good, Lord Caterham. I'll go there at once."

Battle found his way to the Blue Morning room without difficulty. He was already familiar with the geography of the house.

"Ah, there you are, Battle," said Lomax.

He was striding impatiently up and down the carpet. There was one other person in the room, a big man sitting in a chair by the fireplace. He was dressed in very correct English shooting clothes which nevertheless sat strangely upon him. He had a fat yellow face, and black eyes, as impenetrable as those of a cobra. There was a generous curve to the big nose and power in the square lines of the vast jaw.

"Come in, Battle," said Lomax irritably. "And shut the door behind you. This is Mr. Herman Isaacstein."

Battle inclined his head respectfully.

He knew all about Mr. Herman Isaacstein, and though the great financier sat there silent, whilst Lomax strode up and down and talked, he knew who was the real power in the room.

"We can speak more freely now," said Lomax. "Before Lord Caterham and Colonel Melrose, I was anxious not to say too much. You understand, Battle? These things mustn't get about."

"Ah!" said Battle. "But they always do, more's the pity."

Just for a second he saw a trace of a smile on the fat yellow face. It disappeared as suddenly as it had come.

"Now, what do you really think of this young fellow—this Anthony Cade?" continued George. "Do you still assume him to be innocent?"

Battle shrugged his shoulders very slightly.

"He tells a straight story. Part of it we shall be able to verify. On the face of it, it accounts for his presence here last night. I shall cable to South Africa, of course, for information about his antecedents."

"Then you regard him as cleared of all complicity?"

Battle raised a large square hand.

"Not so fast, sir. I never said that."

"What is your idea about the crime, Superintendent Battle?" asked Isaacstein, speaking for the first time.

His voice was deep and rich, and had a certain compelling quality about it. It had stood him in good stead at board meetings in his younger days.

"It's rather too soon to have ideas, Mr. Isaacstein. I've not got beyond asking myself the first question."

"What is that?"

"Oh, it's always the same. Motive. Who benefits by the death of Prince Michael? We've got to answer that before we can get anywhere."

"The Revolutionary party of Herzoslovakia—" began George.

Superintendent Battle waved him aside with something less than his usual respect.

"It wasn't the Comrades of the Red Hand, sir, if you're thinking of them."

"But the paper—with the scarlet hand on it?"

"Put there to suggest the obvious solution."

George's dignity was a little ruffled.

"Really, Battle, I don't see how you can be so sure of that."

"Bless you, Mr. Lomax, we know all about the Comrades of the Red Hand. We've had our eye on them ever since Prince Michael landed in England. That sort of thing is the elementary work of the department. They'd never be allowed to get within a mile of him."

"I agree with Superintendent Battle," said Isaacstein. "We must look elsewhere."

"You see, sir," said Battle, encouraged by this support, "we do know a little about the case. If we don't know who gains by his death, we do know who loses by it."

"Meaning?" said Isaacstein.

His black eyes were bent upon the detective. More than ever, he reminded Battle of a hooded cobra.

"You and Mr. Lomax, not to mention the Loyalist party of Herzoslovakia. If you'll pardon the expression, sir, you're in the soup."

"Really, Battle," interposed George, shocked to the core.

"Go on, Battle," said Isaacstein. "In the soup describes the situation very accurately. You're an intelligent man."

"You've got to have a king. You've lost your king—like that!" He snapped his large fingers. "You've got to find another in a hurry, and that's not an easy job. No, I don't want to know the details of your scheme, the bare outline is enough for me, but, I take it, it's a big deal?"

Isaacstein bent his head slowly.

"It's a very big deal."

"That brings me to my second question. Who is the next heir to the throne of Herzoslovakia?"

Isaacstein looked across at Lomax. The latter answered the question, with a certain reluctance, and a good deal of hesitation:

"That would be—I should say—yes, in all probability Prince Nicholas would be the next heir."

"Ah!" said Battle. "And who is Prince Nicholas?"

"A first cousin of Prince Michael's."

"Ah!" said Battle. "I should like to hear all about Prince Nicholas, especially where he is at present."

"Nothing much is known of him," said Lomax. "As a young man, he was most peculiar in his ideas, consorted with Socialists and Republicans, and acted in a way highly unbecoming to his position. He was sent down from Oxford, I believe, for some wild escapade. There was a rumour of his death two years later in the Congo, but it was only a rumour. He turned up a few months ago when news of the royalist reaction got about."

"Indeed?" said Battle. "Where did he turn up?"

"In America."

"America!"

Battle turned to Isaacstein with one laconic word:

"Oil?"

The financier nodded.

"He represented that if the Herzoslovakians chose a king, they would prefer him to Prince Michael as being more in sympathy with modern enlightened ideas, and he drew attention to his early democratic views and his sympathy with Republican ideals. In return for financial support, he was prepared to grant concessions to a certain group of American financiers."

Superintendent Battle so far forgot his habitual impassivity as to give vent to a prolonged whistle.

"So that is it," he muttered. "In the meantime, the Loyalist party supported Prince Michael, and you felt sure you'd come out on top. And then this happens!"

"You surely don't think—" began George.

"It was a big deal," said Battle. "Mr. Isaacstein says so. And I should say that what he calls a big deal *is* a big deal."

"There are always unscrupulous tools to be got hold of," said Isaacstein quietly. "For the moment, Wall Street wins. But they've not done with me yet. Find out who killed Prince Michael, Superintendent Battle, if you want to do your country a service."

"One thing strikes me as highly suspicious," put in George.

"Why did the equerry, Captain Andrassy, not come down with the Prince yesterday?"

"I've inquired into that," said Battle. "It's perfectly simple. He stayed in town to make arrangements with a certain lady, on behalf of Prince Michael, for next weekend. The Baron rather frowned on such things, thinking them injudicious at the present stage of affairs, so His Highness had to go about them in a hole-and-corner manner. He was, if I may say so, inclined to be a rather—er—dissipated young man."

"I'm afraid so," said George ponderously. "Yes, I'm afraid so."

"There's one other point we ought to take into account, I think," said Battle, speaking with a certain amount of hesitation. "King Victor's supposed to be in England."

"King Victor?"

Lomax frowned in an effort at recollection.

"Notorious French crook, sir. We've had a warning from the Sûreté in Paris."

"Of course," said George. "I remember now. Jewel thief, isn't he? Why, that's the man—"

He broke off abruptly. Isaacstein, who had been frowning abstractedly at the fireplace, looked up just too late to catch the warning glance telegraphed from Superintendent Battle to the other. But being a man sensitive to vibrations in the atmosphere, he was conscious of a sense of strain.

"You don't want me any longer, do you, Lomax?" he inquired.

"No, thank you, my dear fellow."

"Would it upset your plans if I returned to London, Superintendent Battle?"

"I'm afraid so, sir," said the superintendent civilly. "You see, if you go, there will be others who'll want to go also. And that would never do."

"Quite so."

The great financier left the room, closing the door behind him.

"Splendid fellow, Isaacstein," murmured George Lomax perfunctorily.

"Very powerful personality," agreed Superintendent Battle.

George began to pace up and down again.

"What you say disturbs me greatly," he began. "King Victor! I thought he was in prison?"

"Came out a few months ago. French police meant to keep on his heels, but he managed to give them the slip straightaway. He would too. One of the coolest customers that ever lived. For some reason or other, they believe he's in England, and have notified us to that effect."

"But what should he be doing in England?"

"That's for you to say, sir," said Battle significantly.

"You mean?—You think?—You know the story, of course—ah, yes, I can see you do. I was not in office, of course, at the time, but I heard the whole story from the late Lord Caterham. An unparalleled catastrophe."

"The Koh-i-noor," said Battle reflectively.

"Hush, Battle!" George glanced suspiciously round him. "I beg of you, mention no names. Much better not. If you must speak of it, call it the K."

The superintendent looked wooden again.

"You don't connect King Victor with this crime, do you, Battle?"

"It's just a possibility, that's all. If you cast your mind back, sir, you'll remember that there were four places where a—er—certain royal visitor might have concealed the jewel. Chimneys was one of them. King Victor was arrested in Paris three days after the—disappearance, if I may call it that, of the K. It was always hoped that he would some day lead us to the jewel."

"But Chimneys has been ransacked and overhauled a dozen times."

"Yes," said Battle sapiently. "But it's never much good looking when you don't know where to look. Only suppose now, that this King Victor came here to look for the thing, was surprised by Prince Michael, and shot him."

"It's possible," said George. "A most likely solution of the crime."

"I wouldn't go as far as that. It's possible, but not much more."

"Why is that?"

"Because King Victor has never been known to take a life," said Battle seriously.

"Oh, but a man like that—a dangerous criminal—"

But Battle shook his head in a dissatisfied manner.

"Criminals always act true to type, Mr. Lomax. It's surprising. All the same—"

"Yes?"

"I'd rather like to question the Prince's servant. I've left him purposely to the last. We'll have him in here, sir, if you don't mind."

George signified his assent. The superintendent rang the bell. Tredwell answered it, and departed with his instructions.

He returned shortly accompanied by a tall fair man with high cheekbones, and very deep-set blue eyes, and an impassivity of countenance, which almost rivalled Battle's.

"Boris Anchoukoff?"

"Yes."

"You were valet to Prince Michael?"

"I was His Highness' valet, yes."

The man spoke good English, though with a markedly harsh foreign accent.

"You know that your master was murdered last night?"

A deep snarl, like the snarl of a wild beast, was the man's only answer. It alarmed George, who withdrew prudently towards the window.

"When did you see your master last?"

"His Highness retired to bed at half past ten. I slept, as always, in the anteroom next to him. He must have gone down to the room downstairs by the other door, the door that gave on the corridor. I did not hear him go. It may be that I was drugged. I have been an unfaithful servant, I slept while my master woke. I am accursed."

George gazed at him, fascinated.

"You loved your master, eh?" said Battle, watching the man closely.

Boris' features contracted painfully. He swallowed twice. Then his voice came, harsh with emotion.

"I say this to you, English policeman, I would have died for him! And since he is dead, and I still live, my eyes shall not know sleep, or my heart rest, until I have avenged him. Like a dog will I nose out his murderer and when I have discovered him—Ah!" His eyes lit up. Suddenly he drew an immense knife from beneath his coat and brandished it aloft. "Not all at once will I kill him—oh no!—first I will slit his nose, and cut off his ears and put out his eyes, and then—then, into his black heart, I will thrust this knife."

Swiftly he replaced the knife, and turning, left the room. George Lomax, his eyes always protuberant, but now goggling almost out of his head, stared at the closed door.

"Purebred Herzoslovakian, of course," he muttered. "Most uncivilized people. A race of brigands."

Superindentent Battle rose alertly to his feet.

"Either that man's sincere," he remarked, "or he's the best bluffer I've ever seen. And if it's the former, God help Prince Michael's murderer when that human bloodhound gets hold of him."

# Fifteen

## THE FRENCH STRANGER

Virginia and Anthony walked side by side down the path which led to the lake. For some minutes after leaving the house they were silent. It was Virginia who broke the silence at last with a little laugh.

"Oh, dear," she said, "isn't it dreadful? Here I am so bursting with the things I want to tell you, and the things I want to know, that I simply don't know where to begin. First of all"—she lowered her voice—"*What have you done with the body?* How awful it sounds, doesn't it! I never dreamt that I should be so steeped in crime."

"I suppose it's quite a novel sensation for you," agreed Anthony.

"But not for you?"

"Well, I've never disposed of a corpse before, certainly."

"Tell me about it."

Briefly and succinctly, Anthony ran over the steps he had taken on the previous night. Virginia listened attentively.

"I think you were very clever," she said approvingly when he had finished. "I can pick up the trunk again when I go back to Paddington. The only difficulty that might arise is if you had to give an account of where you were yesterday evening."

"I can't see that can arise. The body can't have been found until late last night—or possibly this morning. Otherwise there would have been something about it in this morning's papers. And whatever you may imagine from reading detective stories, doctors aren't such magicians that they can tell you exactly how many hours a man has been dead. The exact time of his death will be pretty vague. An alibi for last night would be far more to the point."

"I know. Lord Caterham was telling me all about it. But the Scotland Yard man is quite convinced of your innocence now, isn't he?"

Anthony did not reply at once.

"He doesn't look particularly astute," continued Virginia.

"I don't know about that," said Anthony slowly. "I've an impression that there are no flies on Superintendent Battle. He appears to be convinced of my innocence—but I'm not sure. He's stumped at present by my apparent lack of motive."

"Apparent?" cried Virginia. "But what possible reason could you have for murdering an unknown foreign count?"

Anthony darted a sharp glance at her.

"You were at one time or other in Herzoslovakia, weren't you?" he asked.

"Yes. I was there with my husband, for two years, at the Embassy."

"That was just before the assassination of the King and Queen. Did you ever run across Prince Michael Obolovitch?"

"Michael? Of course I did. Horrid little wretch! He suggested, I remember, that I should marry him morganatically."

"Did he really? And what did he suggest you should do about your existing husband?"

"Oh, he had a sort of David and Uriah scheme all made out."

"And how did you respond to this amiable offer?"

"Well," said Virginia, "unfortunately one had to be diplomatic. So poor little Michael didn't get it as straight from the shoulder as he might have done. But he retired hurt all the same. Why all this interest about Michael?"

"Something I'm getting at in my own blundering fashion. I take it that you didn't meet the murdered man?"

"No. To put it like a book he 'retired to his own apartments immediately on arrival.'"

"And of course you haven't seen the body?"

Virginia, eyeing him with a good deal of interest, shook her head.

"Could you get to see it, do you think?"

"By means of influence in high places—meaning Lord Caterham—I daresay I could. Why? Is it an order?"

"Good Lord, no," said Anthony, horrified. "Have I been as dictatorial as all that? No, it's simply this. Count Stanislaus was the incognito of Prince Michael of Herzoslovakia."

Virginia's eyes opened very wide.

"I see." Suddenly her face broke into its fascinating one-sided smile. "I hope you don't suggest that Michael went to his rooms simply to avoid seeing me?"

"Something of the kind," admitted Anthony. "You see, if I'm right in my mind that someone wanted to prevent your coming to

Chimneys, the reason seems to lie in your knowing Herzoslovakia. Do you realize that you're the only person here who knew Prince Michael by sight?"

"Do you mean that this man who was murdered was an imposter?" asked Virginia abruptly.

"That is the possibility that crossed my mind. If you can get Lord Caterham to show you the body, we can clear up that point at once."

"He was shot at 11:45," said Virginia thoughtfully. "The time mentioned on that scrap of paper. The whole thing's horribly mysterious."

"That reminds me. Is that your window up there? The second from the end over the Council Chamber?"

"No, my room is in the Elizabethan wing, the other side. Why?"

"Simply because as I walked away last night, after thinking I heard a shot, the light went up in that room."

"How curious! I don't know who has that room, but I can find out by asking Bundle. Perhaps they heard the shot?"

"If so, they haven't come forward to say so. I understood from Battle that nobody in the house heard the shot fired. It's the only clue of any kind that I've got, and I daresay it's a pretty rotten one, but I mean to follow it up for what it's worth."

"It's curious, certainly," said Virginia thoughtfully.

They had arrived at the boathouse by the lake, and had been leaning against it as they talked.

"And now for the whole story," said Anthony. "We'll paddle gently about on the lake, secure from the prying ears of Scotland Yard, American visitors, and curious housemaids."

"I've heard something from Lord Caterham," said Virginia. "But not nearly enough. To begin with, which are you really, Anthony Cade or Jimmy McGrath?"

For the second time that morning, Anthony unfolded the history of the last six weeks of his life—with this difference that the account given to Virginia needed no editing. He finished up with his own astonished recognition of "Mr. Holmes."

"By the way, Mrs. Revel," he ended, "I've never thanked you for imperilling your mortal soul by saying that I was an old friend of yours."

"Of course you're an old friend," cried Virginia. "You don't suppose I'd lumber you with a corpse, and then pretend you were a mere acquaintance next time I met you? No, indeed!"

She paused.

"Do you know one thing that strikes me about all this?" she went on. "That there's some extra mystery about those memoirs that we haven't fathomed yet."

"I think you're right," agreed Anthony. "There's one thing I'd like you to tell me," he continued.

"What's that?"

"Why did you seem so surprised when I mentioned the name of Jimmy McGrath to you yesterday at Pont Street? Had you heard it before?"

"I had, Sherlock Holmes. George—my cousin, George Lomax, you know—came to see me the other day, and suggested a lot of frightfully silly things. His idea was that I should come down here and make myself agreeable to this man, McGrath, and Delilah the memoirs out of him somehow. He didn't put it like that, of course. He talked a lot of nonsense about English gentlewomen, and things like that, but his real meaning was never obscure for a moment. It was just the sort of rotten thing poor old George would think of. And then I wanted to know too much, and he tried to put me off with lies that wouldn't have deceived a child of two."

"Well, his plan seems to have succeeded, anyhow," observed Anthony. "Here am I, the James McGrath he had in mind, and here are you being agreeable to me."

"But alas, for poor old George, no memoirs! Now I've got a question for you. When I said I hadn't written those letters, you said you knew I hadn't—you couldn't know any such thing?"

"Oh, yes, I could," said Anthony, smiling. "I've got a good working knowledge of psychology."

"You mean your belief in the sterling worth of my moral character was such that—"

But Anthony was shaking his head vigorously.

"Not at all. I don't know anything about your moral character. You might have a lover, and you might write to him. But you'd never lie down to be blackmailed. The Virginia Revel of those letters was scared stiff. You'd have fought."

"I wonder who the real Virginia Revel is—where she is, I mean. It makes me feel as though I had a double somewhere."

Anthony lit a cigarette.

"You know that one of the letters was written from Chimneys?" he asked at last.

"What?" Virginia was clearly startled. "When was it written?"

"It wasn't dated. But it's odd, isn't it?"

"I'm perfectly certain no other Virginia Revel has ever stayed at Chimneys. Bundle or Lord Caterham would have said something about the coincidence of the name if she had."

"Yes. It's rather queer. Do you know, Mrs. Revel, I am beginning to disbelieve profoundly in this other Virginia Revel."

"She's very elusive," agreed Virginia.

"Extraordinarily elusive. I am beginning to think that the person who wrote those letters deliberately used your name."

"But why?" cried Virginia. "Why should they do such a thing?"

"Ah, that's just the question. There's the devil of a lot to find out about everything."

"Who do you really think killed Michael?" asked Virginia suddenly. "The Comrades of the Red Hand?"

"I suppose they might have done so," said Anthony in a dissatisfied voice. "Pointless killing would be rather characteristic of them."

"Let's get to work," said Virginia. "I see Lord Caterham and Bundle strolling together. The first thing to do is to find out definitely whether the dead man is Michael or not."

Anthony paddled to shore and a few moments later they had joined Lord Caterham and his daughter.

"Lunch is late," said his lordship in a depressed voice.

"Battle has insulted the cook, I expect."

"This is a friend of mine, Bundle," said Virginia. "Be nice to him."

Bundle looked earnestly at Anthony for some minutes, and then addressed a remark to Virginia as though he had not been there.

"Where do you pick up these nice-looking men, Virginia? 'How do you do it?' says she enviously."

"You can have him," said Virginia generously. "I want Lord Caterham."

She smiled upon the flattered peer, slipped her hand through his arm and they moved off together.

"Do you talk?" asked Bundle. "Or are you just strong and silent?"

"Talk?" said Anthony. "I babble. I murmur. I burble—like the running brook, you know. Sometimes I even ask questions."

"As, for instance?"

"Who occupies the second room on the left from the end?"

He pointed to it as he spoke.

"What an extraordinary question!" said Bundle. "You intrigue me greatly. Let me see—yes—that's Mademoiselle Brun's room. The French governess. She endeavours to keep my young sisters in order. Dulcie and Daisy—like the song, you know. I daresay they'd have called the next one Dorothy May. But mother got tired of having nothing but girls and died. Thought someone else could take on the job of providing an heir."

"Mademoiselle Brun," said Anthony thoughtfully. "How long has she been with you?"

"Two months. She came to us when we were in Scotland."

"Ha!" said Anthony. "I smell a rat."

"I wish I could smell some lunch," said Bundle. "Do I ask the Scotland Yard man to have lunch with us, Mr. Cade? You're a man of the world, you know about the etiquette of such things. We've never had a murder in the house before. Exciting, isn't it. I'm sorry your character was so completely cleared this morning. I've always wanted to meet a murderer and see for myself if they're as genial and charming as the Sunday papers always say they are. God! what's that?"

"That" seemed to be a taxi approaching the house. It's two occupants were a tall man with a bald head and a black beard, and a smaller and younger man with a black moustache. Anthony recognized the former, and guessed that it was he—rather than the vehicle which contained him—that had rung the exclamation of astonishment from his companion's lips.

"Unless I much mistake," he remarked, "that is my old friend, Baron Lollipop."

"Baron what?"

"I call him Lollipop for convenience. The pronouncing of his own name tends to harden the arteries."

"It nearly wrecked the telephone this morning," remarked Bundle. "So that's the Baron, is it? I foresee he'll be turned on to me this afternoon—and I've had Isaacstein all the morning. Let George do his own dirty work, say I, and to hell with politics. Excuse me leaving you, Mr. Cade, but I must stand by poor old Father."

Bundle retreated rapidly to the house.

Anthony stood looking after her for a minute or two and thoughtfully lighted a cigarette. As he did so, his ear was caught by a stealthy sound quite near him. He was standing by the boathouse, and the sound seemed to come from just round the corner. The mental picture conveyed to him was that of a man vainly trying to stifle a sudden sneeze.

"Now I wonder—I very much wonder who's behind the boathouse," said Anthony to himself. "We'd better see, I think."

Suiting the action to the word, he threw away the match he had just blown out, and ran lightly and noiselessly round the corner of the boathouse.

He came upon a man who had evidently been kneeling on the ground and was just struggling to rise to his feet. He was tall, wore a light-coloured overcoat and glasses, and for the rest, had a short pointed black beard and slightly foppish manner. He was between thirty and forty years of age, and altogether of a most respectable appearance.

"What are you doing here?" asked Anthony.

He was pretty certain that the man was not one of Lord Cater-ham's guests.

"I ask your pardon," said the stranger, with a marked foreign accent and what was meant to be an engaging smile. "It is that I wish to return to the Jolly Cricketers and I have lost my way. Would Monsieur be so good as to direct me?"

"Certainly," said Anthony. "But you don't go there by water, you know."

"Eh?" said the stranger, with the air of one at a loss.

"I said," repeated Anthony, with a meaning glance at the boat-house, "that you won't get there by water. There's a right of way across the park—some distance away, but all this is the private part. You're trespassing."

"I am most sorry," said the stranger. "I lost my direction en-tirely. I thought I would come up here and inquire."

Anthony refrained from pointing out that kneeling behind a boathouse was a somewhat peculiar manner of prosecuting inquir-ies. He took the stranger kindly by the arm.

"You go this way, he said. "Right round the lake and straight on—you can't miss the path. When you get on it, turn to the left, and it will lead you to the village. You're staying at the Cricketers, I suppose?"

"I am, monsieur. Since this morning. Many thanks for your kindness in directing me."

"Don't mention it," said Anthony. "I hope you haven't caught cold."

"Eh?" said the stranger.

"From kneeling on the damp ground, I mean," explained Anthony. "I fancied I heard you sneezing."

"I may have sneezed," admitted the other.

"Quite so," said Anthony. "But you shouldn't suppress a sneeze, you know. One of the most eminent doctors said so only the other day. It's frightfully dangerous. I don't remember exactly what it does to you—whether it's an inhibition or whether it hardens your arteries, but you must never do it. Good morning."

"Good morning, and thank you, monsieur, for setting me on the right road."

"Second suspicious stranger from village inn," murmured Anthony to himself, as he watched the other's retreating form. "And one that I can't place, either. Appearance that of a French commercial traveller. I don't quite see him as a Comrade of the Red Hand. Does he represent yet a third party in the harassed state of Herzoslovakia? The French governess has the second window from the end. A mysterious Frenchman is found slinking round the grounds, listening to conversations that are not meant for his ears. I'll bet my hat there's something in it."

Musing thus, Anthony retraced his steps to the house. On the terrace, he encountered Lord Caterham, looking suitably depressed, and two new arrivals. He brightened a little at the sight of Anthony.

"Ah, there you are," he remarked. "Let me introduce you to Baron—er—er—and Captain Andrassy. Mr. Anthony Cade."

The Baron stared at Anthony with growing suspicion.

"Mr. Cade?" he said stiffly. "I think not."

"A word alone with you, Baron," said Anthony. "I can explain everything."

The Baron bowed, and the two men walked down the terrace together.

"Baron," said Anthony. "I must throw myself upon your mercy. I have so far strained the honour of an English gentleman as to travel to this country under an assumed name. I represented myself to you as Mr. James McGrath—but you must see for yourself that the deception involved was infinitesimal. You are doubtless acquainted with the works of Shakespeare, and his remarks about the unimportance of the nomenclature of roses? This case is the same. The man you wanted to see was the man in possession of the memoirs. I was that man. As you know only too well, I am no longer in possession of them. A neat trick, Baron, a very neat trick. Who thought of it, you or your principal?"

"His Highness' own idea it was. And for anyone but him to carry it out he would not permit."

"He did it jolly well," said Anthony, with approval. "I never took him for anything but an Englishman."

"The education of an English gentleman did the Prince receive," explained the Baron. "The custom of Herzoslovakia it is."

"No professional could have pinched those papers better," said Anthony. "May I ask, without indiscretion, what has become of them?"

"Between gentlemen," began the Baron.

"You are too kind, Baron," murmured Anthony. "I've never been called a gentleman so often as I have in the last forty-eight hours."

"I to you say this—I believe them to be burnt."

"You believe, but you don't know, eh? Is that it?"

"His Highness in his own keeping retained them. His purpose it was to read them and then by the fire destroy them."

"I see," said Anthony. "All the same, they are not the kind of light literature you'd skim through in half an hour."

"Among the effects of my martyred master they have not discovered been. It is clear, therefore, that burnt they are."

"Hm!" said Anthony. "I wonder?"

He was silent for a minute or two and then went on.

"I have asked you these questions, Baron, because, as you may have heard, I myself have been implicated in the crime. I must clear myself absolutely, so that no suspicion attaches to me."

"Undoubtedly," said the Baron. "Your honour demands it."

"Exactly," said Anthony. "You put these things so well. I haven't got the knack of it. To continue, I can only clear myself by discovering the real murderer, and to do that I must have all the facts. This question of the memoirs is very important. It seems to me possible that to gain possession of them might be the motive of the crime. Tell me, Baron, is that a very far-fetched idea?"

The Baron hesitated for a moment or two.

"You yourself the memoirs have read?" he asked cautiously at length.

"I think I am answered," said Anthony, smiling. "Now, Baron, there's just one thing more. I should like to give you fair warning that it is still my intention to deliver that manuscript to the publishers on Wednesday next, the 13th of October."

The Baron stared at him.

"But you have no longer got it?"

"On Wednesday next, I said. Today is Friday. That gives me five days to get hold of it again."

"But if it is burnt?"

"I don't think it is burnt. I have good reasons for not believing so."

As he spoke they turned the corner of the terrace. A massive figure was advancing towards them. Anthony, who had not yet seen the great Mr. Herman Isaacstein, looked at him with considerable interest.

"Ah, Baron," said Isaacstein, waving a big black cigar he was smoking, "this is a bad business—a very bad business."

"My good friend, Mr. Isaacstein, it is indeed," cried the Baron. "All our noble edifice in ruins is."

Anthony tactfully left the two gentlemen to their lamentations, and retraced his steps along the terrace.

Suddenly he came to a halt. A thin spiral of smoke was rising into the air apparently from the very centre of the yew hedge.

"It must be hollow in the middle," reflected Anthony "I've heard of such things before."

He looked swiftly to right and left of him. Lord Caterham was at the farther end of the terrace with Captain Andrassy. Their backs were towards him. Anthony bent down and wriggled his way through the massive yew.

He had been quite right in his supposition. The yew hedge was really not one, but two, a narrow passage divided them. The entrance to this was about halfway up, on the side of the house. There was no mystery about it, but no one seeing the yew hedge from the front would have guessed at the probability.

Anthony looked down the narrow vista. About halfway down, a man was reclining in a basket chair. A half-smoked cigar rested on the arm of the chair, and the gentleman himself appeared to be asleep.

"Hm!" said Anthony to himself. "Evidently Mr. Hiram Fish prefers sitting in the shade."

# Sixteen

## Tea in the Schoolroom

Anthony regained the terrace with the feeling uppermost in his mind that the only safe place for private conversations was the middle of the lake.

The resonant boom of a gong sounded from the house, and Tredwell appeared in a stately fashion from a side door "Luncheon is served, my lord."

"Ah!" said Lord Caterham, brisking up a little. "Lunch!"

At that moment two children burst out of the house. They were high-spirited young women of twelve and ten, and though their names might be Dulcie and Daisy, as Bundle had affirmed, they appeared to be more generally known as Guggle and Winkle. They executed a kind of war dance, interspersed with shrill whoops till Bundle emerged and quelled them.

"Where's Mademoiselle?" she demanded.

"She's got the migraine, the migraine, the migraine!" chanted Winkle.

"Hurrah!" said Guggle, joining in.

Lord Caterham had succeeded in shepherding most of his guests into the house. Now he laid a restraining hand on Anthony's arm.

"Come to my study," he breathed. "I've got something rather special there."

Slinking down the hall, far more like a thief than like the master of the house, Lord Caterham gained the shelter of his sanctum. Here he unlocked a cupboard and produced various bottles.

"Talking to foreigners always makes me so thirsty," he explained apologetically. "I don't know why it is."

There was a knock on the door, and Virginia popped her head round the corner of it.

"Got a special cocktail for me?" she demanded.

"Of course," said Lord Caterham hospitably. "Come in."

The next few minutes were taken up with serious rites.

"I needed that," said Lord Caterham with a sigh, as he replaced his glass on the table. "As I said just now, I find talking to foreigners particularly fatiguing. I think it's because they're so polite. Come along. Let's have some lunch."

He led the way to the dining room. Virginia put her hand on Anthony's arm, and drew him back a little.

"I've done my good deed for the day," she whispered. "I got Lord Caterham to take me to see the body."

"Well?" demanded Anthony eagerly.

One theory of his was to be proved or disproved.

Virginia was shaking her head.

"You were wrong," she whispered. "It's Prince Michael right."

"Oh!" Anthony was deeply chagrined.

"And Mademoiselle had the migraine," he added aloud, in a dissatisfied tone.

"What has that got to do with it?"

"Probably nothing, but I wanted to see her. You see, I've found out that Mademoiselle has the second room from the end—the one where I saw the light go up last night."

"That's interesting."

"Probably there's nothing in it. All the same, I mean to see Mademoiselle before the day is out."

Lunch was somewhat of an ordeal. Even the cheerful impartiality of Bundle failed to reconcile the heterogeneous assembly. The Baron and Andrassy were correct, formal, full of etiquette, and had the air of attending a meal in a mausoleum. Lord Catherham was lethargic and depressed. Bill Eversleigh stared longingly at Virginia. George, very mindful of the trying position in which he found himself, conversed weightily with the Baron and Mr. Isaacstein. Guggle and Winkle, completely beside themselves with joy at having a murder in the house, had to be continually checked and kept under, whilst Mr. Hiram Fish slowly masticated his food, and drawled out dry remarks in his own peculiar idiom. Superintendent Battle had considerately vanished, and nobody knew what had become of him.

"Thank God that's over," murmured Bundle to Anthony, as they left the table. "And George is taking the foreign contingent over to the Abbey this afternoon to discuss State secrets."

"That will possibly relieve the atmosphere," agreed Anthony.

"I don't mind the American so much," continued Bundle. "He and Father can talk first editions together quite happily in some secluded spot. Mr. Fish"—as the object of their conversation drew near—"I'm planning a peaceful afternoon for you."

The American bowed.

"That's too kind of you, Lady Eileen."

"Mr. Fish," said Anthony, "had quite a peaceful morning."

Mr. Fish shot a quick glance at him.

"Ah, you observed me, then, in my secluded retreat? There are moments, sir, when far from the madding crowd is the only motto for a man of quiet tastes."

Bundle had drifted on, and the American and Anthony were left together. The former dropped his voice a little.

"I opine," he said, "that there is considerable mystery about this little dustup?"

"Any amount of it," said Anthony.

"That guy with the bald head was perhaps a family connexion?"

"Something of the kind."

"These Central European nations beat the band," declared Mr. Fish. "It's kind of being rumoured around that the deceased gentleman was a Royal Highness. Is that so, do you know?"

"He was staying here as Count Stanislaus," replied Anthony evasively.

To this Mr. Fish offered no further rejoinder than the somewhat cryptic:

"Oh, boy!"

After which he relapsed into silence for some moments.

"This police captain of yours," he observed at last. "Battle, or whatever his name is, is he the goods all right?"

"Scotland Yard think so," replied Anthony dryly.

"He seems kind of hidebound to me," remarked Mr. Fish. "No hustle to him. This big idea of his, letting no one leave the house, what is there to it?"

He darted a very sharp look at Anthony as he spoke.

"Everyone's got to attend the inquest tomorrow morning, you see."

"That's the idea is it? No more to it than that? No question of Lord Caterham's guests being suspected?"

"My dear Mr. Fish!"

"I was getting a mite uneasy—being a stranger in this country. But of course it was an outside job—I remember now. Window found unfastened, wasn't it?"

"It was," said Anthony, looking straight in front of him.

Mr. Fish sighed. After a minute or two he said in a plaintive tone:

"Young man, do you know how they get the water out of a mine?"

"How?"

"By pumping—but it's almighty hard work! I observe the figure of my genial host detaching itself from the group over yonder. I must join him."

Mr. Fish walked gently away, and Bundle drifted back again.

"Funny Fish, isn't he?" she remarked.

"He is."

"It's no good looking for Virginia," said Bundle sharply.

"I wasn't."

"You were. I don't know how she does it. It isn't what she says, I don't even believe it's what she looks. But, oh, boy! she gets there everytime. Anyway, she's on duty elsewhere for the time. She told me to be nice to you, and I'm going to be nice to you—by force if necessary."

"No force required," Anthony assured her. "But, if it's all the same to you, I'd rather you were nice to me on the water, in a boat."

"It's not a bad idea," said Bundle meditatively.

They strolled down to the lake together.

"There's just one question I'd like to ask you," said Anthony as he paddled gently out from the shore, "before we turn to really interesting topics. Business before pleasure."

"Whose bedroom do you want to know about now?" asked Bundle with weary patience.

"Nobody's bedroom for the moment. But I would like to know where you got your French governess from."

"The man's bewitched," said Bundle. "I got her from an agency, and I pay her a hundred pounds a year, and her Christian name is Geneviève. Anything more you want to know?"

"We'll assume the agency," said Anthony. "What about her references?"

"Oh, glowing! She lived for ten years with the Countess of What Not."

"What Not being?—"

"The Comtesse de Breteuil, Château de Breteuil, Dinard."

"You didn't actually see the Comtesse yourself? It was all done by letter?"

"Exactly."

"Hm!" said Anthony.

"You intrigue me," said Bundle. "You intrigue me enormously. Is it love or crime?"

"Probably sheer idiocy on my part. Let's forget it."

" 'Let's forget it,' says he negligently, having extracted all the information he wants. Mr. Cade, who do you suspect? I rather suspect Virginia as being the most unlikely person. Or possibly Bill."

"What about you?"

"Member of the aristocracy joins in secret the Comrades of the Red Hand. It would create a sensation all right."

Anthony laughed. He liked Bundle, though he was a little afraid of the shrewd penetration of her sharp grey eyes.

"You must be proud of all this," he said suddenly, waving his hand towards the great house in the distance.

Bundle screwed up her eyes and tilted her head on one side.

"Yes—it means something, I suppose. But one's too used to it. Anyway, we're not here very much—too deadly dull. We've been at Cowes and Deauville all the summer after town, and then up to Scotland. Chimneys has been swathed in dust sheets for about five months. Once a week they take the dust sheets off and coaches full of tourists come and gape and listen to Tredwell. 'On your right is the portrait of the fourth Marchioness of Caterham, painted by Sir Joshua Reynolds,' etc, and Ed or Bert, the humorist of the party, nudges his girl and says, 'Eh! Gladys, they've got two pennyworth of pictures here, right enough.' And then they go and look at more pictures and yawn and shuffle their feet and wish it was time to go home."

"Yet history has been made here once or twice, by all accounts."

"You've been listening to George," said Bundle sharply. "That's the kind of thing he's always saying."

But Anthony had raised himself on his elbow, and was staring at the shore.

"Is that a third suspicious stranger I see standing disconsolately by the boathouse? Or is it one of the house party?"

Bundle lifted her head from the scarlet cushion.

"It's Bill," she said.

"He seems to be looking for something."

"He's probably looking for me," said Bundle, without enthusiasm.

"Shall we row quickly in the opposite direction?"

"That's quite the right answer, but it should be delivered with more enthusiasm."

"I shall row with double vigour after that rebuke."

"Not at all," said Bundle. "I have my pride. Row me to where that young ass is waiting. Somebody's got to look after him, I suppose. Virginia must have given him the slip. One of these days, inconceivable as it seems, I might want to marry George, so I might as well practise being 'one of our well-known political hostesses.'"

Anthony pulled obediently towards the shore.

"And what's to become of me, I should like to know?" he complained. "I refuse to be the unwanted third. Is that the children I see in the distance?"

"Yes. Be careful, or they'll rope you in."

"I'm rather fond of children," said Anthony. "I might teach them some nice quiet intellectual game."

"Well, don't say I didn't warn you."

Having relinquished Bundle to the care of the disconsolate Bill, Anthony strolled off to where various shrill cries disturbed the peace of the afternoon. He was received with acclamation."

"Are you any good at playing Red Indians?" asked Guggle sternly.

"Rather," said Anthony. "You should hear the noise I make when I'm being scalped. Like this." He illustrated.

"Not so bad," said Winkle grudgingly. "Now do the scalper's yell."

Anthony obliged with a bloodcurdling noise. In another minute the game of Red Indians was in full swing.

About an hour later, Anthony wiped his forehead, and ventured to inquire after Mademoiselle's migraine. He was pleased to hear that that lady had entirely recovered. So popular had he become that he was urgently invited to come and have tea in the schoolroom.

"And then you can tell us about the man you saw hung," urged Guggle.

"Did you say you'd got a bit of the rope with you?" asked Winkle.

"It's in my suitcase," said Anthony solemnly. "You shall each have a piece of it."

Winkle immediately let out a wild Indian yell of satisfaction.

"We'll have to go and get washed, I suppose," said Guggle gloomily. "You will come to tea, won't you? You won't forget?"

Anthony swore solemnly that nothing should prevent him keeping the engagement. Satisfied, the youthful pair beat a retreat towards the house. Anthony stood for a minute looking after them, and, as he did so, he became aware of a man leaving the other side of a little copse of trees and hurrying away across the park. He felt almost sure that it was the same black-bearded stranger he had encountered that morning. Whilst he was hesitating whether to go after him or not the trees just ahead of him were parted and

Mr. Hiram Fish stepped out into the open. He started slightly when he saw Anthony.

"A peaceful afternoon, Mr. Fish?" inquired the latter.

"I thank you, yes."

Mr. Fish did not look as peaceful as usual however. His face was flushed, and he was breathing hard as though he had been running. He drew out his watch and consulted it.

"I guess," he said softly, "it's just about time for your British institution of afternoon tea."

Closing his watch with a snap, Mr. Fish ambled gently away in the direction of the house.

Anthony stood in a brown study and awoke with a start to the fact that Superintendent Battle was standing beside him. Not the faintest sound had heralded his approach, and he seemed literally to have materialized from space.

"Where did you spring from?" asked Anthony irritably.

With a slight jerk of his head, Battle indicated the little copse of trees behind them.

"It seems a popular spot this afternoon," remarked Anthony.

"You were very lost in thought, Mr. Cade."

"I was indeed. Do you know what I was doing, Battle? I was trying to put two and one and five and three together so as to make four. And it can't be done, Battle, it simply can't be done."

"There's difficulties that way," agreed the detective.

"But you're just the man I wanted to see. Battle, I want to go away. Can it be done?"

True to his creed, Superintendent Battle showed neither emotion nor surprise. His reply was easy and matter of fact.

"That depends, sir, as to where you want to go."

"I'll tell you exactly, Battle. I'll lay my cards upon the table. I want to go Dinard, to the château of Madame la Comtesse de Breteuil. Can it be done?"

"When do you want to go, Mr. Cade?"

"Say tomorrow after the inquest. I could be back here by Sunday evening."

"I see," said the superintendent, with peculiar solidity.

"Well, what about it?"

"I've no objection, provided you go where you say you're going, and come straight back here."

"You're a man in a thousand, Battle. Either you have taken an extraordinary fancy to me or else you're extraordinarily deep. Which is it?"

Superintendent Battle smiled a little, but did not answer.

"Well, well," said Anthony, "I expect you'll take your precautions. Discreet minions of the law will follow my suspicious footsteps. So be it. But I do wish I knew what it was all about."

"I don't get you, Mr. Cade."

"The memoirs—what all the fuss is about. Were they only memoirs? Or have you got something up your sleeve?"

Battle smiled again.

"Take it like this. I'm doing you a favour because you've made a favourable impression on me, Mr. Cade. I'd like you to work in with me over this case. The amateur and the professional, they go well together. The one has the intimacy, so to speak, and the other the experience."

"Well," said Anthony slowly, "I don't mind admitting that I've always wanted to try my hand at unravelling a murder mystery."

"Any ideas about the case at all, Mr. Cade?"

"Plenty of them," said Anthony. "But they're mostly questions."

"As, for instance?"

"Who steps into the murdered Michael's shoes? It seems to me that that is important?"

A rather wry smile came over Superintendent Battle's face.

"I wondered if you'd think of that, sir. Prince Nicholas Obolovitch is the next heir—first cousin of this gentleman."

"And where is he at the present moment?" asked Anthony, turning away to light a cigarette. "Don't tell me you don't know, Battle, because I shan't believe you."

We've reason to believe that he's in the United States. He was until quite lately, at all events. Raising money on his expectations."

Anthony gave vent to a surprised whistle.

"I get you," said Anthony. "Michael was backed by England, Nicholas by America. In both countries a group of financiers are anxious to obtain the oil concessions. The Loyalist party adopted Michael as their candidate—now they'll have to look elsewhere. Gnashing of teeth on the part of Isaacstein and Co. and Mr. George Lomax. Rejoicings in Wall Street. Am I right?"

"You're not far off," said Superintendent Battle.

"Hm!" said Anthony. "I almost dare swear that I know what you were doing in that copse."

The detective smiled, but made no reply.

"International politics are very fascinating," said Anthony, "but I fear I must leave you. I have an appointment in the schoolroom."

He strode briskly away towards the house. Inquiries of the dignified Tredwell showed him the way to the schoolroom. He tapped on the door and entered, to be greeted by squeals of joy.

Guggle and Winkle immediately rushed at him and bore him in triumph to be introduced to Mademoiselle.

For the first time, Anthony felt a qualm. Mademoiselle Brun was a small, middle-aged woman with a sallow face, pepper-and-salt hair, and a budding moustache!

As the notorious foreign adventuress she did not fit into the picture at all.

"I believe," said Anthony to himself, "I'm making the most utter fool of myself. Never mind, I must go through with it now."

He was extremely pleasant to Mademoiselle, and she, on her part, was evidently delighted to have a good-looking young man invade her schoolroom. The meal was a great success.

But that evening, alone in the charming bedchamber that had been allotted to him, Anthony shook his head several times.

"I'm wrong," he said to himself. "For the second time, I'm wrong. Somehow or other, I can't get the hang of this thing."

He stopped in his pacing of the floor.

"What the devil—" began Anthony.

The door was being softly opened. In another minute a man had slipped into the room, and stood deferentially by the door.

He was a big fair man, squarely built, with high Slavonic cheekbones, and dreamy fanatic eyes.

"Who the devil are you?" asked Anthony, staring at him.

The man replied in perfect English.

"I am Boris Anchoukoff."

"Prince Michael's servant, eh?"

"That is so. I served my master. He is dead. Now I serve you."

"It's very kind of you," said Anthony. "But I don't happen to want a valet."

"You are my master now. I will serve you faithfully."

"Yes—but—look—here—I don't need a valet. I can't afford one."

Boris Anchoukoff looked at him with a touch of scorn.

"I do not ask for money. I served my master. So will I serve you—to the death!"

Stepping quickly forward, he dropped on one knee, caught Anthony's hand and placed it on his forehead. Then he rose swiftly and left the room as suddenly as he had come.

Anthony stared after him, his face a picture of astonishment.

"That's damned odd," he said to himself. "A faithful sort of dog. Curious the instincts these fellows have."

He rose and paced up and down.

"All the same," he muttered, "it's awkward—damned awkward—just at present."

# Seventeen

## A Midnight Adventure

The inquest took place on the following morning. It was extraordinarily unlike the inquests as pictured in sensational fiction. It satisfied even George Lomax in its rigid suppression of all interesting details. Superintendent Battle and the coroner, working together with the support of the chief constable, had reduced the proceedings to the lowest level of boredom.

Immediately after the inquest, Anthony took an unostentatious departure.

His departure was the one bright spot in the day for Bill Eversleigh. George Lomax, obsessed with the fear that something damaging to his department might leak out, had been exceedingly trying. Miss Oscar and Bill had been in constant attendance. Everything useful and interesting had been done by Miss Oscar. Bill's part had been to run to and fro with countless messages, to decode telegrams, and to listen by the hour to George's repeating himself.

It was a completely exhausted young man who retired to bed on Saturday night. He had had practically no chance to talk to Virginia all day, owing to George's exactions, and he felt injured and ill-used. Thank goodness, that Colonial fellow had taken himself off. He had monopolized far too much of Virginia's society, anyway. And of course if George Lomax went on making an ass of himself like this—His mind seething with resentment, Bill fell asleep. And, in dreams, came consolation. For he dreamt of Virginia.

It was an heroic dream, a dream of burning timbers in which he played the part of the gallant rescuer. He brought down Virginia from the topmost storey in his arms. She was unconscious. He laid her on the grass. Then he went off to find a packet of sandwiches. It was most important that he should find that packet of sandwiches. George had it but instead of giving it up to Bill, he began to dictate telegrams. They were now in the vestry of a church, and any minute Virginia might arrive to be married to him. Horror! He was wearing pyjamas. He must get home at once and find his proper clothes. He rushed out to the car. The car would not start. No petrol in the tank! He was getting desperate. And then a big General bus drew up and Virginia got out of it on the arm of the baldheaded Baron. She was deliciously cool, and exquisitely dressed in grey. She came over to him and shook him by the shoulders playfully. "Bill," she said. "Oh, Bill." She shook him harder. "Bill," she said. "Wake up. Oh, do wake up!"

Very dazed, Bill woke up. He was in his bedroom at Chimneys. But part of the dream was with him still. Virginia was leaning over him, and was repeating the same words with variations.

"Wake up, Bill. Oh, do wake up! Bill."

"Hullo!" said Bill, sitting up in bed. "What's the matter?"

Virginia gave a sigh of relief.

"Thank goodness. I thought you'd never wake up. I've been shaking you and shaking you. Are you properly awake now?"

"I think so," said Bill doubtfully.

"You great lump," said Virginia. "The trouble I've had! My arms are aching."

"These insults are uncalled for," said Bill, with dignity. "Let me say, Virginia, that I consider your conduct most unbecoming. Not at all that of a pure young widow."

"Don't be an idiot, Bill. Things are happening."

"What kind of things?"

"Queer things. In the Council Chamber. I thought I heard a door bang somewhere, and I came down to see. And then I saw a light in the Council Chamber. I crept along the passage, and peeped through the crack of the door. I couldn't see much, but what I could see was so extraordinary that I felt I must see more. And then, all of a sudden, I felt that I should like a nice, big strong man with me. And you were the nicest and biggest and strongest man I could think of, so I came in and tried to wake you up quietly. But I've been ages doing it."

"I see," said Bill. "And what do you want me to do now? Get up and tackle the burglars?"

Virginia wrinkled her brows.

"I'm not sure that they are burglars. Bill, it's very queer—But don't let's waste time talking. Get up."

Bill slipped obediently out of bed.

"Wait while I don a pair of boots—the big ones with nails in them. However big and strong I am. I'm not going to tackle hardened criminals with bare feet."

"I like your pyjamas, Bill," said Virginia dreamily. "Brightness without vulgarity."

"While we're on the subject," remarked Bill, reaching for his second boot, "I like that thingummybob of yours. It's a pretty shade of green. What do you call it? It's not just a dressing gown, is it?"

"It's a negligé," said Virginia. "I'm glad you've led such a pure life, Bill."

"I haven't, said Bill indignantly.

"You've just betrayed the fact. You're very nice, Bill, and I like you. I daresay that tomorrow morning—say about ten o'clock, a good safe hour for not unduly exciting the emotions—I might even kiss you."

"I always think these things are best carried out on the spur of the moment," suggested Bill.

"We've other fish to fry," said Virginia. "If you don't want to put on a gas mask and a shirt of chain mail, shall we start?"

"I'm ready," said Bill.

He wriggled into a lurid silk dressing gown, and picked up a poker.

"The orthodox weapon," he observed.

"Come on," said Virginia, "and don't make a noise."

They crept out of the room and along the corridor, and then down the wide double staircase. Virginia frowned as they reached the bottom of it.

"Those boots of yours aren't exactly domes of silence, are they, Bill?"

"Nails will be nails," said Bill. "I'm doing my best."

"You'll have to take them off," said Virginia firmly.

Bill groaned.

"You can carry them in your hand. I want to see if you can make out what's going on in the Council Chamber. Bill, it's awfully mysterious. Why should burglars take a man in armour to pieces?"

"Well, I suppose they can't take him away whole very well. They disarticulate him, and pack him neatly."

Virginia shook her head, dissatisfied.

"What should they want to steal a mouldy old suit of armour for? Why, Chimneys is full of treasures that are much easier to take away."

Bill shook his head.

"How many of them are there?" he asked, taking a firmer grip of his poker.

"I couldn't see properly. You know what a keyhole is. And they only had a flashlight."

"I expect they've gone by now," said Bill hopefully.

He sat on the bottom stair and drew off his boots. Then, holding them in his hand, he crept along the passage that led to the Council Chamber, Virginia close behind him. They halted outside the massive oak door. All was silent within, but suddenly Virginia pressed his arm, and he nodded. A bright light had shown for a minute through the keyhole.

Bill went down on his knees, and applied his eye to the orifice. What he saw was confusing in the extreme. The scene of the drama that was being enacted inside was evidently just to the left, out of his line of vision. A subdued chink every now and then seemed to point to the fact that the invaders were still dealing with the figure in armour. There were two of these, Bill remembered. They stood together by the wall just under the Holbein portrait. The light of the electric torch was evidently being directed upon the operations in progress. It left the rest of the room nearly in darkness. Once a figure flitted across Bill's line of vision, but there was not sufficient light to distinguish anything about it. It might have been that of a man or a woman. In a minute or two it flitted back again and then the subdued chinking sounded again. Presently there came a new sound, a faint tap-tap as of knuckles on wood.

Bill sat back on his heels suddenly.

"What is it?" whispered Virginia.

"Nothing. It's no good going on like this. We can't see anything, and we can't guess what they're up to. I must go in and tackle them."

He drew on his boots and stood up.

"Now, Virginia, listen to me. We'll open the door as softly as possible. You know where the switch of the electric light is?"

"Yes, just by the door."

"I don't think there are more than two of them. There may be only one. I want to get well into the room. Then, when I say 'Go' I want you to switch on the lights. Do you understand?"

"Perfectly."

"And don't scream or faint or anything. I won't let anyone hurt you."

"My hero!" murmured Virginia.

Bill peered at her suspiciously through the darkness. He heard a faint sound which might have been either a sob or a laugh. Then he grasped the poker firmly and rose to his feet. He felt that he was fully alive to the situation.

Very softly, he turned the handle of the door. It yielded and swung gently inwards. Bill felt Virginia close beside him. Together they moved noiselessly into the room.

At the farther end of the room, the torch was playing upon the Holbein picture. Silhouetted against it was the figure of a man, standing on a chair and gently tapping on the panelling. His back, of course, was to them, and he merely loomed up as a monstrous shadow.

What more they might have seen cannot be told, for at that moment Bill's nails squeaked upon the parquet floor. The man swung round, directing the powerful torch full upon them and almost dazzling them with the sudden glare.

Bill did not hesitate.

"Go," he roared to Virginia, and sprang for his man, as she obediently pressed down the switch of the electric lights.

The big chandelier should have been flooded with light; but instead, all that happened was the click of the switch. The room remained in darkness.

Virginia heard Bill curse freely. The next minute the air was filled with panting, scuffling sounds. The torch had fallen to the ground and extinguished itself in the fall. There was the sound of a desperate struggle going on in the darkness, but as to who was getting the better of it, and indeed as to who was taking part in it, Virginia had no idea. Had there been anyone else in the room besides the man who was tapping the panelling? There might have been. Their glimpse had been only a momentary one.

Virginia felt paralysed. She hardly knew what to do. She dared not try to join in the struggle. To do so might hamper and not aid Bill. Her one idea was to stay in the doorway, so that anyone trying to escape should not leave the room that way. At the same time, she disobeyed Bill's express instructions and screamed loudly and repeatedly for help.

She heard doors opening upstairs, and a sudden gleam of light from the hall and the big staircase. If only Bill could hold his man until help came.

But at that minute there was a final terrific upheaval. They must have crashed into one of the figures in armour, for it fell to the ground with a deafening noise. Virginia saw dimly a figure springing for the window, and at the same time heard Bill cursing and disengaging himself from fragments of armour.

For the first time, she left her post, and rushed wildly for the figure at the window. But the window was already unlatched. The intruder had no need to stop and fumble for it. He sprang out and raced away down the terrace and round the corner of the house. Virginia raced after him. She was young and athletic, and she turned the corner of the terrace not many seconds after her quarry.

But there she ran headlong into the arms of a man who was emerging from a small side door. It was Mr. Hiram P. Fish.

"Gee! It's a lady," he exclaimed. "Why, I beg your pardon, Mrs. Revel. I took you for one of the thugs fleeing from justice."

"He's just passed this way," cried Virginia breathlessly. "Can't we catch him?"

But even as she spoke, she knew it was too late. The man must have gained the park by now, and it was a dark night with no moon. She retraced her steps to the Council Chamber, Mr. Fish by her side, discoursing in a soothing monotone upon the habits of burglars in general, of which he seemed to have a wide experience.

Lord Caterham, Bundle and various frightened servants were standing in the doorway of the Council Chamber.

"What the devil's the matter?" asked Bundle. "Is it burglars? What are you and Mr. Fish doing, Virginia? Taking a midnight stroll?"

Virginia explained the events of the evening.

"How frightfully exciting," commented Bundle. "You don't usually get a murder and a burglary crowded into one weekend. What's the matter with the lights in here? They're all right everywhere else."

That mystery was soon explained. The bulbs had simply been removed and laid in a row against the wall. Mounted on a pair of steps, the dignified Tredwell, dignified even in undress, restored illumination to the stricken apartment.

"If I am not mistaken," said Lord Caterham in his sad voice as he looked around him, "this room has recently been the centre of somewhat violent activity."

There was some justice in the remark. Everything that could have been knocked over had been kocked over. The floor was littered with splintered chairs, broken china, and fragments of armour.

"How many of them were there?" asked Bundle. "It seems to have been a desperate fight."

"Only one, I think," said Virginia. But, even as she spoke she hesitated a little. Certainly only one person—a man—had passed out through the window. But as she had rushed after him, she had a vague impression of a rustle somewhere close at hand. If so, the second occupant of the room could have escaped through the door. Perhaps, though, the rustle had been an effect of her own imagination.

Bill appeared suddenly at the window. He was out of breath and panting hard.

"Damn the fellow!" he exclaimed wrathfully. "He's escaped. I've been hunting all over the place. Not a sign of him."

"Cheer up, Bill," said Virginia, "better luck next time."

"Well," said Lord Caterham, "what do you think we'd better do now? Go back to bed? I can't get hold of Badgworthy at this time of night. Tredwell, you know the sort of thing that's necessary. Just see to it, will you?"

"Very good, my lord."

With a sigh of relief, Lord Caterham prepared to retreat.

"That beggar, Isaacstein, sleeps soundly," he remarked, with a touch of envy. "You'd have thought all this row would have brought him down." He looked across at Mr. Fish. "You found time to dress, I see," he added.

"I flung on a few articles of clothing, yes," admitted the American.

"Very sensible of you," said Lord Caterham. "Damned chilly things, pyjamas."

He yawned. In a rather depressed mood, the house party retired to bed.

# Eighteen

## SECOND MIDNIGHT ADVENTURE

The first person that Anthony saw as he alighted from his train on the following afternoon was Superintendent Battle. His face broke into a smile.

"I've returned according to contract," he remarked. "Did you come down here to assure yourself of the fact?"

Battle shook his head.

"I wasn't worrying about that, Mr. Cade. I happen to be going to London, that's all."

"You have such a trustful nature, Battle."

"Do you think so, sir?"

"No. I think you're deep—very deep. Still waters, you know, and all that sort of thing. So you're going to London?"

"I am, Mr. Cade."

"I wonder why."

The detective did not reply.

"You're so chatty," remarked Anthony. "That's what I like about you."

A far-off twinkle showed in Battle's eyes.

"What about your own little job, Mr. Cade?" he inquired. "How did that go off?"

"I've drawn blank, Battle. For the second time I've been proved hopelessly wrong. Galling, isn't it?"

"What was the idea, sir, if I may ask?"

"I suspected the French governess, Battle. A: upon the grounds of her being the most unlikely person, according to the canons of the best fiction. B: because there was a light in her room on the night of the tragedy."

"That wasn't much to go upon."

"You are quite right. It was not. But I discovered that she had only been here a short time, and I also found a suspicious Frenchman spying round the place. You know all about him, I suppose?"

"You mean the man who calls himself, M. Chelles? Staying at the Cricketers? A traveller in silk."

"That's it, is it? What about him? What does Scotland Yard think?"

"His actions have been suspicious," said Superintendent Battle expressionlessly.

"Very suspicious, I should say. Well, I put two and two together. French governess in the house, French stranger outside. I decided that they were in league together, and I hurried off to interview the lady with whom Mademoiselle Brun had lived for the last ten years. I was fully prepared to find that she had never heard of any such person as Mademoiselle Brun, but I was wrong, Battle. Mademoiselle is the genuine article."

Battle nodded.

"I must admit," said Anthony, "that as soon as I spoke to her I had an uneasy conviction that I was barking up the wrong tree. She seemed so absolutely the governess."

Again Battle nodded.

"All the same, Mr. Cade, you can't always go by that. Women especially can do a lot with makeup. I've seen quite a pretty girl with the colour of her hair altered, a sallow complexion stain, slightly reddened eyelids and, most efficacious of all, dowdy clothes, who would fail to be identified by nine people out of ten who had seen her in her former character. Men haven't got quite the same pull. You can do something with the eyebrows, and of course different sets of false teeth alter the whole expression. But there are always the ears—there's an extraordinary lot of character in ears, Mr. Cade."

"Don't look so hard at mine, Battle," complained Anthony. "You make me quite nervous."

"I'm not talking of false beards and greasepaint," continued the superintendent. "That's only for books. No, there are very few men who can escape identification and put it over on you. In fact there's only one man I know who has a positive genius for impersonation. King Victor. Ever heard of King Victor, Mr. Cade?"

There was something so sharp and sudden about the way the detective put the question that Anthony checked the words that were rising to his lips.

"King Victor?" he said reflectively instead. "Somehow, I seem to have heard the name."

"One of the most celebrated jewel thieves in the world. Irish father, French mother. Can speak five languages at least. He's been serving a sentence, but his time was up a few months ago."

"Really? And where is he supposed to be now?"

"Well, Mr. Cade, that's what we'd rather like to know."

"The plot thickens," said Anthony lightly. "No chance of his turning up here, is there? But I suppose he wouldn't be interested in political memoirs—only in jewels."

"There's no saying," said Superintendent Battle. "For all we know, he may be here already."

"Disguised as the second footman? Splendid. You'll recognize him by his ears and cover yourself with glory."

"Quite fond of your little joke, aren't you, Mr. Cade? By the way, what do you think of that curious business at Staines?"

"Staines?" said Anthony. "What's been happening at Staines?"

"It was in Saturday's papers. I thought you might have seen about it. Man found by the roadside shot. A foreigner. It was in the papers again today, of course."

"I did see something about it," said Anthony carelessly. "Not suicide, apparently."

"No. There was no weapon. As yet the man hasn't been identified."

"You seem very interested," said Anthony, smiling. "No connexion with Prince Michael's death, is there?"

His hand was quite steady. So were his eyes. Was it his fancy that Superintendent Battle was looking at him with peculiar intentness?

"Seems to be quite an epidemic of that sort of thing," said Battle. "But, well, I daresay there's nothing in it."

He turned away, beckoning to a porter as the London train came thundering in. Anthony drew a faint sigh of relief.

He strolled across the park in an unusually thoughtful mood. He purposely chose to approach the house from the same direction as that from which he had come on the fateful Thursday night, and as he drew near to it he looked up at the windows cudgelling his brains to make sure of the one where he had seen the light. Was he quite sure that it was the second from the end?

And, doing so, he made a discovery. There was an angle at the corner of the house in which was a window set farther back. Standing on one spot, you counted this window as the first, and the first one built out over the Council Chamber as the second, but move a few yards to the right and the part built out over the Council Chamber appeared to be the end of the house. The first window was invisible, and the two windows of the rooms over the Council Chamber would have appeared the first and second from the end. Where exactly had he been standing when he had seen the light flash up?

Anthony found the question very hard to determine. A matter of a yard or so made all the difference. But one point was made abundantly clear. It was quite possible that he had been mistaken in describing the light as ocurring in the second room from the end. It might equally well have been the *third*.

Now who occupied the third room? Anthony was determined to find that out as soon as possible. Fortune favoured him. In the hall Tredwell had just set the massive silver urn in its place on the tea tray. Nobody else was there.

"Hullo, Tredwell," said Anthony. "I wanted to ask you something. Who has the third room from the end on the west side? Over the Council Chamber, I mean."

Tredwell reflected for a minute or two.

"That would be the American gentleman's room, sir. Mr. Fish."

"Oh, is it? Thank you."

"Not at all, sir."

Tredwell prepared to depart, then paused. The desire to be the first to impart news makes even pontifical butlers human.

"Perhaps you have heard, sir, of what occurred last night?"

"Not a word," said Anthony. "What did occur last night?"

"An attempt at robbery, sir!"

"Not really? Was anything taken?"

"No sir. The thieves were dismantling the suits of armour in the Council Chamber when they were surprised and forced to flee. Unfortunately they got clear away."

"That's very extraordinary," said Anthony. "The Council Chamber again. Did they break in that way?"

"It is supposed, sir, that they forced the window."

Satisfied with the interest his information had aroused, Tredwell resumed his retreat, but brought up short with a dignified apology.

"I beg your pardon, sir. I didn't hear you come in, and didn't know you were standing just behind me."

Mr. Isaacstein, who had been the victim of the impact, waved his hand in a friendly fashion.

"No harm done, my good fellow. I assure you no harm done."

Tredwell retired looking contemptuous, and Isaacstein came forward and dropped into an easy chair.

"Hullo, Cade, so you're back again. Been hearing all about last night's little show?"

"Yes," said Anthony. "Rather an exciting weekend, isn't it?"

"I should imagine that last night was the work of local men," said Isaacstein. "It seems a clumsy, amateurish affair."

"Is there anyone about here who collects armour?" asked Anthony. "It seems a curious thing to select."

"Very curious," agreed Mr. Isaacstein. He paused a minute, and then said slowly: "The whole position here is very unfortunate."

There was something almost menacing in his tone.

"I don't quite understand," said Anthony.

"Why are we all being kept here in this way? The inquest was over yesterday. The Prince's body will be removed to London, where it is being given out that he died of heart failure. And still nobody is allowed to leave the house. Mr. Lomax knows no more than I do. He refers me to Superintendent Battle."

"Superintendent Battle has something up his sleeve," said Anthony thoughtfully. "And it seems the essence of his plan that nobody should leave."

"But, excuse me, Mr. Cade, you have been away."

"With a string tied to my leg. I've no doubt that I was shadowed the whole time. I shouldn't have been given a chance of disposing of the revolver or anything of that kind."

"Ah, the revolver," said Isaacstein thoughtfully. "That has not yet been found, I think?"

"Not yet."

"Possibly thrown into the lake in passing."

"Very possibly."

"Where is Superintendent Battle? I have not seen him this afternoon."

"He's gone to London. I met him at the station."

"Gone to London? Really? Did he say when he would be back?"

"Early tomorrow, so I understand."

Virginia came in with Lord Caterham and Mr. Fish. She smiled a welcome at Anthony.

"So you're back, Mr. Cade. Have you heard all about our adventures last night?"

"Why, trooly, Mr. Cade," said Hiram Fish. "It was a night of strenuous excitement. Did you hear that I mistook Mrs. Revel for one of the thugs?"

"And in the meantime," said Anthony, "the thug?—"

"Got clear away," said Mr. Fish mournfully.

"Do pour out," said Lord Caterham to Virginia. "I don't know where Bundle is."

Virginia officiated. Then she came and sat down near Anthony.

"Come to the boathouse after tea," she said in a low voice. "Bill and I have got a lot to tell you."

Then she joined lightly in the general conversation.

The meeting at the boathouse was duly held.

Virginia and Bill were bubbling over with their news. They agreed that a boat in the middle of the lake was the only safe place for confidential conversation. Having paddled out a sufficient distance, the full story of last night's adventure was related to Anthony. Bill looked a little sulky. He wished Virginia would not insist on bringing this Colonial fellow into it.

"It's very odd," said Anthony, when the story was finished. "What do you make of it?" he asked Virginia.

"I think they were looking for something," she returned promptly. "The burglar idea is absurd."

"They thought the something, whatever it was, might be concealed in the suits of armour, that's clear enough. But why tap the panelling? That looks more as though they were looking for a secret staircase, or something of that kind."

"There's a priest's hole at Chimneys, I know," said Virginia. "And I believe there's a secret staircase as well. Lord Caterham would tell us all about it. What I want to know is, what can they have been looking for?"

"It can't be the memoirs," said Anthony. "They're a great bulky package. It must have been something small."

"George knows, I expect," said Virginia. "I wonder whether I could get it out of him. All along I've felt there was something behind all this."

"You say there was only one man," pursued Anthony, "but that there might possibly be another, as you thought you heard someone going towards the door as you sprang to the window."

"The sound was very slight," said Virginia. "It might have been just my imagination."

"That's quite possible, but in case it wasn't your imagination the second person must have been an inmate of the house. I wonder now—"

"What are you wondering at?" asked Virginia.

"The thoroughness of Mr. Hiram Fish, who dresses himself completely when he hears screams for help downstairs."

"There's something in that," agreed Virginia. "And then there's

Isaacstein, who sleeps throught it all. That's suspicious too. Surely he couldn't?"

"There's that fellow Boris," suggested Bill. "He looks an unmitigated ruffian. Michael's servant, I mean."

"Chimneys is full of suspicious characters," said Virginia. "I daresay the others are just as suspicious of us. I wish Superintendent Battle hadn't gone to London. I think it's rather stupid of him. By the way, Mr. Cade, I've seen that peculiar-looking Frenchman about once or twice, spying round the park."

"It's a mix-up," confessed Anthony. "I've been away on a wild-goose chase. Made a thorough ass of myself. Look here, to me the whole question seems to resolve itself into this: did the men find what they were looking for last night?"

"Supposing they didn't?" said Virginia. "I'm pretty sure they didn't, as a matter of fact."

"Just this, I believe they'll come again. They know, or they soon will know, that Battle's in London. They'll take the risk and come again tonight."

"Do you really think so?"

"It's a chance. Now we three will form a little syndicate. Eversleigh and I will conceal ourselves with due precautions in the Council Chamber—"

"What about me?" interrupted Virginia. "Don't think you're going to leave me out of it."

"Listen to me, Virginia," said Bill. "This is men's work—"

"Don't be an idiot, Bill. I'm in on this. Don't you make any mistake about it. The syndicate will keep watch tonight."

It was settled thus, and the details of the plan were laid. After the party had retired to bed, first one and then another of the syndicate crept down. They were all armed with powerful electric torches, and in the pocket of Anthony's coat lay a revolver.

Anthony had said that he believed another attempt to resume the search would be made. Nevertheless, he did not expect that the attempt would be made from outside. He believed that Virginia had been correct in her guess that someone had passed her in the dark the night before, and as he stood in the shadow of an old oak dresser it was towards the door and not the window that his eyes were directed. Virginia was crouching behind a figure in armour on the opposite wall, and Bill was by the window.

The minutes passed, at interminable length. One o'clock chimed, then the half hour, then two, then half hour. Anthony felt stiff and cramped. He was coming slowly to the conclusion that he had been wrong. No attempt would be made tonight.

And then he stiffened suddenly, all his senses on the alert. He had heard a footstep on the terrace outside. Silence again, and then a low scratching noise at the window. Suddenly it ceased, and the window swung open. A man stepped across the still into the room. He stood quite still for a moment, peering round as though listening. After a minute or two, seemingly satisfied, he switched on a torch he carried, and turned it rapidly round the room. Apparently he saw nothing unusual. The three watchers held their breath.

He went over to the same bit of panelled wall he had been examining the night before.

And then a terrible knowledge smote Bill. He was going to sneeze! The wild race through the dew-laden park the night before had given him a chill. All day he had sneezed intermittently. A sneeze was due now, and nothing on earth would stop it.

He adopted all the remedies he could think of. He pressed his upper lip, swallowed hard, threw back his head and looked at the ceiling. As a last resort he held his nose and pinched it violently. It was of no avail. He sneezed.

A stifled, checked, emasculated sneeze, but a startling sound in the deadly quiet of the room.

The stranger sprang round, and in the same minute, Anthony acted. He flashed on his torch, and jumped full for the stranger. In another minute they were down on the floor together.

"Lights," shouted Anthony.

Virginia was ready at the switch. The lights came on true and full tonight. Anthony was on top of his man. Bill leant down to give him a hand.

"And now," said Anthony, "let's see who you are, my fine fellow."

He rolled his victim over. It was the neat, dark-bearded stranger from the Cricketers.

"Very nice indeed," said an approving voice.

They all looked up startled. The bulky form of Superintendent Battle was standing in the open doorway.

"I thought you were in London, Superintendent Battle," said Anthony.

Battle's eyes twinkled.

"Did you sir?" he said. "Well, I thought it would be a good thing if I was thought to be going."

"And it has been," agreed Anthony, looking down at his prostrate foe.

To his surprise there was a slight smile on the stranger's face.

"May I get up, gentlemen?" he inquired. "You are three to one."

Anthony kindly hauled him on to his legs. The stranger settled his coat, pulled up his collar, and directed a keen look at Battle.

"I demand pardon," he said, "but do I understand that you are a representative from Scotland Yard?"

"That's right," said Battle.

"Then I will present to you my credentials." He smiled rather ruefully. "I would have been wise to do so before."

He took some papers from his pocket and handed them to the Scotland Yard detective. At the same time, he turned back the lapel of his coat and showed something pinned there.

Battle gave an exclamation of astonishment. He looked through the papers and handed them back with a little bow.

"I'm sorry you've been manhandled, monsieur," he said, "but you brought it on yourself, you know."

He smiled, noting the astonished expression on the faces of the others.

"This is a colleague we have been expecting for some time," he said. "M. Lemoine, of the Sûreté in Paris."

# Nineteen

## SECRET HISTORY

They all stared at the French detective, who smiled back at them.

"But yes," he said, "it is true."

There was a pause for a general readjusting of ideas. Then Virginia turned to Battle.

"Do you know what I think, Superintendent Battle?"

"What do you think, Mrs. Revel?"

"I think the time has come to enlighten us a little."

"To enlighten you? I don't quite understand, Mrs. Revel."

"Superintendent Battle, you understand perfectly. I daresay Mr. Lomax has hedged you about with recommendations of secrecy—George would, but surely it's better to tell us than have us stumbling on the secret all by ourselves, and perhaps doing untold harm. M. Lemoine, don't you agree with me?"

"Madame, I agree with you entirely."

"You can't go on keeping things dark forever," said Battle,

"I've told Mr. Lomax so. Mr. Eversleigh is Mr. Lomax's secretary, there's no objection to his knowing what there is to know. As for Mr. Cade, he's been brought into the thing willy-nilly, and I consider he's a right to know where he stands. But—"

Battle paused.

"I know," said Virginia. "Women are so indiscreet! I've often heard George say so."

Lemoine had been studying Virginia attentively. Now he turned to the Scotland Yard man.

"Did I hear you just now address Madame by the name of Revel?"

"That is my name," said Virginia.

"Your husband was in the Diplomatic Service, was he not? And you were with him in Herzoslovakia just before the assassination of the late King and Queen."

"Yes."

Lemoine turned again.

"I think Madame has a right to hear the story. She is indirectly concerned. Moreover"—his eyes twinkled a little—"Madame's reputation for discretion stands very high in diplomatic circles."

"I'm glad they give me a good character," said Virginia, laughing. "And I'm glad I'm not going to be left out of it."

"What about refreshments?" said Anthony. "Where does the conference take place? Here?"

"If you please, sir," said Battle, "I've a fancy for not leaving this room until morning. You'll see why when you've heard the story."

"Then I'll go and forage," said Anthony.

Bill went with him and they returned with a tray of glasses, siphons and other necessaries of life.

The augmented syndicate established itself comfortably in the corner by the window, being grouped round a long oak table.

"It's understood, of course," said Battle, "that anything that's said here is said in strict confidence. There must be no leakage. I've always felt it would come out one of these days. Gentlemen like Mr. Lomax who want everything hushed up take bigger risks than they think. The start of this business was just over seven years ago. There was a lot of what they call reconstruction going on—especially in the Near East. There was a good deal going on in England, strictly on the QT with that old gentleman, Count Stylptitch, pulling the strings. All the Balkan States were interested parties, and there were a lot of royal personages in England just then. I'm not going into details but Something disappeared—disappeared in a way that seemed incredible unless you admitted two things—that the thief was a royal personage and that at the same time it was the work of a high-class professional. M. Lemoine here will tell you how that well might be."

The Frenchman bowed courteously and took up the tale.

"It is possible that you in England may not even have heard of our famous and fantastic King Victor. What his real name is, no one knows, but he is a man of singular courage and daring, one who speaks five languages and is unequalled in the art of disguise. Though his father is known to have been either English or Irish, he himself has worked chiefly in Paris. It was there, nearly eight years ago, that he was carrying out a daring series of robberies and living under the name of Captain O'Neill."

A faint exclamation escaped Virginia. M. Lemoine darted a keen glance at her.

"I think I understand what agitates Madame. You will see in a

minute. Now we of the Sûreté had our suspicions that this Captain
O'Neill was none other than 'King Victor,' but we could not obtain
the necessary proof. There was also in Paris at the time a clever
young actress, Angèle Mory, of the Folies Bergères. For some time
we had suspected that she was associated with the operations of
King Victor. But again no proof was forthcoming.

"About that time, Paris was preparing for the visit of the young
King Nicholas IV of Herzoslovakia. At the Sûreté we were given
special instructions as to the course to be adopted to ensure the
safety of His Majesty. In particular we were warned to superintend
the activities of a certain Revolutionary organization which called
itself the Comrades of the Red Hand. It is fairly certain now that
the Comrades approached Angèle Mory and offered her a huge
sum if she would aid them in their plans. Her part was to infatu-
ate the young King, and decoy him to some spot agreed upon with
them. Angèle Mory accepted the bribe and promised to perform
her part.

"But the young lady was cleverer and more ambitious than her
employers suspected. She succeeded in captivating the King who
fell desperately in love with her and loaded her with jewels. It was
then that she conceived the idea of being—not a king's mistress, but
a queen! As everyone knows, she realized her ambition. She was
introduced into Herzoslovakia as the Countess Varaga Popoleffsky,
an offshoot of the Romanoffs, and became eventually Queen Varaga
of Herzoslovakia. Not bad for a little Parisian actress! I have always
heard that she played the part extremely well. But her triumph was
not to be long-lived. The Comrades of the Red Hand, furious at
her betrayal, twice attempted her life. Finally they worked up the
country to such a pitch that a revolution broke out in which both

the King and Queen perished. Their bodies, horribly mutilated and hardly recognizable, were recovered, attesting to the fury of the populace against the lowborn foreign Queen.

"Now, in all this, it seems certain that Queen Varaga still kept in with her confederate, King Victor. It is possible that the bold plan was his all along. What is known is that she continued to correspond with him, in a secret code, from the Court of Herzoslovakia. For safety the letters were written in English, and signed with the name of an English lady then at the Embassy. If any inquiry had been made, and the lady in question had denied her signature, it is possible that she would not have been believed, for the letters were those of a guilty woman to her lover. It was your name she used, Mrs. Revel."

"I know," said Virginia. Her colour was coming and going unevenly. "So that is the truth of the letters! I have wondered and wondered."

"What a blackguardly trick," cried Bill indignantly.

"The letters were addressed to Captain O'Neill at his rooms in Paris, and their principal purpose may have light shed upon it by a curious fact which came to light later. After the assassination of the King and Queen, many of the crown jewels which had fallen, of course, into the hands of the mob, found their way to Paris, and it was discovered that in nine cases out of ten the principal stones had been replaced by paste—and mind you, there were some very famous stones among the jewels of Herzoslovakia. So as a queen, Angèle Mory still practised her former activities.

"You see now where we have arrived. Nicholas IV and Queen Varaga came to England and were the guests of the late Marquis of Caterham, then Secretary of State for Foreign Affairs. Herzoslovakia is a small country, but it could not be left out. Queen Varaga was necessarily received. And there we have a royal personage and at the same time an expert thief. There is also no doubt that the—er—substitute which was so wonderful as to deceive anyone but an expert could only have been fashioned by King Victor, and indeed the whole plan, in its daring and audacity, pointed to him as the author."

"What happened?" asked Virginia.

"Hushed up," said Superintendent Battle laconically. "Not a mention of it's ever been made public to this day. We did all that could be done on the quiet—and that was a good deal more than you'd ever imagine, by the way. We've got methods of our own that would surprise. That jewel didn't leave England with the Queen of Herzoslovakia—I can tell you that much. No, Her Majesty hid it somewhere—but where we've never been able to discover. But I shouldn't wonder"—Superintendent Battle let his eyes wander gently round—"if it wasn't somewhere in this room."

Anthony leapt to his feet.

"What? After all these years?" he cried incredulously. "Impossible."

"You do not know the peculiar circumstances, monsieur," said the Frenchman quickly. "Only a fortnight later, the revolution in Herzoslovakia broke out, and the King and Queen were murdered. Also, Captain O'Neill was arrested in Paris and sentenced on a minor charge. We hoped to find the packet of code letters in his house, but it appears that this had been stolen by some Herzoslovakian go-between. The man turned up in Herzoslovakia just before the revolution, and then disappeared completely."

"He probably went abroad," said Anthony thoughtfully. "To

Africa as likely as not. And you bet he hung on to that packet. It was as good as a gold mine to him. It's odd how things come about. They probably called him Dutch Pedro or something like that out there."

He caught Superintendent Battle's expressionless glance bent upon him, and smiled.

"It's not really clairvoyance, Battle," he said, "though it sounds like it. I'll tell you presently."

"There is one thing that you have not explained," said Virginia. "Where does this link up with the memoirs? There must be a link, surely?"

"Madame is very quick," said Lemoine approvingly. "Yes, there is a link. Count Stylptitch was also staying at Chimneys at the time."

"So that he might have known about it?"

"*Parfaitement.*"

"And, of course," said Battle, "if he's blurted it out in his precious memoirs, the fat will be in the fire. Especially after the way the whole thing was hushed up."

Anthony lit a cigarette.

"There's no possibility of there being a clue in the memoirs as to where the stone was hidden?" he asked.

"Very unlikely," said Battle decisively. "He was never in with the Queen—opposed the marriage tooth and nail. She's not likely to have taken him into her confidence."

"I wasn't suggesting such a thing for a minute," said Anthony. "But by all accounts he was a cunning old boy. Unknown to her, he may have discovered where she hid the jewel. In that case, what would he have done, do you think?"

"Sat tight," said Battle, after a moment's reflection.

"I agree," said the Frenchman. "It was a ticklish moment, you see. To return the stone anonymously would have presented great difficulties. Also, the knowledge of its whereabouts would give him great power—and he liked power, that strange old man. Not only did he hold the Queen in the hollow of his hand, but he had a powerful weapon to negotiate with at any time. It was not the only secret he possessed—oh, no!—he collected secrets like some men collect rare pieces of china. It is said that, once or twice before his death, he boasted to people of the things he could make public if the fancy took him. And once at least he declared that he intended to make some startling revelations in his memoirs. Hence"—the Frenchman smiled rather dryly—"the general anxiety to get hold of them. Our own secret police intended to seize them, but the Count took the precaution to have them conveyed away before his death."

"Still, there's no real reason to believe that he knew this particular secret," said Battle.

"I beg your pardon," said Anthony quietly. "There are his own words."

"What?"

Both detectives stared at him as though unable to believe their ears.

"When Mr. McGrath gave me that manuscript to bring to England, he told me the circumstances of his one meeting with Count Stylptitch. It was in Paris. At some considerable risk to himself. Mr. McGrath rescued the Count from a band of Apaches. He was, I understand—shall we say a trifle—exhilarated? Being in that condition, he made two rather interesting remarks. One of them was to the effect that he knew where the Koh-i-noor was—a statement to which my friend paid very little attention. He also said that the gang in question were King Victor's men. Taken together, those two remarks are very significant."

"Good lord," ejaculated Superintendent Battle. "I should say they were. Even the murder of Prince Michael wears a different aspect."

"King Victor has never taken a life," the Frenchman reminded him.

"Supposing he were surprised when he was searching for the jewel?"

"Is he in England, then?" asked Anthony sharply. "You say that he was released a few months ago. Didn't you keep track of him?"

A rather rueful smile overspread the French detective's face.

"We tried to, monsieur. But he is a devil, that man. He gave us the slip at once—at once. We thought, of course, that he would make straight for England. But no. He went—where do you think?"

"Where?" said Anthony.

He was staring intently at the Frenchman, and absentmindedly fingers played with a box of matches.

"To America. To the United States."

"What?"

There was sheer amazement in Anthony's tone.

"Yes, and what do you think he called himself? What part do you think he played over there? The part of Prince Nicholas of Herzoslovakia."

The matchbox fell from Anthony's hand, but his amazement was fully equalled by that of Battle.

"Impossible."

"Not so, my friend. You, too, will get the news in the morning. It has been the most colossal bluff. As you know, Prince Nicholas was rumoured to have died in the Congo years ago. Our friend, King Victor, seizes on that—difficult to prove a death of that kind. He resurrects Prince Nicholas, and plays him to such purpose that he gets away with a tremendous haul of American dollars—all on account of the supposed oil concessions. But by a mere accident, he was unmasked, and had to leave the country hurriedly. This time he did come to England. And that is why I am here. Sooner or later he will come to Chimneys. That is, if he is not already here!"

"You think—that?"

"I think he was here the night Prince Michael died, and again last night."

"It was another attempt, eh?" said Battle.

"It was another attempt."

"What has bothered me," continued Battle, "was wondering what had become of M. Lemoine here. I'd had word from Paris that he was on his way over to work with me, and couldn't make out why he hadn't turned up."

"I must indeed apologize," said Lemoine. "You see, I arrived on the morning after the murder. It occurred to me at once that it would be as well for me to study things from an unofficial standpoint without appearing officially as your colleague. I thought that great possibilities lay that way. I was, of course, aware that I was bound to be an object of suspicion, but that in a way furthered my plan since it would not put the people I was after on their guard. I can assure you that I have seen a good deal that is interesting on the last two days."

"But look here," said Bill, "what really did happen last night?"

"I am afraid," said M. Lemoine, "that I gave you rather violent exercise."

"It was you I chased, then?"

"Yes. I will recount things to you. I came up here to watch, convinced that the secret had to do with this room since the Prince had been killed here. I stood outside on the terrace. Presently I became aware that someone was moving about in this room. I could see the flash of a torch now and again. I tried the middle window and found it unlatched. Whether the man had entered that way earlier, or whether he had left it so as a blind in case he was disturbed, I do not know. Very gently, I pushed it back and slipped inside the room. Step by step I felt my way until I was in a spot where I could watch operations without likelihood of being discovered myself. The man himself I could not see clearly. His back was to me, of course, and he was silhouetted against the light of the torch so that his outline only could be seen. But his actions filled me with surprise. He took to pieces first one and then the other of those two suits of armour, examining each one piece by piece. When he had convinced himself that what he sought was not there, he began tapping the panelling of the wall under that picture. What he would have done next, I do not know. The interruption came. *You* burst in—" He looked at Bill.

"Our well-meant interference was really rather a pity," said Virginia thoughtfully.

"In a sense, madame, it was. The man switched out his torch, and I, who had no wish as yet to be forced to reveal my identity, sprang for the window. I collided with the other two in the dark, and fell headlong. I sprang up and out through the window. Mr. Eversleigh, taking me for his assailant, followed."

"I followed you first," said Virginia. "Bill was only second in the race."

"And the other fellow had the sense to stay still and sneak out through the door. I wonder he didn't meet the rescuing crowd."

"That would present no difficulties," said Lemoine. "He would be a rescuer in advance of the rest, that was all."

"Do you really think this Arsène Lupin fellow is actually among the household now?" asked Bill, his eyes sparkling.

"Why not?" said Lemoine. "He could pass perfectly as a servant. For all we may know, he may be Boris Anchoukoff, the trusted servant of the late Prince Michael."

"He is an odd-looking bloke," agreed Bill.

But Anthony was smiling.

"That's hardly worthy of you, M. Lemoine," he said gently.

The Frenchman smiled too.

"You've taken him on as your valet now, haven't you, Mr. Cade?" asked Superintendent Battle.

"Battle, I take off my hat to you. You know everything. But just as a matter of detail, he's taken me on, not I him."

"Why was that, I wonder, Mr. Cade?"

"I don't know," said Anthony lightly. "It's a curious taste, but perhaps he may have liked my face. Or he may think I murdered his master and wish to establish himself in a handy position for executing revenge upon me."

He rose and went over to the windows, pulling the curtains.

"Daylight," he said, with a slight yawn. "There won't be any more excitements now."

Lemoine rose also.

"I will leave you," he said. "We shall perhaps meet again later in the day."

With a graceful bow to Virginia, he stepped out of the window.

"Bed," said Virginia, yawning. "It's all been very exciting. Come on, Bill, go to bed like a good little boy. The breakfast table will see us not, I fear."

Anthony stayed at the window looking after the retreating form of M. Lemoine.

"You wouldn't think it," said Battle behind him, "but that's supposed to be the cleverest detective in France."

"I don't know that I wouldn't," said Anthony thoughtfully. "I rather think I would."

"Well," said Battle, "he was right about the excitements of this night being over. By the way, do you remember my telling you about that man they'd found shot near Staines?"

"Yes. Why?"

"Nothing. They've identified him, that's all. It seems he was called Giuseppe Manuelli. He was a waiter at the Blitz in London. Curious, isn't it?"

# Twenty

## BATTLE AND ANTHONY CONFER

Anthony said nothing. He continued to stare out of the window. Superintendent Battle looked for some time at his motionless back.

"Well, goodnight, sir," he said at last, and moved to the door.

Anthony stirred.

"Wait a minute, Battle."

The superintendent halted obediently. Anthony left the window. He drew out a cigarette from his case and lighted it. Then, between two puffs of smoke, he said:

"You seem very interested in this business at Staines?"

"I wouldn't go as far as that, sir. It's unusual, that's all."

"Do you think the man was shot where he was found, or do you think he was killed elsewhere and the body brought to that particular spot afterwards?"

"I think he was shot somewhere else, and the body brought there in a car."

"I think so too," said Anthony.

Something in the emphasis of his tone made the dectective look up sharply.

"Any ideas of your own, sir? Do you know who brought him there?"

"Yes," said Anthony. "I did."

He was a little annoyed at the absolutely unruffled calm preserved by the other.

"I must say you take these shocks very well, Battle," he remarked.

" 'Never display emotion.' That was a rule that was given to me once, and I've found it very useful."

"You live up to it, certainly," said Anthony. "I can't say I've ever seen you ruffled. Well, do you want to hear the whole story?"

"If you please, Mr. Cade."

Anthony pulled up two of the chairs, both men sat down, and Anthony recounted the events of the preceding Thursday night.

Battle listened immovably. There was a far-off twinkle in his eyes as Anthony finished.

"You know, sir," he said, "you'll get into trouble one of these days."

"Then, for the second time, I'm not to be taken into custody?"

"We always like to give a man plenty of rope," said Superintendent Battle.

"Very delicately put," said Anthony. "Without unduly stressing the end of the proverb."

"What I can't make out, sir," said Battle, "is why you decided to come across with this now?"

"It's rather difficult to explain," said Anthony. "You see, Battle,

I've come to have really a very high opinion of your abilities. When the moment comes, you're always there. Look at tonight. And it occurred to me that, in withholding this knowledge of mine, I was seriously cramping your style. You deserve to have access to all the facts. I've done what I could, and up to now I've made a mess of things. Until tonight, I couldn't speak for Mrs. Revel's sake. But now that those letters have been definitely proved to have nothing whatever to do with her, any idea of her complicity becomes absurd. Perhaps I advised her badly in the first place, but it struck me that her statement of having paid this man money to suppress the letters, simply as a whim, might take a bit of believing."

"It might, by a jury," agreed Battle. "Juries never have any imagination."

"But you accept it quite easily?" said Anthony, looking curiously at him.

"Well, you see, Mr. Cade, most of my work has lain amongst these people. What they call the upper classes, I mean. You see, the majority of people are always wondering what the neighbours will think. But tramps and aristocrats don't—they just do the first thing that comes into their heads, and they don't bother to think what anyone thinks of them. I'm not meaning just the idle rich, the people who give big parties, and so on. I mean those that have had it born and bred in them for generations that nobody else's opinion counts but their own. I've always found the upper classes the same—fearless, truthful, and sometimes extraordinarily foolish."

"This is a very interesting lecture, Battle. I suppose you'll be writing your reminiscences one of these days. They ought to be worth reading too."

The detective acknowledged the suggestion with a smile, but said nothing.

"I'd like rather to ask you one question," continued Anthony. "Did you connect me at all with the Staines affair? I fancied, from your manner, that you did."

"Quite right. I had a hunch that way. But nothing definite to go upon. Your manner was very good, if I may say so, Mr. Cade. You never overdid the carelessness."

"I'm glad of that," said Anthony. "I've a feeling that ever since I met you you've been laying little traps for me. On the whole I've managed to avoid falling into them, but the strain has been acute."

Battle smiled grimly.

"That's how you get a crook in the end, sir. Keep him on the run, to and fro, turning and twisting. Sooner or later, his nerve goes, and you've got him."

"You're a cheerful fellow, Battle. When will you get me, I wonder?"

"Plenty of rope, sir," quoted the superintendent, "plenty of rope."

"In the meantime," said Anthony. "I am still the amateur assistant?"

"That's it, Mr. Cade."

"Watson to your Sherlock, in fact?"

"Detective stories are mostly bunkum," said Battle unemotionally. "But they amuse people," he added, as an afterthought. "And they're useful sometimes."

"In what way?" asked Anthony curiously.

"They encourage the universal idea that the police are stupid. When we get an amateur crime, such as a murder, that's very useful indeed."

Anthony looked at him for some minutes in silence. Battle sat quite still, blinking now and then, with no expression whatsoever on his square placid face. Presently he rose.

"Not much good going to bed now," he observed. "As soon as he's up, I want to have a few words with his lordship. Anyone who wants to leave the house can do so now. At the same time I should be much obliged to his lordship if he'll extend an informal invitation to his guests to stay on. You'll accept it, sir, if you please, and Mrs. Revel also."

"Have you ever found the revolver?" asked Anthony suddenly.

"You mean the one Prince Michael was shot with? No, I haven't. Yet it must be in the house or grounds. I'll take a hint from you, Mr. Cade, and send some boys up bird's-nesting. If I could get hold of the revolver, we might get forward a bit. That, and the bundle of letters. You say that a letter with the heading 'Chimneys' was amongst them? Depend upon it that was the last one written. The instructions for finding the diamond are written in code in that letter."

"What's your theory of the killing of Giuseppe?" asked Anthony.

"I should say he was a regular thief, and that he was got hold of, either by King Victor or by the Comrades of the Red Hand, and employed by them. I shouldn't wonder at all if the Comrades and King Victor aren't working together. The organization has plenty of money and power, but it isn't very strong in brain. Giuseppe's task was to steal the memoirs—they couldn't have known that you had the letters—it's a very odd coincidence that you should have, by the way."

"I know," said Anthony. "It's amazing when you come to think of it."

"Giuseppe gets hold of the letters instead. Is at first vastly chagrined. Then sees the cutting from the paper and has the brilliant idea of turning them to account on his own by blackmailing the lady. He has, of course, no idea of their real significance. The Comrades find out what he is doing, believe that he is deliberately double-crossing them, and decree his death. They're very fond of executing traitors. It has a picturesque element which seems to appeal to them. What I can't quite make out is the revolver with 'Virginia' engraved upon it. There's too much finesse about that for the Comrades. As a rule, they enjoy plastering their Red Hand sign about—in order to strike terror into other would-be traitors. No, it looks to me as though King Victor had stepped in there. But what his motive was, I don't know. It looks like a very deliberate attempt to saddle Mrs. Revel with the murder, and, on the surface, there doesn't seem any particular point in that."

"I had a theory," said Anthony. "But it didn't work out according to plan."

He told Battle of Virginia's recognition of Michael. Battle nodded his head.

"Oh, yes, no doubt as to his identity. By the way, that old Baron has a very high opinion of you. He speaks of you in most enthusiastic terms."

"That's very kind of him," said Anthony. "Especially as I've given him full warning that I mean to do my utmost to get hold of the missing memoirs before Wednesday next."

"You'll have a job to do that," said Battle.

"Y-es. You think so? I suppose King Victor and Co. have got the letters."

Battle nodded.

"Pinched them off Giuseppe that day in Pont Street. Prettily planned piece of work, that. Yes, they've got 'em all right, and they've decoded them, and they know where to look."

Both men were on the point of passing out of the room.

"In here?" said Anthony, jerking his head back.

"Exactly, in here. But they haven't found the prize yet, and they're going to run a pretty risk trying to get it."

"I suppose," said Anthony. "That you've got a plan in that subtle head of yours?"

Battle returned no answer. He looked particularly stolid and unintelligent. Then, very slowly, he winked.

"Want my help?" asked Anthony.

"I do. And I shall want someone else's."

"Who is that?"

"Mrs. Revel's. You may have noticed it, Mr. Cade, but she's a lady who has a particularly beguiling way with her."

"I've noticed it all right," said Anthony.

He glanced at his watch.

"I'm inclined to agree with you about bed, Battle. A dip in the lake and a hearty breakfast will be far more to the point."

He ran lightly upstairs to his bedroom. Whistling to himself, he discarded, his evening clothes, and picked up a dressing gown and a bath towel.

Then suddenly he stopped dead in front of the dressing table, staring at the object that reposed demurely in front of the looking glass.

For a moment he could not believe his eyes. He took it up, examined it closely. Yes, there was no mistake.

It was the bundle of letters signed Virginia Revel. They were intact. Not one missing.

Anthony dropped into a chair, the letters in his hand.

"My brain must be cracking," he murmured. "I can't understand a quarter of what is going on in this house. Why should the letters reappear like a damned conjuring trick? Who put them on my dressing table? Why?"

And to all these very pertinent questions he could find no satisfactory reply.

# Twenty-one

## MR. ISAACSTEIN'S SUITCASE

At ten o'clock that morning, Lord Caterham and his daughter were breakfasting. Bundle was looking very thoughtful.

"Father," she said at last.

Lord Caterham, absorbed in *The Times*, did not reply.

"Father," said Bundle again, more sharply.

Lord Caterham, torn from his interested perusal of forthcoming sales of rare books, looked up absentmindedly.

"Eh?" he said. "Did you speak?"

"Yes. Who is it who's had breakfast?"

She nodded towards a place that had evidently been occupied. The rest were all expectant.

"Oh, what's-his-name."

"Fat Iky?"

Bundle and her father had enough sympathy between them to comprehend each other's somewhat misleading observations.

"That's it."

"Did I see you talking to the detective this morning before breakfast?"

Lord Caterham sighed.

"Yes, he buttonholed me in the hall. I do think the hours before breakfast should be sacred. I shall have to go abroad. The strain on my nerves—"

Bundle interrupted unceremoniously.

"What did he say?"

"Said everyone who wanted to could clear out."

"Well," said Bundle, "that's all right. That's what you've been wanting."

"I know. But he didn't leave it at that. He went on to say that nevertheless he wanted me to ask everyone to stay on."

"I don't understand," said Bundle, wrinkling her nose.

"So confusing and contradictory," complained Lord Caterham. "And before breakfast too."

"What did you say?"

"Oh, I agreed, of course. It's never any good arguing with these people. Especially before breakfast," continued Lord Caterham, reverting to his principal grievance.

"Who have you asked so far?"

"Cade. He was up very early this morning. He's going to stop on. I don't mind that. I can't quite make the fellow out; but I like him—I like him very much."

"So does Virginia," said Bundle, drawing a pattern on the table with her fork.

"Eh?"

"And so do I. But that doesn't seem to matter."

"And I asked Isaacstein," continued Lord Caterham.

"Well?"

"But fortunately he's got to go back to town. Don't forget to order the car for the 10:50, by the way."

"All right."

"Now if I can only get rid of Fish too," continued Lord Caterham, his spirits rising.

"I thought you liked talking to him about your mouldy old books."

"So I do, so I do. So I did, rather. But it gets monotonous when one finds that one is always doing all the talking. Fish is very interested, but he never volunteers any statements of his own."

"It's better than doing all the listening," said Bundle. "Like one does with George Lomax."

Lord Caterham shuddered at the remembrance.

"George is all very well on platforms," said Bundle. "I've clapped him myself, though of course I know all the time that he's talking balderdash. And anyway, I'm a Socialist—"

"I know, my dear, I know," said Lord Caterham hastily.

"It's all right," said Bundle. "I'm not going to bring politics into the home. That's what George does—public speaking in private life. It ought to be abolished by Act of Parliament."

"Quite so," said Lord Caterham.

"What about Virginia?" asked Bundle. "Is she to be asked to stop on?"

"Battle said everybody."

"Says he firmly! Have you asked her to be my stepma yet?"

"I don't think it would be any good," said Lord Caterham mournfully. "Although she did call me a darling last night. But that's the worst of these attractive young women with affectionate dispositions. They'll say anything, and they mean absolutely nothing by it."

"No," agreed Bundle. "It would have been much more hopeful if she'd thrown a boot at you or tried to bite you."

"You modern young people seem to have such unpleasant ideas about lovemaking," said Lord Caterham plaintively.

"It comes from reading *The Sheik*," said Bundle. "Desert love. Throw her about, etc."

"What is *The Sheik?*" asked Lord Caterham simply. "Is it a poem?"

Bundle looked at him with commiserating pity. Then she rose and kissed the top of his head.

"Dear old Daddy," she remarked, and sprang lightly out of the window.

Lord Caterham went back to the salerooms.

He jumped when addressed suddenly by Mr. Hiram Fish, who had made his usual noiseless entry.

"Good morning, Lord Caterham."

"Oh, good morning," said Lord Caterham. "Good morning. Nice day."

"The weather is delightful," said Mr. Fish.

He helped himself to coffee. By way of food, he took a piece of dry toast.

"Do I hear correctly that the embargo is removed?" he asked after a minute or two. "That we are all free to depart?"

"Yes—er—yes," said Lord Caterham "As a matter of fact, I hoped, I mean, that I shall be delighted"—his conscience drove him on—"only too delighted if you will stay on for a little."

"Why, Lord Caterham—"

"It's been a beastly visit, I know," Lord Caterham hurried on. "Too bad. Shan't blame you for wanting to run away."

"You misjudge me, Lord Caterham. The associations have been painful, no one could deny that point. But the English country life, as lived in the mansions of the great, has a powerful attraction for me. I am interested in the study of those conditions. It is a thing we lack completely in Amercia. I shall be only too delighted to accept your vurry kind invitation and stay on."

"Oh, well," said Lord Caterham, "that's that. Absolutely delighted, my dear fellow, absolutely delighted."

Spurring himself on to a false geniality of manner, Lord Caterham murmured something about having to see his bailiff and escaped from the room.

In the hall, he saw Virginia just descending the staircase.

"Shall I take you in to breakfast?" asked Lord Caterham tenderly.

"I've had it in bed, thank you, I was frightfully sleepy this morning."

She yawned.

"Had a bad night, perhaps?"

"Not exactly a bad night. From one point of view decidedly a good night. Oh, Lord Caterham"—she slipped her hand inside his arm and gave it a squeeze—"I *am* enjoying myself. You were a darling to ask me down."

"You'll stop on for a bit then, won't you? Battle is lifting the— the embargo, but I want you to stay particularly. So does Bundle."

"Of course I'll stay. It's sweet of you to ask me."

"Ah!" said Lord Caterham.

He sighed.

"What is your secret sorrow?" asked Virginia. "Has anyone bitten you?"

"That's just it," said Lord Caterham mournfully.

Virginia looked puzzled.

"You don't feel, by any chance, that you want to throw a boot at me? No, I can see you don't. Oh, well, it's of no consequence."

Lord Caterham drifted sadly away, and Virginia passed out through a side door into the garden.

She stood there for a moment, breathing in the crisp October air which was infinitely refreshing to one in her slightly jaded state.

She started a little to find Superintendent Battle at her elbow. The man seemed to have an extraordinary knack of appearing out of space without the least warning.

"Good morning, Mrs. Revel. Not too tired, I hope?"

Virginia shook her head.

"It was a most exciting night," she said. "Well worth the loss of a little sleep. The only thing is, today seems a trifle dull after it."

"There's a nice shady place down under that cedar tree," remarked the superintendent. "Shall I take a chair down to it for you?"

"If you think it's the best thing for me to do," said Virginia solemnly.

"You're very quick, Mrs. Revel. Yes, it's quite true, I do want a word with you."

He picked up a long wicker chair and carried it down the lawn. Virginia followed him with a cushion under her arm.

"Very dangerous place, that terrace," remarked the detective. "That is, if you want to have a private conversation."

"I'm getting excited again, Superintendent Battle."

"Oh, it's nothing important." He took out a big watch and glanced at it. "Half past ten. I'm starting for Wyvern Abbey in ten minutes to report to Mr. Lomax. Plenty of time. I only wanted to know if you could tell me a little more about Mr. Cade."

"About Mr. Cade?"

Virginia was startled.

"Yes, where you first met him, and how long you've known him and so forth."

Battle's manner was easy and pleasant enough. He even refrained from looking at her and the fact that he did so made her vaguely uneasy.

"It's more difficult than you think," she said at last. "He did me a great service once—"

Battle interrupted her.

"Before you go any further, Mrs. Ravel, I'd just like to say something. Last night, after you and Mr. Eversleigh had gone to bed, Mr. Cade told me all about the letters and the man who was killed in your house."

"He did?" gasped Virginia.

"Yes, and very wisely too. It clears up a lot of misunderstanding. There's only one thing he didn't tell me—how long he had known you. Now I've a little idea of my own about that. You shall tell me if I'm right or wrong. I think that the day he came to your house in Pont Street was the first time you had ever seen him. Ah! I see I'm right. It was so."

Virginia said nothing. For the first time she felt afraid of this stolid man with the expressionless face. She understood what Anthony had meant when he said there were no flies on Superintendent Battle.

"Has he ever told you anything about his life." the detective continued. "Before he was in South Africa, I mean. Canada? Or before that, the Sudan? Or about his boyhood?"

Virginia merely shook her head.

"And yet I'd bet he's got something worth telling. You can't mistake the face of a man who's led a life of daring and adventure. He could tell you some interesting tales if he cared to."

"If you want to know about his past life, why don't you cable to that friend of his, Mr. McGrath?" Virginia asked.

"Oh, we have. But it seems he's up-country somewhere. Still, there's no doubt Mr. Cade was in Bulawayo when he said he was. But I wondered what he'd been doing before he came to South Africa. He'd only had that job with Castle's about a month." He took out his watch again. "I must be off. The car will be waiting."

Virginia watched him retreat to the house. But she did not move from her chair. She hoped that Anthony might appear and join her. Instead came Bill Eversleigh, with a prodigious yawn.

"Thank God, I've got a chance to speak to you at last, Virginia," he complained.

"Well, speak to me very gently, Bill darling, or I shall burst into tears."

"Has someone been bullying you?"

"Not exactly bullying me. Getting inside my mind and turning it inside out. I feel as though I'd been jumped on by an elephant."

"Not Battle?"

"Yes, Battle. He's a terrible man really."

"Well, never mind Battle. I say, Virginia, I do love you so awfully—"

"Not this morning, Bill. I'm not strong enough. Anyway, I've always told you the best people don't propose before lunch."

"Good Lord," said Bill. "I could propose to you before breakfast."

Virginia shuddered.

"Bill, be sensible and intelligent for a minute. I want to ask your advice."

"If you'd once make up your mind to it, and say you'd marry me, you'd feel miles better, I'm sure. Happier, you know, and more settled down."

"Listen to me, Bill. Proposing to me is your *idée fixe*. All men propose when they're bored and can't think of anything to say. Remember my age and my widowed state, and go and make love to a pure young girl."

"My darling Virginia—Oh, Blast! here's that French idiot bearing down on us."

It was indeed M. Lemoine, black-bearded and correct of demeanour as ever.

"Good morning, madame. You are not fatigued, I trust?"

"Not in the least."

"That is excellent. Good morning, Mr. Eversleigh."

"How would it be if we promenaded ourselves a little, the three of us?" suggested the Frenchman.

"How about it, Bill?" said Virginia.

"Oh, all right," said the unwilling young gentleman by her side.

He heaved himself up from the grass, and the three of them walked slowly along. Virginia between the two men. She was sen-

sible at once of a strange undercurrent of excitement in the Frenchman, though she had no clue as to what caused it.

Soon, with her usual skill, she was putting him at his ease,
asking him questions, listening to his answers, and gradually drawing him out. Presently he was telling them anecdotes of the famous
King Victor. He talked well, albeit with a certain bitterness as he
described the various ways in which the detective bureau had been
outwitted.

But all the time, despite the real absorption of Lemoine in his
own narrative, Virginia had a feeling that he had some other object
in view. Moreover, she judged that Lemoine, under cover of his
story, was deliberately striking out his own course across the park.
They were not just strolling idly. He was deliberately guiding them
in a certain direction.

Suddenly, he broke off his story and looked round. They were
standing just where the drive intersected the park before turning an
abrupt corner by a clump of trees. Lemoine was staring at a vehicle
approaching them from the direction of the house.

Virginia's eyes followed his.

"It's the luggage cart," she said, "taking Isaacstein's luggage and
his valet to the station."

"Is that so?" said Lemoine. He glanced down at his own watch
and started. "A thousand pardons. I have been longer here than I
meant—such charming company. Is it possible, do you think, that
I might have a lift to the village?"

He stepped out on to the drive and signalled with his arm.
The luggage cart stopped, and after a word or two of explanation
Lemoine climbed in behind. He raised his hat politely to Virginia,
and drove off.

The other two stood and watched the cart disappearing with puzzled expressions. Just as the cart swung round the bend, a suitcase fell off into the drive. The cart went on.

"Come on," said Virginia to Bill. "We're going to see something interesting. That suitcase was thrown out."

"Nobody's noticed it," said Bill.

They ran down the drive towards the fallen piece of luggage. Just as they reached it, Lemoine came round the corner of the bend on foot. He was hot from walking fast.

"I was obliged to descend," he said pleasantly. "I found that I had left something behind."

"This?" said Bill, indicating the suitcase.

It was a handsome case of heavy pigskin, with the initials H. I. on it.

"What a pity!" said Lemoine gently. "It must have fallen out. Shall we lift it from the road?"

Without waiting for a reply, he picked up the suitcase, and carried it over to the belt of trees. He stooped over it, something flashed in his hand, and the lock slipped back.

He spoke, and his voice was totally different, quick and commanding.

"The car will be here in a minute," he said. "Is it in sight?"

Virginia looked back towards the house.

"No."

"Good."

With deft fingers he tossed the things out of the suitcase. Gold-topped bottle, silk pyjamas, a variety of socks. Suddenly his whole figure stiffened. He caught up what appeared to be a bundle of silk underwear, and unrolled it rapidly.

A slight exclamation broke from Bill. In the centre of the bundle was a heavy revolver.

"I hear the horn," said Virginia.

Like lightning, Lemoine repacked the suitcase. The revolver he wrapped in a silk handkerchief of his own, and slipped into his pocket. He snapped the locks of the suitcase, and turned quickly to Bill.

"Take it. Madame will be with you. Stop the car, and explain that it fell off the luggage cart. Do not mention me."

Bill stepped quickly down to the drive just as the big Lanchester limousine with Isaacstein inside it came round the corner. The chauffeur slowed down, and Bill swung the suitcase up to him.

"Fell off the luggage cart," he explained. "We happened to see it."

He caught a momentary glimpse of a startled yellow face as the financier stared at him, and then the car swept on again.

They went back to Lemoine. He was standing with the revolver in his hand, and a look of gloating satisfaction in his face.

"A long shot," he said. "A very long shot. But it came off."

# Twenty-two

## The Red Signal

Superintendent Battle was standing in the library at Wyvern Abbey.

George Lomax, seated before a desk overflowing with papers, was frowning portentously.

Superintendent Battle had opened proceedings by making a brief and businesslike report. Since then, the conversation had lain almost entirely with George, and Battle had contented himself with making brief and usually monosyllabic replies to the other's questions.

On the desk, in front of George, was the packet of letters Anthony had found on his dressing table.

"I can't understand it at all," said George irritably, as he picked up the packet. "They're in code, you say?"

"Just so, Mr. Lomax."

"And where does he say he found them—on his dressing table?"

Battle repeated, word for word, Anthony Cade's account of how he had come to regain possession of the letters.

"And he brought them at once to you? That was quite proper—quite proper. But who could have placed them in his room?"

Battle shook his head.

"That's the sort of thing you ought to know," complained George. "It sounds to me very fishy—very fishy indeed. What do we know about this man Cade, anyway? He appears in a most mysterious manner—under highly suspicious circumstances—and we know nothing whatever about him. I may say that I, personally, don't care for his manner at all. You've made inquiries about him, I suppose?"

Superintendent Battle permitted himself a patient smile.

"We wired at once to South Africa, and his story has been confirmed on all points. He was in Bulawayo with Mr. McGrath at the time he stated. Previous to their meeting, he was employed by Messrs. Castle, the tourist agents."

"Just what I should have expected," said George. "He has the kind of cheap assurance that succeeds in a certain type of employment. But about these letters—steps must be taken at once—at once—"

The great man puffed himself out and swelled importantly.

Superintendent Battle opened his mouth, but George forestalled him.

"There must be no delay. These letters must be decoded without any loss of time. Let me see, who is the man? There is a man—connected with the British Museum. Knows all there is to know about ciphers. Ran the department for us during the war. Where is Miss Oscar? She will know. Name something like Win—Win—"

"Professor Wynwood," said Battle.

"Exactly. I remember perfectly now. He must be wired to immediately."

"I have done so, Mr. Lomax, an hour ago. He will arrive by the 12:10."

"Oh, very good, very good. Thank heaven, something is off my mind. I shall have to be in town today. You can get along without me, I suppose?"

"I think so, sir."

"Well, do your best, Battle, do your best. I am terribly rushed just at present."

"Just so, sir."

"By the way, why did not Mr. Eversleigh come over with you?"

"He was still asleep, sir. We've been up all night, as I told you."

"Oh, quite so. I am frequently up nearly the whole night myself. To do the work of thirty-six hours in twenty-four, that is my constant task! Send Mr. Eversleigh over at once when you get back, will you, Battle?"

"I will give him your message, sir."

"Thank you, Battle. I realize perfectly that you had to repose a certain amount of confidence in him. But do you think it was strictly necessary to take my cousin, Mrs. Revel, into your confidence also?"

"In view of the name signed to those letters, I do, Mr. Lomax."

"An amazing piece of effrontery," murmured George, his brow darkened as he looked at the bundle of letters. "I remember the late King of Herzoslovakia. A charming fellow, but weak—deplorably weak. A tool in the hands of an unscrupulous woman. Have you any theory as to how these letters came to be restored to Mr. Cade?"

"It's my opinion," said Battle, "that if people can't get a thing one way—they try another."

"I don't quite follow you," said George.

"This crook, this King Victor, he's well aware by now that the Council Chamber is watched. So he'll let us have the letters, and let us do the decoding, and let us find the hiding place. And then— trouble! But Lemoine and I between us will attend to that."

"You've got a plan, eh?"

"I wouldn't go so far as to say I've got a plan. But I've got an idea. It's a very useful thing sometimes, an idea."

Thereupon Superintendent Battle took his departure.

He had no intention of taking George any further into his confidence.

On the way back, he passed Anthony on the road and stopped. "Going to give me a lift back to the house?" asked Anthony. "That's good."

"Where have you been, Mr. Cade?"

"Down to the station to inquire about trains."

Battle raised his eyebrows.

"Thinking of leaving us again?" he inquired.

"Not just at present," laughed Anthony. "By the way, what's upset Isaacstein? He arrived in the car just as I left, and he looked as though something had given him a nasty jolt."

"Mr. Isaacstein?"

"Yes."

"I can't say, I'm sure. I fancy it would take a good deal to jolt him."

"So do I," agreed Anthony. "He's quite one of the strong silent yellow men of finance."

Suddenly Battle leant forward and touched the chauffeur on the shoulder.

"Stop, will you? And wait for me here."

He jumped out of the car, much to Anthony's surprise. But in a minute or two, the latter perceived M. Lemoine advancing to meet the English detective, and gathered that it was a signal from him which had attracted Battle's attention.

There was a rapid colloquy between them, and then the superintendent returned to the car and jumped in again, bidding the chauffeur drive on.

His expression had completely changed.

"They've found the revolver," he said suddenly and curtly.

"What?"

Anthony gazed at him in great surprise.

"Where?"

"In Isaacstein's suitcase."

"Oh, impossible!"

"Nothing's impossible," said Battle. "I ought to have remembered that."

He sat perfectly still, tapping his knee with his hand.

"Who found it?"

Battle jerked his head over his shoulder.

"Lemoine. Clever chap. They think no end of him at the Sûreté."

"But doesn't this upset all your ideas?"

"No," said Superintendent Battle very slowly. "I can't say it does. It was a bit of a surprise, I admit, at first. But it fits in very well with one idea of mine."

"Which is?"

But the superintendent branched off on to a totally different subject.

"I wonder if you'd mind finding Mr. Eversleigh for me, sir? There's a message for him from Mr. Lomax. He's to go over to the Abbey at once."

"All right," said Anthony. The car had just drawn up at the great door. "He's probably in bed still."

"I think not," said the detective. "If you'll look, you'll see him walking under the trees there with Mrs. Revel."

"Wonderful eyes you have, haven't you, Battle?" said Anthony as he departed on his errand.

He delivered the message to Bill, who was duly disgusted.

"Damn it all," grumbled Bill to himself, as he strode off to the house, "why can't Codders sometimes leave me alone? And why can't these blasted Colonials stay in their Colonies? What do they want to come over here for, and pick out all the best girls? I'm fed up to the teeth with everything."

"Have you heard about the revolver?" asked Virginia breathlessly, as Bill left them.

"Battle told me. Rather staggering, isn't it? Isaacstein was in a frightful state yesterday to get away, but I thought it was just nerves. He's about the one person I'd have pitched upon as being above suspicion. Can you see any motive for his wanting Prince Michael out of the way?"

"It certainly doesn't fit in," agreed Virginia thoughtfully.

"Nothing fits in anywhere," said Anthony discontentedly. "I rather fancied myself as an amateur detective to begin with, and so far all I've done is to clear the character of the French governess at vast trouble and some little expense."

"Is that what you went to France for?" inquired Virginia.

"Yes, I went to Dinard and had an interview with the Comtesse de Breteuil, awfully pleased with my own cleverness, and fully expecting to be told that no such person as Mademoiselle Brun had ever been heard of.

Instead of which I was given to understand that the lady in question had been the mainstay of the household for the past seven years. So, unless the Comtesse is also a crook, that ingenious theory of mine falls to the ground."

Virginia shook her head.

"Madame de Breteuil is quite above suspicion. I know her quite well, and I fancy I must have come across Mademoiselle at the château. I certainly knew her face quite well—in that vague way one does know governesses and companions and people one sits opposite to in trains. It's awful, but I never really look at them properly. Do you?"

"Only if they're exceptionally beautiful," admitted Anthony.

"Well, in this case—" she broke off. "What's the matter?"

Anthony was staring at a figure which detached itself from the clump of trees and stood there rigidly at attention. It was the Herzoslovakian, Boris.

"Excuse me," said Anthony to Virginia, "I must just speak to my dog a minute."

He went across to where Boris was standing.

"What's the matter? What do you want?"

"Master," said Boris, bowing.

"Yes, that's all very well, but you mustn't keep following me about like this. It looks odd."

Without a word, Boris produced a soiled scrap of paper, evidently torn from a letter, and handed it to Anthony.

"What's this?" said Anthony.

There was an address scrawled on the paper, nothing else.

"He dropped it," said Boris. "I bring it to the master."

"Who dropped it?"

"The foreign gentleman."

"But why bring it to me?"

Boris looked at him reproachfully.

"Well, anyway, go away now," said Anthony. "I'm busy."

Boris saluted, turning sharply on his heel, and marched away. Anthony rejoined Virginia, thrusting the piece of paper into his pocket.

"What did he want?" she asked curiously. "And why do you call him your dog?"

"Because he acts like one," said Anthony, answering the last question first. "He must have been a retriever in his last incarnation, I think. He's just brought me a piece of a letter which he says the foreign gentleman dropped. I suppose he means Lemoine."

"I suppose so," acquiesced Virginia.

"He's always following me round," continued Anthony. "Just like a dog. Says next to nothing. Just looks at me with his big round eyes. I can't make him out."

"Perhaps he meant Isaacstein," suggested Virginia. "Isaacstein looks foreign enough, heaven knows."

"Isaacstein," muttered Anthony impatiently. "Where the devil does he come in?"

"Are you ever sorry that you've mixed yourself up in all this?" asked Virginia suddenly.

"Sorry? Good Lord, no. I love it. I've spent most of my life looking for trouble, you know. Perhaps, this time, I've got a little more than I bargained for."

"But you're well out of the wood now," said Virginia, a little surprised by the unusual gravity of his tone.

"Not quite."

They strolled on for a minute or two in silence.

"There are some people," said Anthony, breaking the silence, "who don't conform to the signals. An ordinary well-regulated locomotive slows down or pulls up when it sees the red light hoisted against it. Perhaps I was born colour-blind. When I see the red signal—I can't help forging ahead. And in the end, you know, that spells disaster. Bound to. And quite right really. That sort of thing is bad for traffic generally."

He still spoke very seriously.

"I suppose," said Virginia, "that you have taken a good many risks in your life?"

"Pretty nearly everyone there is—except marriage."

"That's rather cynical."

"It wasn't meant to be. Marriage, the kind of marriage I mean, would be the biggest adventure of the lot."

"I like that," said Virginia, flushing eagerly.

"There's only one kind of woman I'd want to marry—the kind who is worlds removed from my type of life. What would we do about it? Is she to lead my life, or am I to lead hers?"

"If she loved you—"

"Sentimentality, Mrs. Revel. You know it is. Love isn't a drug that you take to blind you to your surroundings—you can make it that, yes, but it's a pity—love can be a lot more than that. What do you think the King and his beggarmaid thought of married life after they'd been married a year or two? Didn't she regret her rags and her bare feet and her carefree life? You bet she did. Would it have been any good his renouncing his crown for her sake? Not a bit of good, either. He'd have made a damned bad beggar, I'm sure. And no woman respects a man when he's doing a thing thoroughly badly."

"Have you fallen in love with a beggarmaid, Mr. Cade?" inquired Virginia softly.

"It's the other way about with me, but the principle's the same."

"And there's no way out?" asked Virginia.

"There's always a way out," said Anthony gloomily. "I've got a theory that one can always get anything one wants if one will pay the price. And do you know what the price is, nine times out of ten? Compromise. A beastly thing, compromise, but it steals upon you as you near middle age. It's stealing upon me now. To get the woman I want I'd—I'd even take up regular work."

Virginia laughed.

"I was brought up to a trade, you know," continued Anthony.

"And you abandoned it?"

"Yes."

"Why?"

"A matter of principle."

"Oh!"

"You're a very unusual woman," said Anthony suddenly, turning and looking at her.

"Why?"

"You can refrain from asking questions."

"You mean that I haven't asked you what your trade was?"

"Just that."

Again they walked on in silence. They were nearing the house now, passing close by the scented sweetness of the rose garden.

"You understand well enough, I daresay," said Anthony, breaking the silence. "You know when a man's in love with you. I don't suppose you care a hang for me—or for anyone else—but, by God, I'd like to make you care."

"Do you think you could?" asked Virginia, in a low voice.

"Probably not, but I'd have a damned good try."

"Are you sorry you ever met me?" she said suddenly.

"Lord, no. It's the red signal again. When I first saw you—that day in Pont Street, I knew I was up against something that was going to hurt like fun. Your face did that to me—just your face. There's magic in you from head to foot—some women are like that, but I've never known a woman who had so much of it as you have. You'll marry someone respectable and prosperous, I suppose, and I shall return to my disreputable life, but I'll kiss you once before I go—I swear I will."

"You can't do it now," said Virginia softly. "Superintendent Battle is watching us out of the library window."

Anthony looked at her.

"You're rather a devil, Virginia," he said dispassionately. "But rather a dear too."

Then he waved his hand airily to Superintendent Battle.

"Caught any criminals this morning, Battle?"

"Not as yet, Mr. Cade."

"That sounds hopeful."

Battle with an agility surprising in so stolid a man, vaulted out of the library window and joined them on the terrace.

"I've got Professor Wynwood down here," he announced in a whisper. "Just this minute arrived. He's decoding the letters now. Would you like to see him at work?"

His tone suggested that of the showman speaking of some pet exhibit. Receiving a reply in the affirmative, he led them up to the window and invited them to peep inside.

Seated at a table, the letters spread out in front of him and writing busily on a big sheet of paper, was a small red-haired man of middle age. He grunted irritably to himself as he wrote and every now and then rubbed his nose violently until its hue almost rivalled that of his hair.

Presently he looked up.

"That you, Battle? What do you want me down here to unravel this tomfoolery for? A child in arms could do it. A baby of two could do it on his head. Call this thing a cipher? It leaps to the eye, man."

"I'm glad of that, Professor," said Battle mildly. "But we're not all so clever as you are, you know."

"It doesn't need cleverness," snapped the professor. "It's routine work. Do you want the whole bundle done? It's a long business, you know—requires diligent application and close attention and absolutely no intelligence. I've done the one dated 'Chimneys' which you said was important. I might as well take the rest back to London and hand 'em over to one of my assistants. I really can't afford the time myself. I've come away now from a real teaser, and I want to get back to it."

His eyes glistened a little.

"Very well, Professor," assented Battle. "I'm sorry we're such small-fry. I'll explain to Mr. Lomax. It's just this one letter that all the hurry is about. Lord Caterham is expecting you to stay for lunch, I believe."

"Never have lunch," said the professor. "Bad habit, lunch. A banana and a water biscuit is all any sane and healthy man should need in the middle of the day."

He seized his overcoat, which lay across the back of a chair. Battle went round to the front of the house, and a few minutes later Anthony and Virginia heard the sound of a car driving away.

Battle rejoined them, carrying in his hand the half sheet of paper which the Professor had given him.

"He's always like that," said Battle, referring to the departed professor. "In the very deuce of a hurry. Clever man, though. Well, here's the kernel of Her Majesty's letter. Care to have a look at it?"

Virginia stretched out a hand, and Anthony read it over her shoulder. It had been, he remembered, a long epistle, breathing mingled passion and despair. The genius of Professor Wynwood had transformed it into an essentially businesslike communication.

*Operations carried out successfully, but S double-crossed us. Has removed stone from hiding place. Not in his room. I have searched. Found following memorandum which I think refers to it:*
RICHMOND SEVEN STRAIGHT EIGHT LEFT THREE RIGHT.

"S?" said Anthony. "Stylptitch, of course. Cunning old dog. He changed the hiding place."

"Richmond," said Virginia thoughtfully. "Is the diamond concealed somewhere at Richmond, I wonder?"

"It's a favourite spot for royalties," agreed Anthony.

Battle shook his head.

"I still think it's a reference to something in this house."

"I know," cried Virginia suddenly.

Both men turned to look at her.

"The Holbein portrait in the Council Chamber. They were tapping on the wall just below it. And it's a portrait of the Earl of Richmond!"

"You've got it," said Battle, and slapped his leg.

He spoke with an animation quite unwonted.

"That's the starting point, the picture, and the crooks know no more than we do what the figures refer to. Those two men in armour stand directly underneath the picture, and their first idea was that the diamond was hidden in one of them. The measurements might have been inches. That failed, and their next idea was a secret passage or stairway, or a sliding panel. Do you know of any such thing, Mrs. Revel?"

Virginia shook her head.

"There's a priest's hole, and at least one secret passage, I know," she said. "I believe I've been shown them once, but I can't remember much about them now. Here's Bundle, she'll know."

Bundle was coming quickly along the terrace towards them.

"I'm taking the Panhard up to town after lunch," she remarked. "Anyone want a lift? Wouldn't you like to come, Mr. Cade? We'll be back by dinnertime."

"No, thanks," said Anthony. "I'm quite happy and busy down here."

"The man fears me," said Bundle. "Either my driving or my fatal fascination! Which is it?"

"The latter," said Anthony. "Every time."

"Bundle, dear," said Virginia, "is there any secret passage leading out of the Council Chamber?"

"Rather. But it's only a mouldy one. Supposed to lead from Chimneys to Wyvern Abbey. So it did in the old, old days, but it's all blocked up now. You can only get along it for about a hundred yards from this end. The one upstairs in the White Gallery is ever so much more amusing, and the priest's hole isn't half bad."

"We're not regarding them from an artistic standpoint," explained Virginia. "It's business. How do you get into the Council Chamber one?"

"Hinged panel. I'll show it you after lunch if you like."

"Thank you," said Superintendent Battle. "Shall we say at 2:30?"

Bundle looked at him with lifted eyebrows.

"Crook stuff?" she inquired.

Tredwell appeared on the terrace.

Luncheon is served, my lady," he announced.

# Twenty-three

## Encounter in the Rose Garden

At 2:30 a little party met together in the Council Chamber: Bundle, Virginia, Superintendent Battle, M. Lemoine and Anthony Cade.

"No good waiting until we can get hold of Mr. Lomax," said Battle. "This is the kind of business one wants to get on with quickly."

"If you've got any idea that Prince Michael was murdered by someone who got in this way, you're wrong," said Bundle. "It can't be done. The other end's blocked completely."

"There is no question of that, milady," said Lemoine quickly. "It is quite a different search that we make."

"Looking for something, are you?" asked Bundle quickly. "Not the historic whatnot, by any chance?"

Lemoine looked puzzled.

"Explain yourself, Bundle," said Virginia encouragingly. "You can when you try."

"The thingummybob," said Bundle. "The historic diamond of purple princes that was pinched in the dark ages before I grew to years of discretion."

"Who told you this, Lady Eileen?" asked Battle.

"I've always known. One of the footmen told me when I was twelve years old."

"A footman," said Battle. "Lord! I'd like Mr. Lomax to have heard that!"

"Is it one of George's closely guarded secrets?" asked Bundle. "How perfectly screaming! I never really thought it was true. George always was an ass—he must know that servants know everything."

She went across to the Holbein portrait, touched a spring concealed somewhere at the side of it, and immediately, with a creaking noise, a section of the panelling swung inwards, revealing a dark opening.

"*Entrez, messieurs et mesdames,*" said Bundle dramatically. "Walk up, walk up, walk up, dearies. Best show of the season, and only a tanner."

Both Lemoine and Battle were provided with torches. They entered the dark aperture first, the others close on their heels.

"Air's nice and fresh," remarked Battle. "Must be ventilated somehow."

He walked on ahead. The floor was rough uneven stone, but the walls were bricked. As Bundle had said, the passage extended for a bare hundred yards. Then it came to an abrupt end with a fallen heap of masonry. Battle satisfied himself that there was no way of egress beyond, and then spoke over his shoulder.

"We'll go back, if you please. I wanted just to spy out the land, so to speak."

In a few minutes they were back again at the panelled entrance.

"We'll start from here," said Battle. "Seven straight, eight left, three right. Take the first as paces."

He paced seven steps carefully, and bending down examined the ground.

"About right, I should fancy. At one time or another, there's been a chalk mark made here. Now then, eight left. That's not paces, the passage is only wide enough to go Indian file, anyway."

"Say it in bricks," suggested Anthony.

"Quite right, Mr. Cade. Eight bricks from the bottom or the top on the left-hand side. Try from the bottom first—it's easier."

He counted up eight bricks.

"Now three to the right of that. One, two, three—Hullo— Hullo, what's this?"

"I shall scream in a minute," said Bundle, "I know I shall. *What* is it?"

Superintendent Battle was working at the brick with the point of his knife. His practised eye had quickly seen that this particular brick was different from the rest. A minute or two's work, and he was able to pull it right out. Behind was a small dark cavity. Battle thrust in his hand.

Everyone waited in breathless expectancy.

Battle drew out his hand again.

He uttered an exclamation of surprise and anger.

The others crowded round and stared uncomprehendingly at the three articles he held. For a moment it seemed as though their eyes must have deceived them.

A card of small pearl buttons, a square of coarse knitting, and a piece of paper on which were inscribed a row of capital E's!

"Well," said Battle. "I'm—I'm danged. What's the meaning of this?"

"*Mon Dieu*," muttered the Frenchman. "*Ça, c'est un peu trop fort!*"

"But what does it mean?" cried Virginia, bewildered.

"Mean?" said Anthony. "There's only one thing it can mean. The late Count Stylptitch must have had a sense of humour! This is an example of that humour. I may say that I don't consider it particularly funny myself."

"Do you mind explaining your meaning a little more clearly, sir?" said the Superintendent Battle.

"Certainly. This was the Count's little joke. He must have suspected that his memorandum had been read. When the crooks came to recover the jewel, they were to find instead this extremely clever conundrum. It's the sort of thing you pin on to yourself at Book Teas, when people have to guess what you are."

"It has a meaning, then?"

"I should say, undoubtedly. If the Count had meant to be merely offensive, he would have put a placard with 'Sold' on it, or a picture of a donkey or something crude like that."

"A bit of knitting, some capital E's, and a lot of buttons," muttered Battle discontendedly.

"*C'est inouï,*" said Lemoine angrily.

"Cipher No. 2," said Anthony. "I wonder whether Professor Wynwood would be any good at this one?"

"When was this passage last used, milady?" asked the Frenchman of Bundle.

Bundle reflected.

"I don't believe anyone's been into it for over two years. The priest's hole is the show exhibit for Americans and tourists generally."

"Curious," murmured the Frenchman.

"Why curious?"

Lemoine stooped and picked up a small object from the floor.

"Because of this," he said. "This match has not lain here for two years—not even two days."

"Any of you ladies or gentlemen drop this, by any chance?" he asked.

He received a negative all round.

"Well, then," said Superintendent Battle, "we've seen all there is to see. We might as well get out of here."

The proposal was assented to by all. The panel had swung to, but Bundle showed them how it was fastened from the inside. She unlatched it, swung it noiselessly open, and sprang through the opening, alighting in the Council Chamber with a resounding thud.

"Damn!" said Lord Caterham, springing up from an armchair in which he appeared to have been taking forty winks.

"Poor old Father," said Bundle. "Did I startle you?"

"I can't think," said Lord Caterham, "why nobody nowadays ever sits still after a meal. It's a lost art. God knows Chimneys is big enough but even here there doesn't seem to be a single room where I can be sure of a little peace. Good Lord, how many of you are there? Reminds me of the pantomimes I used to go to as a boy when hordes of demons used to pop up out of trapdoors."

"Demon No. 7," said Virginia, approaching him, and patting

him on the head. "Don't be cross. We're just exploring secret passages, that's all."

"There seems to be a positive boom in secret passages today," grumbled Lord Caterham, not yet completely mollified. "I've had to show that fellow Fish round them all this morning."

"When was that?" asked Battle quickly.

"Just before lunch. It seems he'd heard of the one in here. I showed him that, and then took him up to the White Gallery, and we finished up with the priest's hole. But his enthusiasm was waning by that time. He looked bored to death. But I made him go through with it." Lord Caterham chuckled at the remembrance.

Anthony put a hand on Lemoine's arm.

"Come outside," he said softly. "I want to speak to you."

The two men went out together through the window. When they had gone a sufficient distance from the house, Anthony drew from his pocket the scrap of paper that Boris had given him that morning.

"Look here," he said. "Did you drop this?"

Lemoine took it and examined it with some interest.

"No," he said. "I have never seen it before. Why?"

"Quite sure?"

"Absolutely sure, monsieur."

"That's very odd."

He repeated to Lemoine what Boris had said. The other listened with close attention.

"No, I did not drop it. You say he found it in that clump of trees?"

"Well, I assumed so, but he did not actually say so."

"It is just possible that it might have fluttered out of M. Isaacstein's suitcase. Question Boris again." He handed the paper back to Anthony. After a minute or two he said: "What exactly do you know of this man Boris?"

Anthony shrugged his shoulders.

"I understood he was the late Prince Michael's trusted servant."

"It may be so, but make it your business to find out. Ask someone who knows, such as the Baron Lolopretjzyl. Perhaps this man was engaged but a few weeks ago. For myself, I have believed him honest. But who knows? King Victor is quite capable of making himself into a trusted servant at a moment's notice."

"Do you really think—"

Lemoine interrupted him.

"I will be quite frank. With me, King Victor is an obsession. I see him everywhere. At this moment even I ask myself—this man who is talking to me, this M. Cade, is he, perhaps, King Victor?"

"Good Lord," said Anthony, "you have got it badly."

"What do I care for the diamond? For the discovery of the murderer of Prince Michael? I leave those affairs to my colleague of Scotland Yard whose business it is. Me, I am in England for one purpose, and one purpose only, to capture King Victor and capture him red-handed. Nothing else matters."

"Think you'll do it?" asked Anthony, lighting a cigarette.

"How should I know?" said Lemoine, with sudden despondency.

"Hm!" said Anthony.

They had regained the terrace. Superintendent Battle was standing near the French window in a wooden attitude.

"Look at poor old Battle," said Anthony. "Let's go and cheer him up." He paused a minute, and said, "You know, you're an odd fish in some ways, M. Lemoine."

"In what ways, M. Cade?"

"Well," said Anthony, "in your place, I should have been inclined to note down that address that I showed you. It may be of no importance—quite conceivably. On the other hand, it might be very important indeed."

Lemoine looked at him for a minute or two steadily. Then, with a slight smile, he drew back the cuff of his left coat sleeve. Pencilled on the white shirt cuff beneath were the words "Hurstmere, Langly Road, Dover."

"I apologize," said Anthony. "And I retire worsted."

He joined Superintendent Battle.

"You look very pensive, Battle," he remarked.

"I've got a lot to think about, Mr. Cade."

"Yes, I expect you have."

"Things aren't dovetailing. They're not dovetailing at all."

"Very trying," sympathized Anthony. "Never mind, Battle, if the worst comes to the worst, you can always arrest me. You've got my guilty footprints to fall back upon, remember."

But the superintendent did not smile.

"Got any enemies here that you know of, Mr. Cade?" he asked.

"I've an idea that the third footman doesn't like me," replied Anthony lightly. "He does his best to forget to hand me the choicest vegetables. Why?"

"I've been getting anonymous letters," said Superintendent Battle. "Or rather an anonymous letter, I should say."

"About me?"

Without answer Battle took a folded sheet of cheap notepaper from his pocket, and handed it to Anthony. Scrawled on it in an illiterate handwriting were the words:

*Look out for Mr. Cade. He isn't wot he seems.*

Anthony handed it back with a light laugh.

"That all? Cheer up, Battle. I'm really a king in disguise, you know."

He went into the house, whistling lightly as he walked along. But as he entered his bedroom and shut the door behind him, his face changed. It grew set and stern. He sat down on the edge of the bed and stared moodily at the floor.

"Things are getting serious," said Anthony to himself. "Something must be done about it. It's all damned awkward. . . ."

He sat there for a minute or two, then strolled to the window. For a moment or two he stood looking out aimlessly and then his eyes became suddenly focused on a certain spot, and his face lightened.

"Of course," he said. "The rose garden! That's it! The rose garden."

He hurried downstairs again and out into the garden by a side door. He approached the rose garden by a circuitous route. It had a little gate at either end. He entered by the far one, and walked up to the sundial which was on a raised hillock in the exact centre of the garden.

Just as Anthony reached it, he stopped dead and stared at another occupant of the rose garden who seemed equally surprised to see him.

"I didn't know that you were interested in roses, Mr. Fish," said Anthony gently.

"Sir," said Mr. Fish, "I am considerably interested in roses."

They looked at each other warily, as antagonists seek to measure their opponents' strength.

"So am I," said Anthony.

"Is that so?"

"In fact, I dote upon roses," said Anthony airily.

A very slight smile hovered upon Mr. Fish's lips, and at the same time Anthony also smiled. The tension seemed to relax.

"Look at this beauty now," said Mr. Fish, stooping to point out a particularly fine bloom. "Madame Abel Chatenay, I pressoom it to be. Yes, I am right. This white rose, before the war, was known as Frau Carl Drusky. They have, I believe, renamed it. Oversensitive, perhaps, but truly patriotic. The La France is always popular. Do you care for red roses at all, Mr. Cade? A bright scarlet rose now—"

Mr. Fish's slow, drawling voice, was interrupted. Bundle was leaning out of a first-floor window.

"Care for a spin to town, Mr. Fish? I'm just off."

"Thank you, Lady Eileen, but I am vurry happy here."

"Sure you won't change your mind, Mr. Cade?"

Anthony laughed and shook his head. Bundle disappeared.

"Sleep is more in my line," said Anthony, with a wide yawn. "A good after-luncheon nap!" He took out a cigarette. "You haven't got a match, have you?"

Mr. Fish handed him a matchbox. Anthony helped himself, and handed back the box with a word of thanks.

"Roses," said Anthony, "are all very well. But I don't feel particularly horticultural this afternoon."

With a disarming smile, he nodded cheerfully.

A thundering noise sounded from just outside the house.

"Pretty powerful engine she's got in that car of hers," remarked Anthony. "There, off she goes."

They had a view of the car speeding down the long drive.

Anthony yawned again, and strolled towards the house.

He passed in through the door. Once inside, he seemed as though changed to quicksilver. He raced across the hall, out through one of the windows on the farther side, and across the park. Bundle, he knew, had to make a big detour by the lodge gates, and through the village.

He ran desperately. It was a race against time. He reached the park wall just as he heard the car outside. He swung himself up and dropped into the road.

"Hi!" cried Anthony.

In her astonishment, Bundle swerved half across the road. She managed to pull up without accident. Anthony ran after the car, opened the door, and jumped in beside Bundle.

"I'm coming to London with you," he said. "I meant to all along."

"Extraordinary person," said Bundle. "What's that you've got in your hand?"

"Only a match," said Anthony.

He regarded it thoughtfully. It was pink, with a yellow head. He threw away his unlighted cigarette, and put the match carefully into his pocket.

# Twenty-four

## The House at Dover

"You don't mind, I suppose," said Bundle after a minute or two, "if I drive rather fast? I started later than I meant to do."

It had seemed to Anthony that they were proceeding at a terrific speed already, but he soon saw that that was nothing compared to what Bundle could get out of the Panhard if she tried.

"Some people," said Bundle, as she slowed down momentarily to pass through a village, "are terrified of my driving. Poor old Father, for instance. Nothing would induce him to come up with me in this old bus."

Privately, Anthony thought Lord Caterham was entirely justified. Driving with Bundle was not a sport to be indulged in by nervous, middle-aged gentlemen.

"But you don't seem nervous a bit," continued Bundle approvingly, as she swept round a corner on two wheels.

"I'm in pretty good training, you see," explained Anthony

gravely. "Also," he added, as an afterthought, "I'm rather in a hurry myself."

"Shall I speed her up a bit more?" asked Bundle kindly.

"Good Lord, no," said Anthony hastily. "We're averaging about fifty as it is."

"I'm burning with curiosity to know the reason for this sudden departure," said Bundle, after executing a fanfare upon the klaxon which must temporarily have deafened the neighbourhood. "But I suppose I mustn't ask? You're not escaping from justice, are you?"

"I'm not quite sure," said Anthony. "I shall know soon."

"That Scotland Yard man isn't as much of a rabbit as I thought," said Bundle thoughtfully.

"Battle's a good man," agreed Anthony.

"You ought to have been in diplomacy," remarked Bundle. "You don't part with much information, do you?"

"I was under the impression that I babbled."

"Oh! Boy! You're not eloping with Mademoiselle Brun, by any chance?"

"Not guilty!" said Anthony with fervour.

There was a pause of some minutes during which Bundle caught up and passed three other cars. Then she asked suddenly:

"How long have you known Virginia?"

"That's a difficult question to answer," said Anthony, with perfect truth. "I haven't actually met her very often, and yet I seem to have known her a long time."

Bundle nodded.

"Virginia's got brains," she remarked abruptly. "She's always talking nonsense, but she's got brains all right. She was frightfully good out in Herzoslovakia, I believe. If Tim Revel had lived he'd have had a fine career—and mostly owing to Virginia. She worked for him tooth and nail. She did everything in the world she could for him—and I know why, too."

"Because she cared for him?" Anthony sat looking very straight ahead of him.

"No, because she didn't. Don't you see? She didn't love him—she never loved him, and so she did everything on earth she could to make up. That's Virginia all over. But don't you make any mistake about it. Virginia was never in love with Tim Revel."

"You seem very positive," said Anthony, turning to look at her.

Bundle's little hands were clenched on the steering wheel, and her chin was stuck out in a determined manner.

"I know a thing or two. I was only a kid at the time of her marriage, but I heard one or two things, and knowing Virginia I can put them together easily enough. Tim Revel was bowled over by Virginia—he was Irish, you know, and most attractive, with a genius for expressing himself well. Virginia was quite young—eighteen. She couldn't go anywhere without seeing Tim in a state of picturesque misery, vowing he'd shoot himself or take to drink if she didn't marry him. Girls believe these things—or used to—we've advanced a lot in the last eight years. Virginia was carried away by the feeling she thought she'd inspired. She married him—and she was an angel to him always. She wouldn't have been half as much of an angel if she'd loved him. There's a lot of the devil in Virginia. But I can tell you one thing—she enjoys her freedom. And anyone will have a hard time persuading her to give it up."

"I wonder why you tell me all this?" said Anthony slowly.

"It's interesting to know about people, isn't it? Some people, that is."

"I've wanted to know," he acknowledged.

"And you'd never have heard from Virginia. But you can trust me for an inside tip from the stables. Virginia's a darling. Even women like her because she isn't a bit of a cat. And anyway," Bundle ended, somewhat obscurely, "one must be a sport, mustn't one?"

"Oh, certainly," Anthony agreed. But he was still puzzled. He had no idea what had prompted Bundle to give him so much information unasked. That he was glad of it, he did not deny.

"Here are the trams," said Bundle, with a sigh. "Now, I suppose, I shall have to drive carefully."

"It might be as well," agreed Anthony.

His ideas and Bundle's on the subject of careful driving hardly coincided. Leaving indignant suburbs behind them they finally emerged into Oxford Street.

"Not bad going, eh?" said Bundle, glancing at her wristwatch.

Anthony assented fervently.

"Where do you want to be dropped?"

"Anywhere. Which way are you going?"

"Knightsbridge way."

"All right, drop me at Hyde Park Corner."

"Good-bye," said Bundle, as she drew up at the place indicated. "What about the return journey?"

"I'll find my own way back, thanks very much."

"I *have* scared him," remarked Bundle.

"I shouldn't recommend driving with you as a tonic for nervous old ladies, but personally I've enjoyed it. The last time I was in equal danger was when I was charged by a herd of wild elephants."

"I think you're extremely rude," remarked Bundle. "We're not even had one bump today."

"I'm sorry if you've been holding yourself in on my account," retorted Anthony.

"I don't think men are really very brave," said Bundle.

"That's a nasty one," said Anthony. "I retire, humiliated." Bundle nodded and drove on. Anthony hailed a passing taxi. "Victoria Station," he said to the driver as he got in.

When he got to Victoria he paid off the taxi and inquired for the next train to Dover. Unfortunately he had just missed one.

Resigning himself to a wait of something over an hour, Anthony paced up and down, his brows knit. Once or twice he shook his head impatiently.

The journey to Dover was uneventful. Arrived there, Anthony passed quickly out of the station and then, as though suddenly remembering, he turned back again. There was a slight smile on his lips as he asked to be directed to Hurstmere, Langly Road.

The road in question was a long one, leading right out of the town. According to the porter's instructions, Hurstmere was the last house. Anthony trudged along steadily. The little pucker had reappeared between his eyes. Nevertheless there was a new elation in his manner, as always when danger was near at hand.

Hurstmere was, as the porter had said, the last house in Langly Road. It stood well back, enclosed in its own grounds, which were ragged and overgrown. The place, Anthony judged, must have been empty for many years. A large iron gate swung rustily on its hinges, and the name on the gatepost was half obliterated.

"A lonely spot," muttered Anthony to himself, "and a good one to choose."

He hesitated a minute or two, glanced quickly up and down

the road—which was quite deserted—and then slipped quietly past the creaking gate into the overgrown drive. He walked up it a little way, and then stood listening. He was still some distance from the house. Not a sound could be heard anywhere. Some fast-yellowing leaves detached themselves from one of the trees overhead and fell with a soft rustling sound that was almost sinister in the stillness. Anthony started; then smiled.

"Nerves," he murmured to himself. "Never knew I had such things before."

He went on up the drive. Presently, as the drive curved, he slipped into the shrubbery and so continued his way unseen from the house. Suddenly he stood still, peering out through the leaves. Some distance away a dog was barking, but it was a sound nearer at hand that had attracted Anthony's attention.

His keen hearing had not been mistaken. A man came rapidly round the corner of the house, a short square, thickset man, foreign in appearance. He did not pause but walked steadily on, circling the house and disappearing again.

Anthony nodded to himself.

"Sentry," he murmured. "They do the thing quite well."

As soon as he had passed, Anthony went on, diverging to the left, and so following in the footsteps of the sentry.

His own footsteps were quite noiseless.

The wall of the house was on his right, and presently he came to where a broad blur of light fell on the gravelled walk. The sound of several men talking together was clearly audible.

"My God! what double-dyed idiots," murmured Anthony to himself. "It would serve them right to be given a fright."

He stole up to the window, stooping a little so that he should not be seen. Presently he lifted his head very carefully to the level of the sill and looked in.

Half a dozen men were sprawling round a table. Four of them were big thickset men, with high cheekbones, and eyes set in Magyar slanting fashion. The other two were rat-like little men with quick gestures. The language that was being spoken was French, but the four big men spoke it with uncertainty and a hoarse guttural intonation.

"The boss?" growled one of these. "When will he be here?"

One of the smaller men shrugged his shoulders.

"Any time now."

"About time, too," growled the first man. "I have never seen him, this boss of yours, but, oh, what great and glorious work might we not have accomplished in these days of idle waiting!"

"Fool," said the other little man bitingly. "Getting nabbed by the police is all the great and glorious work you and your precious lot would have been likely to accomplish. A lot of blundering gorillas!"

"Aha!" roared another big thickset fellow. "You insult the Comrades? I will soon set the sign of the Red Hand round your throat."

He half rose, glaring ferociously at the Frenchman, but one of his companions pulled him back again.

"No quarrelling," he grunted. "We're to work together. From all I heard, this King Victor doesn't stand for being disobeyed."

In the darkness, Anthony heard the footsteps of the sentry coming his round again, and he drew back behind a bush.

"Who's that?" said one of the men inside.

"Carlo—going his rounds."

"Oh! What about the prisoner?"

"He's all right—coming round pretty fast now. He's recovered well from the crack on the head we gave him."

Anthony moved gently away.

"God! What a lot," he muttered. "They discuss their affairs with an open window, and that fool Carlo goes his round with the tread of an elephant—and the eyes of a bat. And to crown all, the Herzoslovakians and the French are on the point of coming to blows. King Victor's headquarters seem to be in a parlous condition. It would amuse me, it would amuse me very much, to teach them a lesson."

He stood irresolute for a minute, smiling to himself.

From somewhere above his head came a stifled groan.

Anthony looked up. The groan came again.

Anthony glanced quickly from left to right. Carlo was not due round again just yet. He grasped the heavy Virginia creeper and climbed nimbly till he reached the sill of a window. The window was shut, but with a tool from his pocket he soon succeeded in forcing up the catch.

He paused a minute to listen, then sprang lightly inside the room. There was a bed in the far corner and on that bed a man was lying, his figure barely discernible in the gloom.

Anthony went over to the bed, and flashed his pocket torch on the man's face. It was a foreign face, pale and emaciated, and the head was swathed in heavy bandages.

The man was bound hand and foot. He stared up at Anthony like one dazed.

Anthony bent over him, and as he did so he heard a sound behind him and swung round, his hand travelling to his coat pocket.

But a sharp command arrested him.

"Hands up, sonny. You didn't expect to see me here, but I happened to catch the same train as you at Victoria."

It was Mr. Hiram Fish who was standing in the doorway. He was smiling and in his hand was a big blue automatic.

# Twenty-five

## TUESDAY NIGHT AT CHIMNEYS

Lord Caterham, Virginia and Bundle were sitting in the library after dinner. It was Tuesday evening. Some thirty hours had elapsed since Anthony's rather dramatic departure.

For at least the seventh time Bundle repeated Anthony's parting words, as spoken at Hyde Park Corner.

"I'll find my own way back," echoed Virginia thoughtfully. "That doesn't look as though he expected to be away as long as this. And he's left all his things here."

"He didn't tell you where he was going?"

"No," said Virginia, looking straight in front of her. "He told me nothing."

After this, there was a silence for a minute or two. Lord Caterham was the first to break it.

"On the whole," he said, "keeping an hotel has some advantages over keeping a country house."

"Meaning—"

"That little notice they always hang up in your room. Visitors intending departure must give notice before twelve o'clock."

Virginia smiled.

"I daresay," he continued, "that I am old-fashioned and unreasonable. It's the fashion, I know, to pop in and out of a house. Same idea as an hotel—perfect freedom of action, and no bill at the end!"

"You are an old grouser," said Bundle. "You've had Virginia and me. What more do you want?"

"Nothing more, nothing more," Lord Caterham assured them hastily. "That's not it at all. It's the principle of the thing. It gives one such a restless feeling. I'm quite willing to admit that it's been an almost ideal twenty-four hours. Peace—perfect peace. No burglaries or other crimes of violence, no detectives, no Americans. What I complain of is that I should have enjoyed it all so much more if I'd felt really secure. As it is, all the time, I've been saying to myself, 'One or the other of them is bound to turn up in a minute.' And that spoilt the whole thing."

"Well, nobody has turned up," said Bundle. "We've been left severely alone—neglected, in fact. It's odd the way Fish disappeared. Didn't he say anything?"

"Not a word. Last time I saw him he was pacing up and down the rose garden yesterday afternoon, smoking one of those unpleasant cigars of his. After that he seems to have just melted into the landscape."

"Somebody must have kidnapped him," said Bundle hopefully.

"In another day or two, I expect we shall have Scotland Yard dragging the lake to find his dead body," said her father gloomily. "It serves me right. At my time of life, I ought to have gone quietly abroad and taken care of my health, and not allowed myself to be drawn into George Lomax's wildcat schemes. I—"

He was interrupted by Tredwell.

"Well," said Lord Caterham, irritably, "what is it?"

"The French detective is here, my lord, and would be glad if you could spare him a few minutes."

"What did I tell you?" said Lord Caterham. "I knew it was too good to last. Depend up on it, they've found Fish's dead body doubled up in the goldfish pond."

Tredwell, in a strictly respectful manner, steered him back to the point at issue.

"Am I to say that you will see him, my lord?"

"Yes, yes. Bring him in here."

Tredwell departed. He returned a minute or two later announcing in a lugubrious voice:

"Monsieur Lemoine."

The Frenchman came in with a quick, light step. His walk, more than his face, betrayed the fact that he was excited about something.

"Good evening, Lemoine," said Lord Caterham. "Have a drink, won't you?"

"I thank you, no." He bowed punctiliously to the ladies. "At last I make progress. As things are, I felt that you should be acquainted with the discoveries—the very grave discoveries that I have made in the course of the last twenty-four hours."

"I thought there must be something important going on somewhere," said Lord Caterham.

"My lord, yesterday afternoon one of your guests left this house in a curious manner. From the beginning, I must tell you, I have had my suspicions. Here is a man who comes from the wilds. Two months ago he was in South Africa. Before that—where?"

Virginia drew a sharp breath. For a moment the Frenchman's eyes rested on her doubtfully. Then he went on:

"Before that—where? None can say. And he is just such a one as the man I am looking for—gay, audacious, reckless, one who would dare anything. I send cable after cable, but I can get no word as to his past life. Ten years ago he was in Canada, yes, but since then—silence. My suspicions grow stronger. Then I pick up one day a scrap of paper where he has lately passed along. It bears an address—the address of a house in Dover. Later, as though by chance, I drop that same piece of paper. Out of the tail of my eye, I see this Boris, the Herzoslovakian, pick it up and take it to his master. All along I have been sure that this Boris is an emissary of the Comrades of the Red Hand. We know that the Comrades are working in with King Victor over this affair. If Boris recognized his chief in Mr. Anthony Cade, would he not do just what he has done—transferred his allegiance? Why should he attach himself otherwise to an insignificant stranger? It was suspicious, I tell you, very suspicious.

"But almost I am disarmed, for Anthony Cade brings this same paper to me at once and asks me if I have dropped it. As I say, almost I am disarmed—but not quite! For it may mean that he is innocent, or it may mean that he is very, very clever. I deny, of course, that it is mine or that I dropped it. But in the meantime I have set inquiries on foot. Only today I have news. The house at Dover has been precipitately abandoned, but up till yesterday afternoon it was occupied by a body of foreigners. Not a doubt but that it was King Victor's headquarters. Now see the significance of these points. Yesterday afternoon, Mr. Cade clears out from here precipitately. Ever since he dropped that paper, he must know that the game is up. He reaches Dover and immediately the gang is disbanded. What the next move will be, I do not know. What is quite certain is that Mr. Anthony Cade will not return here. But knowing King Victor as I do, I am certain that he will not abandon the game without having one more try for the jewel. And that is when I shall get him!"

Virginia stood up suddenly. She walked across to the mantelpiece and spoke in a voice that rang cold like steel.

"You are leaving one thing out of account, I think, M. Lemoine," she said. "Mr. Cade is not the only guest who disappeared yesterday in a suspicious manner."

"You mean, madame?—"

"That all you have said applies equally well to another person. What about Mr. Hiram Fish?"

"Oh Mr. Fish!"

"Yes, Mr. Fish. Did you not tell us that first night that King Victor had lately come to England from America? So has Mr. Fish come to England from America. It is true that he brought a letter of introduction from a very well-known man, but surely that would be a simple thing for a man like King Victor to manage. He is certainly not what he pretends to be. Lord Caterham has commented on the fact that when it is a question of the first editions he is supposed to have come here to see he is always the listener, never the talker. And there are several suspicious facts against him. There was a light in his window the night of the murder. Then take that evening in the Council Chamber. When I met him on the terrace he was fully dressed. *He* could have dropped the paper. You didn't actually *see* Mr. Cade do so. Mr. Cade may have gone to Dover. If he did it was simply to investigate. He may have been kidnapped there. I say that there is far more suspicion attaching to Mr. Fish's actions than to Mr. Cade's."

The Frenchman's voice rang out sharply:

"From your point of view, that well may be, madame. I do not dispute it. And I agree that Mr. Fish is not what he seems."

"Well, then?"

"But that makes no difference. *You see, madame, Mr. Fish is a Pinkerton's man.*"

"What?" cried Lord Caterham.

"Yes, Lord Caterham. He came over here to trail King Victor. Superintendent Battle and I have known this for some time."

Virginia said nothing. Very slowly she sat down again. With those few words the structure that she had built up so carefully was scattered in ruins about her feet.

"You see," Lemoine was continuing, "we have all known that eventually King Victor would come to Chimneys. It was the one place we were sure of catching him."

Virginia looked up with an odd light in her eyes, and suddenly she laughed.

"You've not caught him yet," she said.

Lemoine looked at her curiously.

"No, madame. But I shall."

"He's supposed to be rather famous for outwitting people, isn't he?"

The Frenchman's face darkened with anger.

"This time, it will be different," he said between his teeth.

"He's a very attractive fellow," said Lord Caterham. "Very attractive. But surely—why, you said he was an old friend of yours, Virginia?"

"That is why," said Virginia composedly, "I think M. Lemoine must be making a mistake."

And her eyes met the detective's steadily, but he appeared in no wise discomfited.

"Time will show, madame," he said.

"Do you pretend that it was he who shot Prince Michael?" she asked presently.

"Certainly."

But Virginia shook her head.

"Oh no!" she said, "Oh, no! That is one thing I am quite sure of. Anthony Cade never killed Prince Michael."

Lemoine was watching her intently.

"There is a possibility that you are right, madame," he said slowly. "A possibility, that is all. It may have been the Herzoslovakian, Boris, who exceeded his orders and fired that shot. Who knows, Prince Michael may have done him some great wrong, and the man sought revenge."

"He looks a murderous sort of fellow," agreed Lord Caterham. "The housemaids, I believe, scream when he passes them in the passages."

"Well," said Lemoine. "I must be going now. I felt it was due to you, my lord, to know exactly how things stand."

"Very kind of you, I'm sure," said Lord Caterham. "Quite certain you won't have a drink? All right, then. Goodnight."

"I hate that man with his prim little black beard and his eyeglasses," said Bundle, as soon as the door had shut behind him. "I hope Anthony *does* snoo him. I'd love to see him dancing with rage. What do you think about it all, Virginia?"

"I don't know," said Virginia. "I'm tired. I shall go up to bed."

"Not a bad idea," said Lord Caterham. "It's half past eleven."

As Virginia was crossing the wide hall, she caught sight of a broad back that seemed familiar to her discreetly vanishing through a side door.

"Superintendent Battle," she called imperiously.

The superintendent, for it was indeed he, retraced his steps with a shade of unwillingness.

"Yes, Mrs. Revel?"

"M. Lemoine has been here. He says—Tell me, is it true, really true, that Mr. Fish is an American detective?"

Superintendent Battle nodded.

"That's right."

"You have known it all along?"

Again Superintendent Battle nodded.

Virginia turned away towards the staircase.

"I see," she said. "Thank you."

Until that minute she had refused to believe.

And now?—

Sitting down before her dressing table in her own room, she faced the question squarely. Every word that Anthony had said came back to her fraught with a new significance.

Was this the "trade" that he had spoken of?

The trade that he had given up. But then—

An unusual sound disturbed the even tenor of her meditations. She lifted her head with a start. Her little gold clock showed the hour to be after one. Nearly two hours she had sat here thinking.

Again the sound was repeated. A sharp tap on the window-pane. Virginia went to the window and opened it. Below on the pathway was a tall figure which even as she looked stooped for another handful of gravel.

For a moment Virginia's heart beat faster—then she recognized the massive strength and square-cut outline of the Herzoslovakian, Boris.

"Yes," she said in a low voice. "What is it?"

At the moment it did not strike her as strange that Boris should be throwing gravel at her window at this hour of the night.

"What is it?" she repeated impatiently.

"I come from the master," said Boris in a low tone which nevertheless carried perfectly. "He has sent for you."

He made the statement in a perfectly matter-of-fact tone.

"Sent for me?"

"Yes, I am to bring you to him. There is a note. I will throw it up to you."

Viriginia stood back a little, and a slip of paper, weighted with a stone, fell accurately at her feet. She unfolded it and read:

*My dear* (Anthony had written)—*I'm in a tight place, but I mean to win through. Will you trust me and come to me?*

For quite two minutes Virginia stood there, immovable, reading those few words over and over again.

She raised her head, looking round the well-appointed luxury of the bedroom as though she saw it with new eyes.

Then she leaned out of the window again.

"What am I to do?" she asked.

"The detectives are the other side of the house, outside the Council Chamber. Come down and out through the side door. I will be there. I have a car waiting outside in the road."

Virginia nodded. Quickly she changed her dress for one of fawn tricot, and pulled on a little fawn leather hat.

Then, smiling a little, she wrote a short note, addressed it to Bundle and pinned it to the pincushion.

She stole quietly downstairs and undid the bolts of the side door. Just a moment she paused, then, with a little gallant toss of the head, the same toss of the head with which her ancestors had gone into action in the Crusades, she passed through.

# Twenty-six

## The 13th of October

At ten o'clock on the morning of Wednesday, the 13th of October, Anthony Cade walked into Harridge's Hotel and asked for Baron Lolopretjzyl who was occupying a suite there.

After suitable and imposing delay, Anthony was taken to the suite in question. The Baron was standing on the hearthrug in a correct and stiff fashion. Little Captain Andrassy, equally correct as to demeanour, but with a slightly hostile attitude, was also present.

The usual bows, clicking of heels, and other formal greetings of etiquette took place. Anthony was, by now, thoroughly conversant with the routine.

"You will forgive this early call I trust, Baron," he said cheerfully, laying down his hat and stick on the table. "As a matter of fact, I have a little business proposition to make to you."

"Ha! Is that so?" said the Baron.

Captain Andrassy, who had never overcome his initial distrust of Anthony, looked suspicious.

"Business," said Anthony, "is based on the well-known principle of supply and demand. You want something, the other man has it. The only thing left to settle is the price."

The Baron looked at him attentively, but said nothing.

"Between a Herzoslovakian nobleman and an English gentleman the terms should be easily arranged," said Anthony rapidly.

He blushed a little as he said it. Such words do not rise easily to an Englishman's lips, but he had observed on previous occasions the enormous effect of such phraseology upon the Baron's mentality. True enough, the charm worked.

"That is so," said the Baron approvingly, nodding his head. "That is entirely so."

Even Captain Andrassy appeared to unbend a little, and nodded his head also.

"Very good," said Anthony. "I won't beat about the bush any more—"

"What is that, you say?" interrupted the Baron. "To beat about the bush? I do not comprehend?"

"A mere figure of speech, Baron. To speak in plain English, *you* want the goods, *we* have them! The ship is all very well, but it lacks a figurehead. By the ship, I mean the Loyalist party of Herzoslovakia. At the present minute you lack the principal plank of your political programme. You are minus a prince! Now supposing—only supposing, that I could supply you with a prince?"

The baron stared.

"I do not comprehend you in the least," he declared.

"Sir," said Captain Andrassy, twirling his moustache fiercely, "you are insulting!"

"Not at all," said Anthony. "I'm trying to be helpful. Supply and demand, you understand. It's all perfectly fair and square. No princes supplied unless genuine—see trademark. If we come to terms, you'll find it's quite all right. I'm offering you the real genuine article—out of the bottom drawer."

"Not in the least," the Baron declared again, "do I comprehend you."

"It doesn't really matter," said Anthony kindly. "I just want you to get used to the idea. To put it vulgarly, I've got something up my sleeve. Just get hold of this. You want a prince. Under certain conditions, I will undertake to supply you with one."

The Baron and Andrassy stared at him. Anthony took up his hat and stick again and prepared to depart.

"Just think it over. Now, Baron, there is one thing further. You must come down to Chimneys this evening—Captain Andrassy also. Several very curious things are likely to happen there. Shall we make an appointment? Say in the Council Chamber at nine o'clock? Thank you, gentlemen, I may rely upon you to be there?"

The Baron took a step forward and looked searchingly in Anthony's face.

"Mr. Cade," he said, not without dignity, "it is not, I hope, that you wish to make fun of me?"

Anthony returned his gaze steadily.

"Baron," he said, and there was a curious note in his voice, "when this evening is over, I think you will be the first to admit that there is more earnest than jest about this business."

Bowing to both men, he left the room.

His next call was in the City where he sent in his card to Mr. Herman Isaacstein.

After some delay, Anthony was received by a pale and exquisitely dressed underling with an engaging manner, and a military title.

"You wanted to see Mr. Isaacstein, didn't you?" said the young man. "I'm afraid he's most awfully busy this morning—board meetings and all that sort of thing, you know. Is it anything that I can do?"

"I must see him personally," said Anthony, and added carelessly, "I've just come up from Chimneys."

The young man was slightly staggered by the mention of Chimneys.

"Oh!" he said doubtfully. "Well, I'll see."

"Tell him it's important," said Anthony.

"Message from Lord Caterham?" suggested the young man.

"Something of the kind," said Anthony, "but it's imperative that I should see Mr. Isaacstein at once."

Two minutes later Anthony was conducted into a sumptuous inner sanctum where he was principally impressed by the immense size and roomy depths of the leather-covered armchairs.

Mr. Isaacstein rose to greet him.

"You must forgive my looking you up like this," said Anthony. "I know that you're a busy man, and I'm not going to waste more of your time than I can help. It's just a little matter of business that I want to put before you."

Isaacstein looked at him attentively for a minute or two out of his beady black eyes.

"Have a cigar," he said unexpectedly, holding out an open box.

"Thank you," said Anthony. "I don't mind if I do."

He helped himself.

"It's about this Herzoslovakian business," continued Anthony as he accepted a match. He noted the momentary flickering of the other's steady gaze. "The murder of Prince Michael must have rather upset the applecart."

Mr. Isaacstein raised one eyebrow, murmured. "Ah?" interrogatively and transferred his gaze to the ceiling.

"Oil," said Anthony, thoughtfully surveying the polished surface of the desk. "Wonderful thing, oil."

He felt the slight start the financier gave.

"Do you mind coming to the point, Mr. Cade?"

"Not at all. I imagine, Mr. Isaacstein, that if those oil concessions are granted to another company you won't be exactly pleased about it?"

"What's the proposition?" asked the other, looking straight at him.

"A suitable claimant to the throne, full of pro-British sympathies."

"Where have you got him?"

"That's my business."

Isaacstein acknowledged the retort by a slight smile, his glance had grown hard and keen.

"The genuine article? I can't stand for any funny business?"

"The absolute genuine article."

"Straight?"

"Straight."

"I'll take your word for it."

"You don't seem to take much convincing?" said Anthony, looking curiously at him.

Herman Isaacstein smiled.

"I shouldn't be where I am now if I hadn't learnt to know whether a man is speaking the truth or not," he replied simply. What terms do you want?"

"The same loan, on the same conditions, that you offered to Prince Michael."

"What about yourself?"

"For the moment, nothing, except that I want you to come down to Chimneys tonight."

"No," said Isaacstein, with some decision. "I can't do that."

"Why?"

"Dining out—rather an important dinner."

"All the same, I'm afraid you'll have to cut it out—for your own sake."

"What do you mean?"

Anthony looked at him for a full minute before he said slowly:

"Do you know that they've found the revolver, the one Michael was shot with? Do you know where they found it? In your suitcase."

"What?"

Isaacstein almost leapt from his chair. His face was frenzied.

"What are you saying? What do you mean?"

"I'll tell you."

Very obligingly, Anthony narrated the occurrences in connexion with the finding of the revolver. As he spoke the other's face assumed a greyish tinge of absolute terror.

"But it's false," he screamed out as Anthony finished.

"I never put it there. I know nothing about it. It is a plot."

"Don't excite yourself," said Anthony soothingly. "If that's the case you'll easily be able to prove it."

"Prove it? How can I prove it?"

"If I were you," said Anthony gently, "I'd come to Chimneys tonight."

Isaacstein looked at him doubtfully.

"You advise it?"

Anthony leant forward and whispered to him. The financier fell back in amazement, staring at him.

"You actually mean—"

"Come and see," said Anthony.

# Twenty-seven

## The 13th of October (*contd*)

The clock in the Council Chamber struck nine.

"Well," said Lord Caterham, with a deep sigh. "Here they all are, just like little Bo-Peep's flock, back again and wagging their tails behind them."

He looked sadly round the room.

"Organ grinder complete with monkey," he murmured, fixing the Baron with his eye. "Nosy Parker of Throgmorton Street—"

"I think you're rather unkind to the Baron," protested Bundle, to whom these confidences were being poured out. "He told me that he considered you the perfect example of English hospitality among the *haute noblesse*."

"I daresay," said Lord Caterham. "He's always saying things like that. It makes him most fatiguing to talk to. But I can tell you I'm not nearly as much of the hospitable English gentleman as I was. As soon as I can I shall let Chimneys to an enterprising American, and go and live in an hotel. There, if anyone worries you, you can just ask for your bill and go."

"Cheer up," said Bundle. "We seem to have lost Mr. Fish for good."

"I always found him rather amusing," said Lord Caterham, who was in a contradictory temper. "It's that precious young man of yours who has let me in for this. Why should I have this board meeting called in my house? Why doesn't he rent The Larches or Elmhurst, or some nice villa residence like that at Streatham, and hold his company meetings there?"

"Wrong atmosphere," said Bundle.

"No one is going to play any tricks on us, I hope?" said her father nervously. "I don't trust that French fellow, Lemoine. The French police are up to all sorts of dodges. Put india rubber bands round your arm, and then reconstruct the crime and make you jump, and it's registered on a thermometer. I know that when they call out 'Who killed Prince Michael?' I shall register a hundred and twenty-two or something perfectly frightful, and they'll haul me off to jail at once."

The door opened and Tredwell announced:

"Mr. George Lomax. Mr. Eversleigh."

"Enter Codders, followed by faithful dog," murmured Bundle.

Bill made a beeline for her, whilst George greeted Lord Caterham in the genial manner he assumed for public occasions.

"My dear Caterham," said George, shaking him by the hand, "I got your message and came over, of course."

"Very good of you, my dear fellow, very good of you. Delighted to see you." Lord Caterham's conscience always drove him on to an excess of geniality when he was conscious of feeling none. "Not that it was my message, but that doesn't matter at all."

In the meantime Bill was attacking Bundle in an undertone.

"I say. What's it all about? What's this I hear about Virginia bolting off in the middle of the night? She's not been kidnapped has she?"

"Oh, no," said Bundle. "She left a note pinned to the pincushion in the orthodox fashion."

"She's not gone off with anyone, has she? Not with that Colonial Johnny? I never liked the fellow, and, from all I hear, there seems to be an idea floating around that he himself is the supercrook. But I don't quite see how that can be?"

"Why not?"

"Well, this King Victor was a French fellow, and Cade's English enough."

"You don't happen to have heard that King Victor was an accomplished linguist, and, moreover, was half Irish?"

"Oh, Lord! Then that's why he's made himself scarce, is it?"

"I don't know about his making himself scarce. He disappeared the day before yesterday, as you know. But this morning we got a wire from him saying he would be down here at 9 p.m. tonight, and suggesting that Codders should be asked over. All these other people have turned up as well—asked by Mr. Cade."

"It is a gathering," said Bill, looking round. "One French detective by window, one English ditto by fireplace. Strong foreign element. The Stars and Stripes don't seem to be represented?"

Bundle shook her head.

"Mr. Fish has disappeared into the blue. Virginia's not here either. But everyone else is assembled, and I have a feeling in my bones, Bill, that we are drawing very near to the moment when somebody says 'James, the footman,' and everything is revealed. We're only waiting now for Anthony Cade to arrive."

"He'll never show up," said Bill.

"Then why call this company meeting, as Father calls it?"

"Ah, there's some deep idea behind that. Depend upon it. Wants us all here while he's somewhere else—you know the sort of thing."

"You don't think he'll come, then?"

"No fear. Run his head into the lion's mouth? Why, the room's bristling with detectives and high officials."

"You don't know much about King Victor, if you think that would deter him. By all accounts, it's the kind of situation he loves above all, and he always manages to come out on top."

Mr. Eversleigh shook his head doubtfully.

"That would take some doing—with the dice loaded against him. He'll never—"

The door opened again and Tredwell announced:

"Mr. Cade."

Anthony came straight across to his host.

"Lord Caterham," he said, "I'm giving you a frightful lot of trouble, and I'm awfully sorry about it. But I really do think that tonight will see the clearing up of the mystery."

Lord Caterham looked mollified. He had always had a secret liking for Anthony.

"No trouble at all," he said heartily.

"It's very kind of you," said Anthony. "We're all here, I see. Then I can get on with the good work."

"I don't understand," said George Lomax weightily. "I don't understand in the least. This is all very irregular. Mr. Cade has no standing—no standing whatever. The position is a very difficult and delicate one. I am strongly of the opinion—"

George's flood of eloquence was arrested. Moving unobtrusively to the great man's side, Superintendent Battle whispered a few words in his ear. George looked perplexed and baffled.

"Very well, if you say so," he remarked grudgingly. Then added in a louder tone, "I'm sure we are all willing to listen to what Mr. Cade has to say."

Anthony ignored the palpable condescension of the other's tone.

"It's just a little idea of mine, that's all," he said cheerfully. "Probably all of you know that we got hold of a certain message in cipher the other day. There was a reference to Richmond, and some numbers." He paused. "Well, we had a shot at solving it—and we failed. Now in the late Count Stylptitch's memoirs (which I happen to have read) there is a reference to a certain dinner—a 'flower' dinner which everyone attended wearing a badge representing a flower. The Count himself wore the exact duplicate of that curious device we found in the cavity in the secret passage. It represented a rose. If you remember, it was all *rows* of things—buttons, letter Es, and finally rows of knitting. Now, gentlemen, what is there in this house that is arranged in rows? Books, isn't that so? Add to that, that in the catalogue of Lord Caterham's library there is a book called *The Life of the Earl of Richmond*, and I think you will get a very fair idea of the hiding place. Starting at the volume in question, and using the numbers to denote shelves and books, I think you will find that the—er—object of our search is concealed in a dummy book, or in a cavity behind a particular book."

Anthony looked round modestly, obviously waiting for applause.

"Upon my word, that's very ingenious," said Lord Caterham.

"Quite ingenious," admitted George condescendingly. "But it remains to be seen—"

Anthony laughed.

"The proof of the pudding's in the eating—eh? Well, I'll soon settle that for you." He sprang to his feet. "I'll go to the library—"

He got no farther. M. Lemoine moved forward from the window.

"Just one moment, Mr. Cade. You permit, Lord Caterham?"

He went to the writing table, and hurriedly scribbled a few lines. He sealed them up in an envelope, and then rang the bell. Tredwell appeared in answer to it. Lemoine handed him the note.

"See that that is delivered at once, if you please."

"Very good, sir," said Tredwell.

With his usual dignified tread he withdrew.

Anthony, who had been standing, irresolute, sat down again.

"What's the big idea, Lemoine?" he asked gently.

There was a sudden sense of strain in the atmosphere.

"If the jewel is where you say it is—well, it has been there for over seven years—a quarter of an hour more does not matter."

"Go on," said Anthony. "That wasn't all you wanted to say?"

"No, it was not. At this juncture it is—unwise to permit any one person to leave the room. Especially if that person has rather questionable antecedents."

Anthony raised his eyebrows and lighted a cigarette.

"I suppose a vagabond life is not very respectable," he mused.

"Two months ago, Mr. Cade, you were in South Africa. That is admitted. Where were you before that?"

Anthony leaned back in his chair, idly blowing smoke rings.

"Canada. Wild Northwest."

"Are you sure you were not in prison? A French prison?"

Automatically, Superintendent Battle moved a step nearer the door, as if to cut off a retreat that way, but Anthony showed no signs of doing anything dramatic.

Instead, he stared at the French detective, and then burst out laughing.

"My poor Lemoine. It is a monomania with you! You do indeed see King Victor everywhere. So you fancy that I am that interesting gentleman?"

"Do you deny it?"

Anthony brushed a fleck of ash from his coat sleeve.

"I never deny anything that amuses me," he said lightly. "But the accusation is really too ridiculous."

"Ah! you think so?" The Frenchman leant forward. His face was twitching painfully, and yet he seemed perplexed and baffled—as though something in Anthony's manner puzzled him. "What if I tell you, monsieur, that this time—this time—I am out to get King Victor, and nothing shall stop me!"

"Very laudable," was Anthony's comment. "You've been out to get him before, though, haven't you, Lemoine? And he's got the better of you. Aren't you afraid that that may happen again? He's a slippery fellow, by all accounts."

The conversation had developed into a duel between the detective and Anthony. Everyone else in the room was conscious of the tension. It was a fight to a finish between the Frenchman, painfully in earnest, and the man who smoked so calmly and whose words seemed to show that he had not a care in the world.

"If I were you, Lemoine," continued Anthony, "I should be very, very careful. Watch your step, and all that sort of thing."

"This time," said Lemoine grimly, "there will be no mistake."

"You seem very sure about it all," said Anthony. "But there's such a thing as evidence, you know."

Lemoine smiled, and something in his smile seemed to attract Anthony's attention. He sat up and stubbed out his cigarette.

"You saw that note I wrote just now?" said the French detective. "It was to my people at the inn. Yesterday I received from France the fingerprints and the Bertillon measurements of King Victor—the so-called Captain O'Neill. I have asked for them to be sent up to me here. In a few minutes we shall *know* whether you are the man!"

Anthony stared steadily at him. Then a little smile crept over his face.

"You're really rather clever, Lemoine. I never thought of that. The documents will arrive, you will induce me to dip my fingers in the ink, or something equally unpleasant, and you will measure my ears and look for my distinguishing marks. And if they agree—"

"Well," said Lemoine, "if they agree—eh?"

Anthony leaned forward in his chair.

"Well, if they do agree," he said very gently, "what then?"

"What then?" The detective seemed taken aback. "But—I shall have proved then that you are King Victor!"

But for the first time, a shade of uncertainty crept into his manner.

"That will doubtless be a great satisfaction to you," said Anthony. "But I don't quite see where it's going to hurt me. I'm not admitting anything, but supposing, just for the sake of argument, that I was King Victor—I might be trying to repent, you know."

"Repent?"

"That's the idea. Put yourself in King Victor's place, Lemoine. Use your imagination. You've just come out of prison. You're getting on in life. You've lost the first fine rapture of the adventurous life. Say, even that you meet a beautiful girl. You think of marrying and settling down somewhere in the country where you can grow vegetable marrows. You decide from henceforth to lead a blameless life. Put yourself in King Victor's place. Can't you imagine feeling like that?"

"I do not think that I should feel like that," said Lemoine with a sardonic smile.

"Perhaps you wouldn't," admitted Anthony. "But then you're not King Victor, are you? You can't possibly know what he feels like."

"But it is nonsense, what you are saying there," spluttered the Frenchman.

"Oh, no, it isn't. Come now, Lemoine, if I'm King Victor, what have you against me after all? You could never get the necessary evidence in the old, old days, remember. I've served my sentence, and that's all there is to it. I suppose you could arrest me for the French equivalent of 'Loitering with intent to commit a felony,' but that would be poor satisfaction, wouldn't it?"

"You forget," said Lemoine. "America! How about this business of obtaining money under false pretences, and passing yourself off as Prince Nicholas Obolovitch?"

"No good, Lemoine," said Anthony, "I was nowhere near America at the time. And I can prove that easily enough. If King Victor impersonated Prince Nicholas in America, then I'm not King Victor. You're sure he *was* impersonated? That it wasn't the man himself?"

Superintendent Battle suddenly interposed.

"The man was an imposter all right, Mr. Cade."

"I wouldn't contradict you, Battle," said Anthony. "You have such a habit of being always right. Are you equally sure that Prince Nicholas died in the Congo?"

Battle looked at him curiously.

"I wouldn't swear to that, sir. But it's generally believed."

"Careful man. What's your motto? Plenty of rope, eh? I've taken a leaf out of your book. I've given M. Lemoine plenty of rope. I've not denied his accusations. But, all the same, I'm afraid he's going to be disappointed. You see I always believe in having something up one's sleeve. Anticipating that some little unpleasantness might arise here, I took the precaution to bring a trump card along with me. It—or rather he—is upstairs."

"Upstairs?" said Lord Caterham, very interested.

"Yes, he's been having rather a trying time of it lately, poor fellow. Got a nasty bump on the head from someone. I've been looking after him."

Suddenly the deep voice of Mr. Isaacstein broke in: "Can we guess who he is?"

"If you like," said Anthony, "but—"

Lemoine interrupted with sudden ferocity:

"All this is foolery. You think to outwit me yet again. It may be true what you say—that you were not in America. You are too clever to say it if it were not true. But there is something else. Murder! Yes, murder. The murder of Prince Michael. He interfered with you that night as you were looking for the jewel."

"Lemoine, have you ever known King Victor do murder?" Anthony's voice rang out sharply. "You know as well—better than I do, that he has never shed blood."

"Who else but you could have murdered him?" cried Lemoine. "Tell me that!"

The last word died on his lips, as a shrill whistle sounded from the terrace outside. Anthony sprang up, all his assumed nonchalance laid aside.

"You ask me who murdered Prince Michael?" he cried. "I won't tell you—I'll *show* you. That whistle was the signal I've been waiting for. The murderer of Prince Michael is in the library now."

He sprang out through the window, and the others followed him as he led the way round the terrace, until they came to the library window. He pushed the window, and it yielded to his touch.

Very softly he held aside the thick curtain, so that they could look into the room.

Standing by the bookcase was a dark figure, hurriedly pulling out and replacing volumes, so absorbed in the task that no outside sound was heeded.

And then, as they stood watching, trying to recognize the figure that was vaguely silhouetted against the light of the electric torch it carried, someone sprang past them with a sound like the roar of a wild beast.

The torch fell to the ground, was extinguished, and the sounds of a terrific struggle filled the room. Lord Caterham groped his way to the lights and switched them on.

Two figures were swaying together. And as they looked the end came. The short sharp crack of a pistol shot, and the small figure crumbled up and fell. The other figure turned and faced them—it was Boris, his eyes alight with rage.

"She killed my master," he growled. "Now she tries to shoot me. I would have taken the pistol from her and shot her, but it went off in the struggle. St. Michael directed it. The evil woman is dead."

"A woman?" cried George Lomax.

They drew nearer. On the floor, the pistol still clasped in her hand, and an expression of deadly malignity on her face, lay—Mademoiselle Brun.

# Twenty-eight

## King Victor

"I suspected her from the first," explained Anthony. "There was a light in her room on the night of the murder. Afterwards, I wavered. I made inquiries about her in Brittany, and came back satisfied that she was what she represented herself to be. I was a fool. Because the Comtesse de Breteuil had employed a Mademoiselle Brun and spoke highly of her, it never occurred to me that the real Mademoiselle Brun might have been kidnapped on her way to her new post, and that it might be a substitute taking her place. Instead I shifted my suspicions to Mr. Fish. It was not until he had followed me to Dover, and we had had a mutual explanation, that I began to see clearly. Once I knew that he was a Pinkerton's man, trailing King Victor, my suspicions swung back again to their original object.

"The thing that worried me most was that Mrs. Revel had definitely recognized the woman. Then I remembered that it was only *after* I had mentioned her being Madame de Breteuil's govern-ess. And all she had said was that that accounted for the fact that the woman's face was familiar to her. Superintendent Battle will tell you that a deliberate plot was formed to keep Mrs. Revel from coming to Chimneys. Nothing more nor less than a dead body, in fact. And though the murder was the work of the Comrades of the Red Hand, punishing supposed treachery on the part of the victim, the staging of it, and the absence of the Comrade's sign manual, pointed to some abler intelligence directing operations. From the first, I suspected some connexion with Herzoslovakia. Mrs. Revel was the only member of the house party who had been to the country. I suspected at first that someone was impersonat-ing Prince Michael, but that proved to be a totally erroneous idea. When I realized the possibility of Mademoiselle Brun's being an imposter, and added to that the fact that her face was familiar to Mrs. Revel, I began to see daylight. It was evidently very important that she should not be recognized, and Mrs. Revel was the only person likely to do so."

"But who was she?" said Lord Caterham. "Someone Mrs. Revel had known in Herzoslovakia?"

"I think the Baron might be able to tell us," said Anthony.

"I?" The Baron stared at him, then down at the motionless figure.

"Look well," said Anthony. "Don't be put off by the makeup. She was an actress once, remember."

The Baron stared again. Suddenly he started.

"God in heaven," he breathed, "it is not possible."

"What is not possible?" asked George. "Who is the lady? You recognize her, Baron?"

"No, no, it is not possible." The Baron continued to mutter. "She was killed. They were both killed. On the steps of the palace. Her body was recovered."

"Mutilated and unrecognizable," Anthony reminded him. "She managed to put up a bluff. I think she escaped to America, and has spent a good many years lying low in deadly terror of the Comrades of the Red Hand. They promoted the revolution, remember, and, to use an expressive phrase, they always had it in for her. Then King Victor was released, and they planned to recover the diamond together. She was searching for it that night when she came suddenly upon Prince Michael, and he recognized her. There was never much fear of her meeting him in the ordinary way of things. Royal guests don't come in contact with governesses, and she could always retire with a convenient migraine, as she did the day the Baron was here.

"However, she met Prince Michael face to face when she least expected it. Exposure and disgrace stared her in the face. She shot him. It was she who placed the revolver in Isaacstein's suitcase, so as to confuse the trail, and she who returned the letters."

Lemoine moved forward.

"She was coming down to search for the jewel that night, you say," he said. "Might she not have been going to meet her accomplice, King Victor, who was coming from outside? Eh? What do you say to that?"

Anthony sighed.

"Still at it, my dear Lemoine? How persistent you are! You won't take my hint that I've got a trump card up my sleeve?"

But George, whose mind worked slowly, now broke in.

"I am still completely at sea. Who was this lady, Baron? You recognize her, it seems?"

But the Baron drew himself up and stood very straight and stiff.

"You are in error, Mr. Lomax. To my knowledge I have not this lady seen before. A complete stranger she is to me."

"But—"

George stared at him—bewildered.

The Baron took him into a corner of the room, and murmured something into his ear. Anthony watched with a good deal of enjoyment, George's face turning slowly purple, his eyes bulging, and all the incipient symptoms of apoplexy. A murmur of George's throaty voice came to him.

"Certainly . . . certainly . . . by all means . . . no need at all . . . complicate situation . . . utmost discretion."

"Ah!" Lemoine hit the table sharply with his hand. "I do not care about all this! The murder of Prince Michael—that was not my affair. I want King Victor."

Anthony shook his head gently.

"I'm sorry for you, Lemoine. You're really a very able fellow. But, all the same, you're going to lose the trick. I'm about to play my trump card."

He stepped across the room and rang the bell. Tredwell answered it.

"A gentlemen arrived with me this evening, Tredwell."

"Yes, sir, a foreign gentleman."

"Quite so. Will you kindly ask him to join us here as soon as possible?"

"Yes, sir."

Tredwell withdrew.

"Entry of the trump card, the mysterious Monsieur X," remarked Anthony. "*Who is he?* Can anyone guess?"

"Putting two and two together," said Herman Isaacstein, "what with your mysterious hints this morning, and your attitude this afternoon, I should say there was no doubt about it. Somehow or other you've managed to get hold of Prince Nicholas of Herzoslovakia."

"You think the same, Baron?"

"I do. Unless yet another impostor you have put forward. But that I will not believe. With me, your dealings most honourable have been."

"Thank you, Baron. I shan't forget those words. So you are all agreed?"

His eyes swept round the circle of waiting faces. Only Lemoine did not respond, but kept his eyes fixed sullenly on the table.

Anthony's quick ears had caught the sound of footsteps outside in the hall.

"And yet, you know," he said with a queer smile, "you're all wrong!"

He crossed swiftly to the door and flung it open.

A man stood on the threshold—a man with a neat black beard, eyeglasses, and a foppish appearance slightly marred by a bandage round the head.

"Allow me to present to you the real Monsieur Lemoine of the Sûreté."

There was a rush and a scuffle, and then the nasal tones of Mr. Hiram Fish rose bland and reassuring from the window:

"No, you don't, sonny—not this way. I have been stationed here this whole evening for the particular purpose of preventing your escape. You will observe that I have you covered well and good with this gun of mine. I came over to get you, and I've got you—but you sure are some lad!"

# Twenty-nine

## FURTHER EXPLANATIONS

"You owe us an explanation, I think, Mr. Cade," said Herman Isaacstein, somewhat later in the evening.

"There's nothing much to explain," said Anthony modestly. "I went to Dover and Fish followed me under the impression that I was King Victor. We found a mysterious stranger imprisoned there, and as soon as we heard his story we knew where we were. The same idea again, you see. The real man kidnapped, and the false one—in this case King Victor himself—takes his place. But it seems that Battle here always thought there was something fishy about his French colleague, and wired to Paris for his fingerprints and other means of identification."

"Ah!" cried the Baron. "The fingerprints. The Bertillon measurements that that scoundrel talked about?"

"It was a clever idea," said Anthony. "I admired it so much that I felt forced to play it up. Besides, my doing so puzzled the false

Lemoine enormously. You see, as soon as I had given the tip about the 'rows' and where the jewel really was, he was keen to pass on the news to his accomplice, and at the same time to keep us all in that room. The note was really to Mademoiselle Brun. He told Tredwell to deliver it at once, and Tredwell did so by taking it upstairs to the schoolroom. Lemoine accused me of being King Victor, by that means creating a diversion and preventing anyone from leaving the room. By the time all that had been cleared up and we adjourned to the library to look for the stone, he flattered himself that the stone would be no longer there to find!"

George cleared his throat.

"I must say, Mr. Cade," he said pompously, "that I consider your action in that matter highly reprehensible. If the slightest hitch had occurred in your plans, one of our national possessions might have disappeared beyond the hope of recovery. It was foolhardy, Mr. Cade, reprehensibly foolhardy."

"I guess you haven't tumbled to the little idea, Mr. Lomax," said the drawling voice of Mr. Fish. "That historic diamond was never behind the books in the library."

"Never?"

"Not on your life."

"You see," explained Anthony, "that little device of Count Stylptitch's stood for what it had originally stood for—a rose. When that dawned upon me on Monday afternoon, I went straight to the rose garden. Mr. Fish had already tumbled to the same idea. If, standing with your back to the sundial, you take seven paces straight forward, then eight to the left and three to the right, you come to some bushes of a bright red rose called Richmond. The house has been ransacked to find the hiding place, but nobody has thought of digging in the garden. I suggest a little digging party tomorrow morning."

"Then the story about the books in the library—"

"An invention of mine to trap the lady. Mr. Fish kept watch on the terrace, and whistled when the psychological moment had arrived. I may say that Mr. Fish and I established martial law at the Dover house, and prevented the Comrades from communicating with the false Lemoine. He sent them an order to clear out, and word was conveyed to him that this had been done. So he went happily ahead with his plans for denouncing me."

"Well, well," said Lord Caterham cheerfully, "everything seems to have been cleared up most satisfactorily."

"Everything but one thing," said Mr. Isaacstein.

"What is that?"

The great financier looked steadily at Anthony.

"What did you get me down here for? Just to assist at a dramatic scene as an interested onlooker?"

Anthony shook his head.

"No, Mr. Isaacstein. You are a busy man whose time is money. Why did you come down here originally?"

"To negotiate a loan."

"With whom?"

"Prince Michael of Herzoslovakia."

"Exactly. Prince Michael is dead. Are your prepared to offer the same loan on the same terms to his cousin Nicholas?"

"Can you produce him? I thought he was killed in the Congo?"

"He was killed all right. I killed him. Oh, no, I'm not a murderer. When I say I killed him, I mean that I spread the report of his death. I promise you a prince, Mr. Isaacstein. Will *I* do?"

"You?"

"Yes, I'm the man. Nicholas Sergius Alexander Ferdinand Obolovitch. Rather long for the kind of life I proposed to live, so I emerged from the Congo as plain Anthony Cade."

Little Captain Andrassy sprang up.

"But this is incredible—incredible," he spluttered. "Have a care, sir, what you say."

"I can give you plenty of proofs," said Anthony quietly. "I think I shall be able to convince the Baron here."

The Baron lifted his hand.

"Your proofs I will examine, yes. But of them for me there is no need. Your word alone sufficient for me is. Besides, your English mother you much resemble. All along have I said: 'This young man on one side or the other most highly born is.'"

"You have always trusted my word, Baron," said Anthony. "I can assure you that in the days to come I shall not forget."

Then he looked over at Superintendent Battle, whose face had remained perfectly expressionless.

"You can understand," said Anthony with a smile, "that my position has been extremely precarious. Of all of those in the house I might be supposed to have the best reason for wishing Michael Obolovitch out of the way, since I was the next heir to the throne. I've been extraordinarily afraid of Battle all along. I always felt that he suspected me, but that he was held up by lack of motive."

"I never believed for a minute that you'd shot him, sir," said Superintendent Battle. "We've got a feeling in such matters. But I knew that you were afraid of something, and you puzzled me. If I'd known sooner who you really were I daresay I'd have yielded to the evidence, and arrested you."

"I'm glad I managed to keep one guilty secret from you. You wormed everything else out of me all right. You're a damned good man at your job Battle. I shall always think of Scotland Yard with respect."

"Most amazing," muttered George. "Most amazing story I ever heard. I—I can really hardly believe it. You are quite sure, Baron, that—"

"My dear Mr. Lomax," said Anthony, with a slight hardness in his tone, "I have no intention of asking the British Foreign Office to support my claim without bringing forward the most convincing documentary evidence. I suggest that we adjourn now, and that you, the Baron, Mr. Isaacstein and myself discuss the terms of the proposed loan."

The Baron rose to his feet, and clicked his heels together.

"It will be the proudest moment of my life, sir," he said solemnly, "when I see you King of Herzoslovakia."

"Oh, by the way, Baron," said Anthony carelessly, slipping his hand through the other's arm, "I forgot to tell you. There's a string tied to this. I'm married, you know."

The Baron retreated a step or two. Dismay overspread his countenance.

"Something wrong I knew there would be," he boomed. "Merciful God in heaven! He has married a black woman in Africa!"

"Come, come, it's not so bad as all that," said Anthony laughing. "She's white enough—white all through, bless her."

"Good. A respectable morganatic affair it can be, then."

"Not a bit of it. She's to play Queen to my King. It's no use shaking your head. She's fully qualified for the post. She's the daughter of an English peer who dates back to the time of the Conqueror. It's very fashionable just now for royalties to marry into the aristocracy—and she knows something of Herzoslovakia."

"My God!" cried George Lomax, startled out of his usual careful speech. "Not—not—Virginia Revel?"

"Yes," said Anthony. "Virginia Revel."

"My dear fellow," cried Lord Caterham, "I mean—sir, I congratulate you. I do indeed. A delightful creature."

"Thank you, Lord Caterham," said Anthony. "She's all you say and more."

But Mr. Isaacstein was regarding him curiously.

"You'll excuse my asking your Highness, but when did this marriage take place?"

Anthony smiled back at him.

"As a matter of fact," he said, "I married her this morning."

# Thirty

## ANTHONY SIGNS ON FOR A NEW JOB

"If you will go on, gentlemen, I will follow you in a minute," said Anthony.

He waited while the others filed out, and then turned to where Superintendent Battle was standing apparently absorbed in examining the panelling.

"Well, Battle? Want to ask me something, don't you?"

"Well, I do, sir, though I don't know how you knew I did. But I always marked you out as being specially quick in the uptake. I take it that the lady who is dead was the late Queen Varaga?"

"Quite right, Battle. It'll be hushed up, I hope. You can understand what I feel about family skeletons."

"Trust Mr. Lomax for that, sir. No one will ever know. That is, a lot of people will know, but it won't get about."

"Was that what you wanted to ask me about?"

"No, sir—that was only in passing. I was curious to know just what made you drop your own name—if I'm not taking too much of a liberty?"

"Not a bit of it. I'll tell you. I killed myself for the purest motives, Battle. My mother was English, I'd been educated in England, and I was far more interested in England than in Herzoslovakia. And I felt an absolute fool knocking about the world with a comic-opera title tacked on to me. You see, when I was very young, I had democratic ideas. Believed in the purity of ideals, and the equality of all men. I especially disbelieved in kings and princes."

"And since then?" asked Battle shrewdly.

"Oh, since then, I've travelled and seen the world. There's damned little equality going about. Mind you, I still believe in democracy. But you've got to force it on people with a strong hand—ram it down their throats. Men don't want to be brothers—they may some day, but they don't now. My belief in the brotherhood of man died the day I arrived in London last week, when I observed people standing in a Tube train resolutely refuse to move up and make room for those who entered. You won't turn people into angels by appealing to their better natures just yet awhile—but by judicious force you can coerce them into behaving more or less decently to one another to go on with. I still believe in the brotherhood of man, but it's not coming yet awhile. Say another ten thousand years or so. It's no good being impatient. Evolution is a slow process."

"I'm very interested in these views of yours, sir," said Battle with a twinkle. "And if you'll allow me to say so, I'm sure you'll make a very fine king out there."

"Thank you, Battle," said Anthony with a sigh.

"You don't seem very happy about it, sir?"

"Oh, I don't know. I daresay it will be rather fun. But it's tying oneself down to regular work. I've always avoided that before."

"But you consider it your duty, I suppose, sir?"

"Good Lord, no! What an idea. It's a woman—it's always a woman, Battle. I'd do more than be a king for her sake."

"Quite so, sir."

"I've arranged it so that the Baron and Isaacstein can't kick. The one wants a king, and the other wants oil. They'll both get what they want, and I've got—oh, Lord, Battle, have you ever been in love?"

"I am much attached to Mrs. Battle, sir."

"Much attached to Mrs.—oh, you don't know what I'm talking about! It's entirely different!"

"Excuse me, sir, that man of yours is waiting outside the window."

"Boris? So he is. He's a wonderful fellow. It's a mercy that pistol went off in the struggle and killed the lady. Otherwise Boris would have wrung her neck as sure as Fate, and then you would have wanted to hang him. His attachment to the Obolovitch dynasty is remarkable. The queer thing was that as soon as Michael was dead he attached himself to me—and yet he couldn't possibly have known who I really was."

"Instinct," said Battle. "Like a dog."

"Very awkward instinct I thought it at the time. I was afraid it might give the show away to you. I suppose I'd better see what he wants."

He went out through the window. Superintendent Battle, left

alone, looked after him for a minute, then apparently addressed the panelling.

"He'll do," said Superintendent Battle.

Outside Boris explained himself.

"Master," he said, and led the way along the terrace.

Anthony followed him, wondering what was forward.

Presently Boris stopped and pointed with his forefinger. It was moonlight, and in front of them was a stone seat on which sat two figures.

"He *is* a dog," said Anthony to himself. "And what's more a pointer!"

He strode forward. Boris melted into the shadows.

The two figures rose to meet him. One of them was Virginia—the other—

"Hullo, Joe," said a well-remembered voice. "This is a great girl of yours."

"Jimmy McGrath, by all that's wonderful," cried Anthony. "How in the name of fortune did you get here?"

"That trip of mine into the interior went phut. Then some dagos came monkeying around. Wanted to buy that manuscript off me. Next thing I as near as nothing got a knife in the back one night. That made me think that I'd handed you out a bigger job than I knew. I thought you might need help, and I came along after you by the very next boat."

"Wasn't it splendid of him?" said Virginia. She squeezed Jimmy's arm. "Why didn't you ever tell me how frightfully nice he was? You are, Jimmy, you're a perfect dear."

"You two seem to be getting along all right," said Anthony.

"Sure thing," said Jimmy. "I was snooping round for news of

you, when I connected with this dame. She wasn't at all what I thought she'd be—some swell haughty society lady that'd scare the life out of me."

"He told me all about the letters," said Virginia. "And I feel almost ashamed not to have been in real trouble over them when he was such a knight-errant."

"If I'd known what you were like," said Jimmy gallantly, "I'd not have given him the letters. I'd have brought them to you myself. Say, young man, is the fun really over? Is there nothing for me to do?"

"By Jove," said Anthony, "there is! Wait a minute."

He disappeared into the house. In a minute or two he returned with a paper package which he cast into Jimmy's arms.

"Go round to the garage and help yourself to a likely looking car. Beat it to London and deliver that parcel at 17 Everdean Square. That's Mr. Balderson's private address. In exchange he'll hand you a thousand pounds."

"What? It's not the memoirs? I understood that they'd been burnt."

"What do you take me for?" demanded Anthony.

"You don't think I'd fall for a story like that, do you? I rang up the publishers at once, found out that the other was a fake call, and arranged accordingly. I made up a dummy package as I'd been directed to do. But I put the real package in the manager's safe and handed over the dummy. The memoirs have never been out of my possession."

"Bully for you, my son," said Jimmy.

"Oh, Anthony," cried Virginia. "You're not going to let them be published?"

"I can't help myself. I can't let a pal like Jimmy down. But you needn't worry. I've had time to wade through them, and I see now why people always hint that bigwigs don't write their own reminiscences but hire someone to do it for them. As a writer, Stylptitch is an insufferable bore. He proses on about statecraft, and doesn't go in for any racy and indiscreet anecdotes. His ruling passion of secrecy held strong to the end. There's not a word in the memoirs from beginning to end to flutter the susceptibilities of the most difficult politician. I rang up Balderson today, and arranged with him that I'd deliver the manuscript tonight before midnight. But Jimmy can do his own dirty work now that he's here."

"I'm off," said Jimmy. "I like the idea of that thousand pounds—especially when I'd made up my mind it was down and out."

"Half a second," said Anthony. "I've got a confession to make to you, Virginia. Something that everyone else knows, but that I haven't yet told you."

"I don't mind how many strange women you've loved so long as you don't tell me about them."

"Women!" said Anthony, with a virtuous air. "Women indeed? You ask James here what kind of women I was going about with the last time he saw me."

"Frumps," said Jimmy solemnly. "Utter frumps. Not one a day under forty-five."

"Thank you, Jimmy," said Anthony, "you're a true friend. No, it's much worse than that. I've deceived you as to my real name."

"Is it very dreadful?" said Virginia, with interest. "It isn't something silly like Pobbles, is it? Fancy being called Mrs. Pobbles."

"You are always thinking the worst of me."

"I admit that I did once think you were King Victor, but only for about a minute and a half."

"By the way, Jimmy, I've got a job for you—gold prospecting in the rocky fastnesses of Herzoslovakia?"

"Is there gold there?" asked Jimmy eagerly.

"Sure to be," said Anthony. "It's a wonderful country."

"So you're taking my advice and going there?"

"Yes," said Anthony. "Your advice was worth more than you knew. Now for the confession. I wasn't changed at nurse, or anything romantic like that, but nevertheless I am really Prince Nicholas Obolovitch of Herzoslovakia."

"Oh, Anthony," cried Virginia. "How perfectly screaming! And I have married you! What are we going to do about it?"

"We'll go to Herzoslovakia and pretend to be kings and queens. Jimmy McGrath once said that the average life of a king or queen out there is under four years. I hope you don't mind?"

"Mind?" cried Virginia. "I shall love it!"

"Isn't she great?" murmured Jimmy.

Then, discreetly, he faded into the night. A few minutes later the sound of a car was heard.

"Nothing like letting a man do his own dirty work," said Anthony with satisfaction. "Besides, I didn't know how else to get rid of him. Since we were married I've not had one minute alone with you."

"We'll have a lot of fun," said Virginia. "Teaching the brigands not to be brigands, and the assassins not to assassinate, and generally improving the moral tone of the country."

"I like to hear these pure ideals," said Anthony. "It makes me feel my sacrifice has not been in vain."

"Rot," said Virginia calmly, "you'll enjoy being a king. It's in your blood, you know. You were brought up to the trade of royalty, and you've got a natural aptitude for it, just like plumbers have a natural bent for plumbing."

"I never think they have," said Anthony. "But, damn it all, don't let's waste time talking about plumbers. Do you know that at this very minute I'm supposed to be deep in conference with Isaacstein and old Lollipop? They want to talk about oil. Oil, my God! They can just await my kingly pleasure. Virginia, do you remember my telling you once that I'd have a damned good try to make you care for me?"

"I remember," said Virginia softly. "But Superintendent Battle was looking out of the window."

"Well, he isn't now," said Anthony.

He caught her suddenly to him, kissing her eyelids, her lips, the green gold of her hair. . . .

"I do love you so, Virginia," he whispered. "I do love you so. Do you love me?"

He looked down at her—sure of the answer.

Her head rested against his shoulder, and very low, in a sweet shaken voice, she answered:

"Not a bit!"

"You little devil," cried Anthony, kissing her again. "Now I know for certain that I shall love you until I die. . . ."

# Thirty-one

## SUNDRY DETAILS

Scene—Chimneys, 11 a.m. Thursday morning.

Johnson, the police constable, with his coat off, digging.

Something in the nature of a funeral feeling seems to be in the air. The friends and relations stand round the grave that Johnson is digging.

George Lomax has the air of the principal beneficiary under the will of the deceased. Superintendent Battle, with his immovable face, seems pleased that the funeral arrangements have gone so nicely. As the undertaker, it reflects credit upon him. Lord Caterham has that solemn and shocked look which Englishmen assume when a religious ceremony is in progress.

Mr. Fish does not fit into the picture so well. He is not sufficiently grave.

Johnson bends to his task. Suddenly he straightens up. A little stir of excitement passes round.

"That'll do, sonny," said Mr. Fish. "We shall do nicely now."

One perceives at once that he is really the family physician.

Johnson retires. Mr. Fish, with due solemnity, stoops over the excavation. The surgeon is about to operate.

He brings out a small canvas package. With much ceremony he hands it to Superintendent Battle. The latter, in his turn, hands it to George Lomax. The etiquette of the situation has now been carefully complied with.

George Lomax unwraps the package, slits up the oilsilk inside it, burrows into further wrapping. For a moment he holds something on the palm of his hand—then quickly shrouds it once more in cottonwool.

He clears his throat.

"At this auspicious moment," he begins, with the clear delivery of the practised speaker.

Lord Caterham beats a precipitate retreat. On the terrace he finds his daughter.

"Bundle, is that car of yours in order?"

"Yes. Why?"

"Then take me up to town in it immediately. I'm going abroad at once—today."

"But, Father—"

"Don't argue with me, Bundle. George Lomax told me when he arrived this morning that he was anxious to have a few words with me privately on a matter of the utmost delicacy. He added that the King of Timbuctoo was arriving in London shortly. I won't go through it again, Bundle, do you hear? Not for fifty George Lomaxes! If Chimneys is so valuable to the nation, let the nation buy it. Otherwise I shall sell it to a syndicate and they can turn it into an hotel."

"Where is Codders now?"

Bundle is rising to the situation.

"At the present minute," replied Lord Caterham, looking at his watch, "he is good for at least fifteen minutes about the Empire."

Another picture.

Mr. Bill Eversleigh, not invited to be present at the graveside ceremony, at the telephone.

"No, really, I mean it . . . I say, don't be huffy . . . Well, you will have supper tonight, anyway? . . . No, I haven't. I've been kept to it with my nose at the grindstone. You've no idea what Codders is like . . . I say, Dolly, you know jolly well what I think about you . . . You know I've never cared for anyone but you . . . Yes, I'll come to the show first. How does the old wheeze go? 'And the little girl tries, Hooks and Eyes'. . . ."

Unearthly sounds. Mr. Eversleigh trying to hum the refrain in question.

And now George's peroration draws to a close.

". . . the lasting peace and prosperity of the British Empire!"

"I guess," said Mr. Hiram Fish *sotto voce* to himself and the world at large, "that this has been a great little old week."

# The *Agatha Christie* Collection

## THE HERCULE POIROT MYSTERIES
### Match your wits with the famous Belgian detective.

The Mysterious Affair at Styles

The Murder on the Links

Poirot Investigates

The Murder of Roger Ackroyd

The Big Four

The Mystery of the Blue Train

Peril at End House

Lord Edgware Dies

Murder on the Orient Express

Three Act Tragedy

Death in the Clouds

The A.B.C. Murders

Murder in Mesopotamia

Cards on the Table

Murder in the Mews

Dumb Witness

Death on the Nile

Appointment with Death

Hercule Poirot's Christmas

Sad Cypress

One, Two, Buckle My Shoe

Evil Under the Sun

Five Little Pigs

The Hollow

The Labors of Hercules

Taken at the Flood

The Under Dog and
Other Stories

Mrs. McGinty's Dead

After the Funeral

Hickory Dickory Dock

Dead Man's Folly

Cat Among the Pigeons

The Clocks

Third Girl

Hallowe'en Party

Elephants Can Remember

Curtain: Poirot's Last Case

Explore more at www.AgathaChristie.com

# The *Agatha Christie*® Collection

## THE MISS MARPLE MYSTERIES

Join the legendary spinster sleuth from
St. Mary Mead in solving murders far and wide.

The Murder at the Vicarage

The Body in the Library

The Moving Finger

A Murder Is Announced

They Do It with Mirrors

A Pocket Full of Rye

4:50 From Paddington

The Mirror Crack'd from
Side to Side

A Caribbean Mystery

At Bertram's Hotel

Nemesis

Sleeping Murder

Miss Marple: The Complete
Short Stories

## THE TOMMY AND TUPPENCE MYSTERIES

Jump on board with the entertaining crime-solving
couple from Young Adventurers Ltd.

The Secret Adversary

Partners in Crime

N or M?

By the Pricking of My Thumbs

Postern of Fate

# The *Agatha Christie* Collection

**Don't miss a single one of Agatha Christie's stand-alone novels and short-story collections.**

The Man in the Brown Suit

The Secret of Chimneys

The Seven Dials Mystery

The Mysterious Mr. Quin

The Sittaford Mystery

Parker Pyne Investigates

Why Didn't They Ask Evans?

Murder Is Easy

The Regatta Mystery and Other Stories

And Then There Were None

Towards Zero

Death Comes as the End

Sparkling Cyanide

The Witness for the Prosecution and Other Stories

Crooked House

Three Blind Mice and Other Stories

They Came to Baghdad

Destination Unknown

Ordeal by Innocence

Double Sin and Other Stories

The Pale Horse

Star over Bethlehem: Poems and Holiday Stories

Endless Night

Passenger to Frankfurt

The Golden Ball and Other Stories

The Mousetrap and Other Plays

The Harlequin Tea Set and Other Stories

Explore more at www.AgathaChristie.com

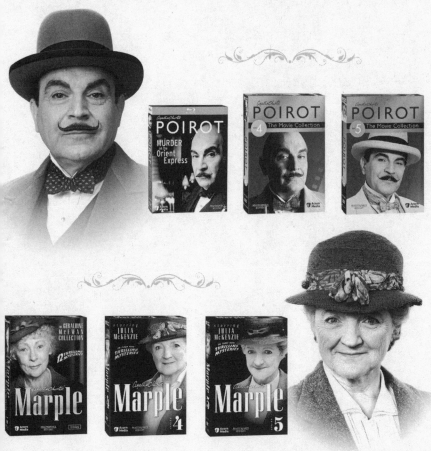

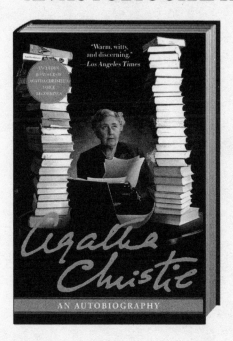